RUNNING THE DISTANCE

RUNNING THE DISTANCE

An Athlete's Year

JACK BUCKNER

HEINEMANN KINGSWOOD

Heinemann Kingswood
Michelin House, 81 Fulham Road, London SW3 6RB

LONDON MELBOURNE AUCKLAND

First published 1989

0 434 98135 4

Printed and bound in Great Britain by
Richard Clay Ltd, Bungay, Suffolk

CONTENTS

ACKNOWLEDGEMENTS

I have quoted from *The Brendan Foster Story* by Brendan Foster and Cliff Temple, *Only A Game* by Eamon Dunphy, *Testament of a Runner* by W. Loader, *Running Free* by Sebastian Coe and David Miller and newspaper articles by the following: Cliff Temple (*Sunday Times*), Neil Wilson (*the Independent*), Pat Butcher (*The Times*), Hugh McIlvanney (*the Observer*) and Ian Wooldridge (*the Daily Mail*). My thanks are due to the above authors and publishers.

I am also grateful to the following: Andy and Izzy Etchells, Dave Bedford and Dr Mike Turner for comments on the manuscript; John Pawsey, Margot Richardson and Derek Wyatt for their professional editing and advice; Mark Shearman for providing the pictures; Mike McNally, Dean Saddington and North Leicestershire ITEC for technical support.

On the athletics side thanks are due to the various medical personnel who have almost kept me on my feet throughout the year; Adidas and Paul Atherton in particular for sponsorship; the training group in Loughborough for shared suffering on the track; my parents, family and friends, for help and encouragement this year and every year.

Lastly a word of appreciation for my two mentors (or are they tormentors?) – coach George Gandy and wife Kerin. George helps and advises me on every aspect of my running career. In the diary when I refer to athletic decisions, I do not give sufficient credit to his guiding influence. Kerin flits in and out of the pages with only passing reference. This is not the case in real life. She deserves far more than the scant praise she receives. However as the book is mainly about running she has been forced to take a back seat for a change! I am indebted to them both.

INTRODUCTION

'So what's it like being a runner?' is a question often levelled at me. It usually leads to a conversation where I begin by explaining to the innocent inquirer that runners do not simply turn up at an athletics track and run fast times. The next stage is to sketch the outline of the runner's life and before long I am holding forth on a variety of topics ranging from the misery of training on a cold winter's night, to the excitement of racing in a packed stadium.

In this diary I have attempted to answer that initial question and provide an insight into the challenges that face the contemporary athlete. I commenced my diary fresh from the heights of a World Championship bronze medal, following my victory in the previous year's European Championships. I was optimistic about my chances in the 1988 Olympics. Unfortunately during the following twelve months I experienced some of the many setbacks that threaten every athlete. My eventual result in Seoul may not have been as glittering as I had hoped, but was achieved despite a number of obstacles.

During the course of the year I have drawn attention to the various off-track dramas that surround athletics and have reflected on them from my own viewpoint. The life of a sportsperson stretches beyond the field of play and I have tried to explain how some of the many changes in athletics have affected me.

Running the Distance is a personal record of a year in athletics. It may not be a balanced, considered view of the year. It is a subjective account of one runner's experiences. With hindsight, perhaps I should have reacted differently to certain situations; perhaps I made mistakes. It is too late to alter anything. This was my athletic year – as it happened.

1

The World Championship 5000m

September 6, 1987. It's the day of the World Championship 5000 metres final and I'm lying on my hotel bed in central Rome. Outside it's raining. The rain has caught even the locals by surprise and on the balconies around the courtyard that I can see from my bed, Italian women are hastily unpegging their washing. Sunday lunch parties have been ruined and I can hear grumbling voices below as the remains of dinner are carted off inside. This is the one day of the year when I've been expecting sunshine, and it rains.

Months before when my coach George Gandy and I examined the British Amateur Athletic Board information pack about the World Championships, one problem was immediately obvious – the climate. In early September the average daytime temperature in Rome is about 28 degrees centigrade, and humidity could be 90 per cent. The 5000m final was scheduled for the late afternoon, so conditions could be uncomfortable, especially for sun-starved British runners. Throughout August I'd spent an hour, four times per week, in an environmental chamber at Loughborough University. I'd sat in temperatures of over 40 degrees centigrade and humidity of 95 per cent. I'd travelled out to Rome a week before the heats of the 5000m to acclimatise further. I was ready for the worst the heat and humidity could throw at me and now it's raining.

The rain is loud and persistent. It's woken me up from my pre-race doze. I am feeling quite relaxed. This morning I jogged around the streets for fifteen minutes. I always jog the morning of a race. It's as much a mental exercise as a physical one. The jog is a reminder to my lethargic body that everything is fine. I may feel weak and listless for the next few hours, but once the gun goes my limbs will spring back to life. However, until that moment my body won't function properly. The jog has gently prodded my memory. All the hard work has been completed. I've reached the World Championship 5000m final and I'm in great shape.

There is less than an hour before we leave the hotel. My wife, Kerin, and her mother Elise are ready in the room next door. George has travelled down from the village and has left me alone to relax. He is probably sheltering somewhere from the rain. The hotel is virtually deserted. It is the final afternoon of the World Championships: the men's 1500m and the women's javelin (how will Crammie and Fatima perform?), the men's marathon, the relays, and of course the 5000m. The final dramatic events in the most prestigious athletic championships. The hotel has been full of supporters of the British team. I was fortunate to find a room here after I'd decided that the overcrowded hectic atmosphere of the Games village was too suffocating.

I'd stayed in the World Championship village for three days. The food was awful and I'd hardly slept. The vast anonymous Princess Hotel built in the fashion of the dreariest Spanish resorts was guarded on every floor by the Italian army, fully equipped with suitably impressive guns. During my second night there, the soldiers discovered a searchlight. This new toy was powered by a noisy electricity generator and the periodic shrieks of laughter indicated that the Italian soldiers were having a great time shining the searchlight around the surrounding deserted fields and onto the windows of the Princess Hotel. I don't think a more effective method of disturbing athletes' sleep could have been devised. I managed to find a room in the hotel where Kerin and Elise were staying, and moved out. Perhaps I was overreacting. I expect I could have survived in the village, but when you have spent most of the previous year preparing for an event, you are not going to allow minor irritations in the last few days to upset your final preparations.

There is less than three hours until my race, time to leave the hotel. A final check of my kit. My spikes, Great Britain vest and wet-suit are all packed just as they were ten minutes ago. The rain appears to be stopping. It's still cool outside so I shall take a spare sweat-shirt. George returns from his walk around Rome. He has avoided the worst of the rain. We collect Kerin and Elise and wander down to the hotel lobby to wait for the taxi. One of the hall porters tries to conduct a conversation regarding my forthcoming performance. Normally this would have been an amiable pidgin English encounter. He wants to have my British vest after the race to display in the hotel foyer. But I am entering my pre-race isolation state and cannot be bothered to converse. Some athletes become excited at the prospect of competition. They crack jokes and act in an extroverted fashion. Others withdraw into themselves becoming quiet and uncommunicative. I am one of the latter. George intervenes, jokes with the porter and relieves me of any social effort.

The taxi driver takes us a different way to the stadium, avoiding the marathon course. The marathon will have just started, and the runners must be delighted with the cool conditions. We travel through the Villa Borghese. I have been training all week around its ancient temples and well-worn footpaths. Usually there are young couples passionately entwined beneath every other tree, but today the wet grass has ruined romance in the park. We roar along the banks of the Tiber, overtaking the congested inner lanes of traffic and cutting across to turn left at the last moment as only taxi drivers can. We arrive at the Rome Olympic Stadium, venue of the second World Athletic Championships. There are large crowds milling around the square in front of the stadium even though the athletics started hours ago and all the tickets have been sold. Kerin and Elise leave for their seats. Kerin kisses me, whispering 'good luck'. There is nothing else to say.

The warm-up area adjacent to the stadium is virtually deserted. The only events left are the 400m relays, the men's 1500 and my 5000m. The remaining field events have already started so there are very few athletes waiting to compete. Earlier in the week the Marble Stadium, as the warm-up area is called after the magnificent marble statues of Roman gods that surround the arena, was packed with nervous athletes from every country in the world. The track had been crowded with sprinters practising starts and runners jogging gently around the grass verge, all anxiously preparing for their competitions. Now there is an end of term atmosphere in the quiet warm-up area. The few remaining officials, their exhaustive duties nearly completed, are chatting and laughing amongst themselves.

A couple of hours and the World Championships will be over. An hour and a half and my race will be over. Already preparations are beginning for the closing ceremony. Youngsters waving flags are parading on the inside of the warm-up track. They are all animated and excited. This is a big day for them, like the athletes. Whatever happens we'll remember today all our lives. These are the important moments of an athlete's career. You remember the races you've won, the hard training sessions and of course the disappointments, but above all you remember the major championships. In a few years' time when the current generation of stars are only memories, the record books will list two details – world records and championship victories. Nothing else will be recorded from anyone's career, however successful.

George and I wait in the British team's changing room. Inside are the team's physiotherapists, the 400m relay runners, and the three British representatives for the 5000m final, Tim Hutchings, Steve Ovett and me. The BBC have fixed up a TV monitor in the changing room and Brendan Foster is saying how the weather conditions will suit 'our boys'. Then the picture cuts to the 1500m. I leave the changing room to start warming up. I jog gently on the grass inside the track. The ground is still wet from the rain, but the skies are clearing and the humidity is increasing.

News quickly filters through about the 1500m. Abdi Bile has won, Crammie was nowhere. Suddenly Cram appears through the tunnel that leads to the Olympic Stadium. He walks alone slowly, disconsolately, across the warm-up track. Daley Thompson and Frank Dick (the BAAB director of coaching) approach him to offer their consolations. Frank throws an arm round him. Crammie looks tired and bemused rather than dejected. He has just suffered the first real disappointment of his entire career. I feel sorry for him, the most successful miler of the 1980s temporarily dethroned, but these sentiments are quickly suppressed as I concentrate on my own challenge.

Aouita is warming up, the favourite, everyone's favourite for my race. Said Aouita, world record holder and Olympic Champion, unbeaten in any race since 1985. I've nearly finished my jogging and the call light above the reporting room is flashing. A group of fifteen distance runners report for the World Championship 5000m final. Once we have reported we are on our own. Coaches and officials must wait outside the room. Inside we have our bags and spikes checked to ensure that only authorised team equipment is taken into the main stadium. Sponsors have paid large sums of money to the various national athletic federations to supply the team kit and these equipment manufacturers don't want individual athletes wearing clothing of a rival company in front of a worldwide television audience. The British team are only permitted to take the official team kit into the arena. My own T-shirts display a different logo so they must be left behind with George. Whilst I am waiting to have my bag searched, Steve Ovett standing behind me comments that despite the rule about officials not being allowed into the report room, Aouita is still surrounded by his entourage of manager and friends. They stay with him until the race. It is a small insignificant matter that doesn't affect the outcome of the competition, but indicates that if you are important enough in athletics you can avoid the rules applied to lesser mortals.

We are led through the tunnel to the main stadium. All the runners are nervous. The huge crowd are applauding the marathon runners. Fatima has won the javelin, Britain's first gold medal of these Championships. I can see her smiling and waving in the distance. Fluttering officials and reporters surround her like moths around a candle. We are passing the final check-point, waiting impatiently to escape onto the track, spikes clacking on the stone floor. Then, a hitch in the organisation. There have been problems all week and we have been warned that at any stage the Italian administration could break down. This is only a minor hitch. A crowd of noisy closing ceremony participants dressed in dinner jackets and ball gowns have entered the tunnel. They are not supposed to be here. Sequined dresses and top hats mingle with running spikes. Shouting officials, nervous athletes and laughing dancers all squeezed into an enclosed space. Before temporary chaos turns into irritation, we runners are ejected onto the track. It is a relief to escape the claustrophobic atmosphere of the tunnel and to stand at long last on the track.

Marathoners are still entering the stadium. The crowd's applause is more muted now, unlike earlier, when an Italian athlete ran onto the track. The noise was so great, we thought he must have broken the world record, but in fact Bordin was finishing third. It is the stragglers, ashen-faced, who are currently struggling around the track. Nevertheless, the crowd's urgency enables the flagging runners to refocus their wandering minds and bodies on the finish. Most manage a final spurt to cross the line. By contrast, we fresh, edgy 5000m competitors are striding out relaxed along the back straight. There is a victory ceremony. Seventy thousand spectators stand. The athletes stop warming up and stand still. The only movements in the stadium are the last few marathon runners on the track and three flags unfurling in the gentle breeze. For a brief moment my nerves vanish, I feel proud and delighted to be part of the World Athletic Championships.

The announcer calls up the competitors for the Men's 5000m final. The biggest cheer is for Aouita. He may be Moroccan but he lives and trains in Italy. Fifteen runners tense on the start line. There is that fortunately brief moment just before the gun goes when your stomach lurches and you wish you were anywhere else in the world other than on an athletics track, and then at long last the race begins.

It is slow. The field is bunched and all fifteen of us are watching our feet. I drift towards the back of the field. There are twelve and a half laps to go, and position is unimportant at the moment. It is a stumbling procession with nobody prepared to lead. I don't want this. I want a genuine, fast, open race like last year's European Championship. That was my kind of race. I won the European Championship in the second-fastest time in the world last year. This year I know I am fitter, but I need a good fast pace if I'm to perform to my best. Two laps drift past and it's still a sedate jog. It would be suicide to try anything myself. I have a plan but I wouldn't even consider leading the race until less than four laps to go. I'm not strong enough to run away from this field any earlier than that. Another couple of laps and the procession continues.

So much for Aouita's claims of a world record. Earlier in the week the outspoken Moroccan told the world's media that he would break his own world record for 'my King and country', but after the slow early pace a fast time is impossible. It is obvious that Aouita will wait and rely on his superior finishing speed to win the race. If it comes down to a last lap dash I'm going to find it tough. I haven't the finishing speed of Ovett, Maree, O'Mara, Aouita, or Délèze. It's nothing to do with confidence, just fact. They are all quicker than me over 1500m and 800m. My personal best for 800m is 1.49, most of them have run close to 1.45. A guy who can run 800m in 1.45 should always outsprint someone who can run 800m in 1.49.

Nearly half-way and Ngugi sweeps into the lead. Ngugi is the World Cross-Country Champion, the unknown factor. He cantered through the qualifying heat in a championship record. The Africans have run well all week. There have been Kenyan victories in the 800m, 10,000m and the Marathon. Ngugi is supposed to be the best Kenyan prospect. He lopes lazily along in front and then suddenly surges. I'm ready for this. It is an African tactic to surge and relax, then surge again. It upsets the rhythm of the race. Kipkoech won the 10,000m this way. I ignore the surge. Only Aouita and O'Mara sprint with Ngugi. Then after about 200m he slows, I gradually catch them up without having to alter my pace. I have run the first lap more economically than the leading trio and have conserved precious energy reserves without losing any ground.

Three weeks ago I won the 5000m in Zurich when Peter Koech, another African, tried to break away from the field in a similar fashion. My performance in Zurich ranks me second in the world for the year. But, fast times are irrelevant if the race is a sprint over the last 400m. Hopefully Ngugi will keep surging and some runners will drop behind. If Ngugi doesn't continue to step up the pace, nobody will struggle and all fifteen of us will be jostling for position at the bell. He is running very wide, almost on the edge of the first lane. I am watching from fourth position. Gradually I've worked my way through the field and I'm now alert and ready to cover any move. It will help my cause if Ngugi keeps leading and upsetting the slow tempo.

We're reaching the 3000m point with five laps left. Ngugi's increased pace has made the last couple of laps quicker, but the overall speed is still desperately slow. The time at 3000m is 8 minutes 16 seconds. I wanted a time of 8 minutes. We're the equivalent of 100 metres slower. A vast difference in a race of this standard. This is the crucial period of the race for me. Ngugi hasn't produced another surge and once again the pace slows as fifteen athletes drift sedately around the running track all watching each other. No one is prepared to commit himself. I have to decide in the course of the next two laps whether to take the lead or whether to follow. If I want to win this race I must go to the front and produce a sustained finishing burst over the last mile. But such a tactic will be foolhardy if I'm not confident of running the last mile in close to four minutes. If I don't attempt this tactic I might as well wait until the last lap sprint and risk my chances in the final headlong dash for the tape. Because if I don't take the lead this is what will surely happen, as I don't think anyone else will try such a gamble. We'll all be jostling and fighting flat out over the last 400m.

There is less than four laps left. I must make my decision in the next 45 seconds. I'm in third position behind Ngugi and Aouita. I feel tired and listless. I don't feel any sense of occasion or pressure, even though I have to make the most important decision in my athletic career now: to risk front running the race, or to wait and chance everything in the lottery of a final sprint.

I'll wait.

The noise of the crowd is increasing as the spectators anticipate the final act of this particular sporting drama. They have sat through ten minutes of minor scenes and only subtle alterations in plot. Now they want the grand finale. But I've decided that I shall be playing a supporting role, watching the action unfold and hoping to grasp glory at the end. I shan't be attempting the heroic conclusion.

Two and a half laps left and the fighting for positions begins. Pierre Délèze, the Swiss athlete, sprints past from the back of the field. I'm in fifth position. Half a lap later I'm sixth as one of the Castro twins races past. The two Castro brothers are both in this 5000m final. They are identical twins and I'm not sure which one has overtaken me.

I'm in a bad position for the last lap of the race, caught on the inside curve behind Ngugi who is obviously tiring. Other athletes are running on my outside and the field that was a long line of runners now becomes a tight group spreading across the width of the track, as we enter the finishing straight on the penultimate lap.

The bell – 400m left. Aouita sprints into the lead. Castro and Délèze follow him. I'm caught behind Ngugi and in the few vital seconds that it takes me to slow, step out, accelerate and pass the fading Kenyan, Aouita, Castro and Délèze are five and then ten metres clear.

It's too late for tactics. I must sprint harder and faster than ever before to catch three athletes who are moving further away from me with every stride.

Into the final bend. I'm making no impression. I can't catch them. I won't win a medal. I'm desperate to win a medal. Drive harder, faster. Aouita will win, Castro and Délèze second and third. The last 100 metres. Rousseau, a Belgian athlete, is on my shoulder. Come on, faster. I'm catching Délèze and Castro. Concentrate and sprint. I'm passing Délèze – bronze, now for Castro . . . too late – it's over.

Aouita has won. Domingos Castro, who I'd beaten by nearly ten seconds a fortnight previously, is second. I'm third. Délèze fourth. I'd overtaken Délèze in the final ten metres of the race to win a medal. (Later I found out that I finished closer to second than fourth. The final times were first, Aouita 13.26.44; second, Domingos Castro 13.27.59. Myself 0.15 seconds behind in 13.27.74. Fourth Pierre Délèze 13.28.06, 0.32 seconds behind me.)

I've won a bronze medal and turn round to congratulate Castro. As I wander over to him, Steve Ovett crosses the finish line. I don't know where he's finished but he looks awful, sweating profusely. He grimaces and we offer each other sympathetic noises of congratulation and consolation. The Castro twins are almost in tears, both delighted with their performances. I grin and join in the general bonhomie, my outward smiles masking inner frustration at losing silver. Aouita is jogging his victory lap. I see George and shrug my shoulders. I wander off down the tunnel. I am tired, my head still pounding from the exertion of the desperate final lap. Slumping onto a bench, I pull on my tracksuit surprised at how hot I feel. Ignatov, the Bulgarian runner, sits down next to me. He appears disappointed and, normally a friendly rival, barely exchanges a glance. A uniformed official pulls my sleeve. She is explaining that I must report for dope testing within the time limit. Fatigued, I ask her to repeat herself. My voice sounds incoherent and distant.

Ahead are the medal ceremony, dope testing, press reporters, TV interviews – all the paraphernalia of sporting success – but none of that matters as I sit exhausted inside the Olympic Stadium.

The race is finished. My challenge of the last twelve months over. All that hard work and the race was finally a disappointment. It was slow, scrappy and tactical. It didn't go according to plan and I hadn't performed to my expectations. But, on the other hand, at least I'd shown tenacity in a furious final lap and salvaged a medal.

Later Aouita described the race as 'as easy as sitting in a cinema'.

Shortly after the World Championships I met Gordon Pirie for the first time. I, like many others, admired and respected his achievements. He didn't bother with any social chit-chat. 'Why didn't you take the lead in Rome then?' And before I'd had the chance to reply, 'The more you've got rid of before the last lap the fewer you'll have to beat in the home straight' or words to that effect. End of conversation.

Later in the year I spoke to Brendan Foster. He put the same case rather more tactfully. How had I felt about my performance in Rome? Not especially pleased, was my reply. Foster's argument was that because I hadn't committed myself in the race, I'd spend the rest of my career wondering what might have happened. If I had taken the lead with four laps left at least I'd have found out. I might have blown up and finished sixth but I could be satisfied that I had tried my hardest and given everything.

One of the attractions of sport is that the participants are forced to make instant decisions. In some sports these decisions have to be made within fractions of a second. Should a batsman leave or play a delivery from a fast bowler? In football, the goalkeeper may have slightly more time to decide whether to stay on his line or rush out to meet the oncoming centre forward. In golf, there is even more time to decide upon which club to use in an awkward lie.

Part of the appeal of sport is that spectators, journalists and pundits can all comment, applaud or criticise the decisions the participants make. 'He should never have played that ball' or 'He'd have been better off using a sand wedge.' In Rome I was forced to make such a crucial decision in the last mile of the race. Should I take the lead or not? Should I attempt to run away from the best 5000m runners in the world over the last four laps of the World Championships or should I wait? I had the luxury of two minutes to reach my decision. It would have been foolhardy to take the lead from further than four laps out and not many top athletes can be dropped in the last two laps of a slow 5000m. At the time, when I was concentrating hard in the race I decided not to take the lead. I didn't feel strong enough. I thought it would have been a mistake and therefore I decided to wait.

George and I discussed the race regularly over the next few weeks. We'd spent most of the year planning for the World Championships. It had been the crucial race of the year, the culmination of months of hard training. George argued that if I genuinely felt incapable of making a decisive move in the race I was sensible not to commit myself. What a futile waste of effort it would have been to foolishly attempt to speed up the last mile in the World Championships and then trail home a distant sixth. In deciding to follow the slow pace I had salvaged a bronze medal. It had been an awkward tactical race, unsuited to my abilities, and yet I'd still finished third. It all hinges on how I felt during those vital two minutes on the track in the Olympic Stadium. I felt tired and uninspired so I waited. But perhaps any athlete, any sportsperson, feels tired and possibly frightened when faced with the major decision? Perhaps the hallmark of greatness is to ignore the tiredness and instead commit yourself completely to the challenge you face?

Postscript to the World Championships. 'These overblown athletic jamborees now carry far too many hazards and opportunities for abuse and are, in any case, fraught with too many doubts about motivation at the national and even the personal level to be remotely identifiable with the idealism that spawned them.' Hugh McIlvanney writing about this summer's Pan American Games, with passing reference to the Olympics.

In the 1987 Rome 'athletic jamboree' there was evidence that the 'opportunity for abuse' McIlvanney refers to existed, even if it was hidden behind the excuse of mistake or inefficiency. For example, there were insufficient entries for the men's 10,000m heats, so the organisers held the final at the scheduled heat time rather than a few days later at its allocated time in the original programme. This upset many of the competitors who were only informed the day before the race. The altered time, incidentally, allowed the Italian favourite Panetta much longer to recover between the 10,000m and the heats of his best event, the 3000m steeplechase. A fortunate coincidence, or deliberate manipulation of the programme to suit the host nation? Later in the week Evangelisti won a surprise bronze medal in the long jump to the delight of the crowd. Television replays clearly showed his supposed medal winning performance was significantly shorter than the measured distance. Had the officials deliberately exaggerated the leap? At a less important level, why was Aouita accompanied into the reporting room by his coach, unlike his fellow 5000m competitors? Were these all legitimate mistakes or examples of abuse?

On the positive side, the second World Athletic Championships was a purely sporting occasion free from the political connotations of the Olympics. Like the football World Cup, these Games avoided any controversy beyond the realms of sport. Already there is a body of opinion within athletics arguing that the World Championships are a more prestigious event than the Oympics because of their political immunity.

But where the two events differ is in their initial conception. The Olympics, as McIlvanney indicates, were based on idealism. The World Athletic Championships were not. The World Athletic Championships are a response to the 1980s not the 1890s. In today's world, the key words are marketing and television – not idealism. Primo Nebiolo, International Amateur Athletics Federation (IAAF) president, in his introduction to the glossy brochure about Rome '87, writes about 'fundamental landmarks of a gradual new promotional, organisational and technical evolution that will come to a head at Rome '87'.

Some of the products of this 'promotional evolution' for

Rome '87 reached the athletes. There was a bewildering assortment of key-rings, note-pads, stickers and pens all bearing the IAAF and Rome logos. These were presumably the items that journalists and sponsors had already received in abundance. The IAAF must have spent vast sums of money on promoting their World Championships. Most of the competitors would have forgone the glossy 'freebies' and settled instead for some respectable accommodation rather than the concrete jungle of the games village. But it is the 'freebies' that epitomise the promotional evolution that Nebiolo writes about.

Athletics has moved into the market place. As the sport has accepted the importance of television, sponsorship and business, so athletics is in danger of becoming divorced from its idealistic roots. There is a delicate balance between satisfying the demands of commerce and pandering to them. It is this balance that is so unsettled in athletics and could lead to further abuse in the sport.

But despite the importance of 'promotion', Nebiolo also mentioned in his address the certainty 'of unchanging realities in the tradition of athletics'. It is these unchanging realities that enable the sport to survive its move into the market place. The unchanging realities were illustrated in Rome by individuals such as Peter Elliott gritting his teeth in the 800m, Paul Kipkoech romping away in the 10,000m and Kostadinova setting a world record in the women's high jump.

The challenge of the sport remains the same. Whatever the arguments about politics and commerce the pure spirit of competition is at the heart of athletics. The World Championships were successful not because of skilful marketing but because of the athletes, those who ran personal bests and still did not make it through the qualifying rounds, as well as the medal winners. We athletes are far from faultless. Of course we want appearance money and our slice of the financial cake. The drugs problem also casts a deep shadow over the sport. But despite the current difficulties athletics is encountering, the healthy spirit of competition remains unchanged.

Next year, for many thousands of young sportspeople, the

challenge will be the Olympic Games in Seoul. It is the same challenge that has inspired sportspeople since 1896. Perhaps amongst the competitors at least, there is still some idealism left in sport.

2

The Last Races of Summer

September 8: Memories of Last Year. My arrival back in England after the World Championships has been very different from last year when I returned from Stuttgart after the European Championships. I had travelled to Stuttgart as an unfancied outsider in the 5000m. Steve Ovett, the recent Commonwealth Champion, was the British favourite for the event. Tim Hutchings and I, second and third in the Commonwealth Games respectively, were largely ignored by the media. The positive aspect of this lack of recognition was that Tim and I competed in Stuttgart without any pressure or expectation other than our own.

The 5000m was the final individual track event on the last afternoon of the Games. In the 1500m that day, Steve Cram outsprinted Seb Coe to record a British 1–2.

Immediately afterwards the 5000m began. It was a hot afternoon and I felt quietly confident. Steve Ovett had beaten me in the Commonwealth Games in early August when I had been recovering from a cold. Since then my fitness had steadily improved and I had cruised comfortably through the qualifying heats three days before. Unlike the recent Rome final the pace in Stuttgart was fast. A succession of athletes contested the lead, eager to stretch a strong field. The persistent tempo left a trail of casualties as the race sped towards its conclusion. Steve Ovett and Markus Ryffel dropped out. Pierre Délèze and Alberto Cova lost contact with the leaders. I worked my way steadily through the field. I was enjoying the fast pace and the crescendo of applause from the German crowd. Two laps left, and Tim Hutchings forged to the front, pushing on still faster. I followed and was aware that there were only a handful of runners left in contention. As the final lap began I took the lead. I glanced at the electronic scoreboard that was projecting pictures of the race and saw that only four of us had survived – Hutchings, myself, Ignatov from Bulgaria and Stefano Mei, the Italian runner who had already won the 10,000m.

With 300m left Mei strained to take the lead. He struggled past me and cut in sharply, forcing me to chop my stride. At that moment I knew I could win. Mei was using his fading strength to overtake me and would not be able to kick again in the finishing straight. I tucked in behind Mei conserving my energy for a final effort. Round the last turn. Sprint. The exertion of a year's hard work was concentrated into those brief seconds. I had run thousands of miles and all that mattered was this last 100 metres. I was alone, clear and accelerating down the last 100m. No one could catch me – I wanted those few seconds to last much longer. Forty metres from the finish I noticed the electronic clock on the infield. I realised that I could break 13.10 if I sprinted desperately for the line. In heady optimism I thought 'I'll break 13.10 another day'. Instead I decided to wave to the world and savour the brief moments of glory. Then, it was all over, I had won – European Champion.

The noise of the crowd intruded into my blissful trance. The vast stadium that fifteen minutes ago had appeared so remote and lonely was now full of friendly faces. The cheers and congratulations all rolled over me as I jogged a victory lap, deliriously happy. I did not feel tired, just intoxicated, the greatest high I had ever experienced. I spotted George waving in the crowd. I ran over to him and shook hands in a typically reserved British gesture. The rest of the day passed in a delightful reverie of congratulation. After my triumph the 400m relay squad obliged with a final gold medal despite the third-leg runner Brian Whittle losing his shoe. On the final afternoon, the British team won three gold medals bringing our total for the week to eight. The following day we returned to Heathrow to face an ecstatic welcome. Kerin and her father were hidden behind a posse of photographers.

There had been interviews and TV appearances. Britain's eight gold medals in Stuttgart had generated excitement and enthusiasm. Athletics was the sport of the moment. Victory in the Europeans had elevated me to minor sporting celebrity and with that accolade came the requisite trappings – *A Question of Sport*, dinner invitations, smart hotels and autograph requests. Overnight my life changed.

A year later and I have finished third in the World Championships. I suppose third in the world and first in Europe are comparable, but bronze doesn't have the same glitter as gold. I have returned home and there is not the same interest in my performance. The telephone answering-machine purchased after my Stuttgart triumph lies redundant. All journalists want to ask me is my opinions on drugs, not about my race in Rome.

Part of this general disinterest stems from the public perception of the World Championships. Last year in Stuttgart, the eight gold medals raised expectations for Rome. The World Championships were always going to be much tougher than the Europeans and Fatima's solitary gold medal appeared meagre after the glories of Stuttgart. This year, of Britain's eight European Champions, Seb Coe and Roger Black were injured, Linford Christie finished fourth in the greatest 100m ever seen, Fatima Whitbread won the javelin, I finished third in the 5000m, whilst the performances of Daley Thompson and Steve Cram in their respective events were disappointing. However there were other outstanding British performances in Rome. Fatima was the star of the show, but Peter Elliott and Jon Ridgeon won silver medals in the 800m and 110m hurdles, whilst John Regis and Colin Jackson came third in the 200m and 110m hurdles. Finally the 4 × 400m relay boys battled through for a silver medal, second only to an exceptional American quartet. So overall the British team performed as well in Rome at the second World Championships, as in the inaugural event in Helsinki.

But this time public expectation was much higher and the two athletes who have dominated their events for several years – Steve Cram and Daley Thompson – for once failed. Cram and Thompson have been the most consistently successful British athletes of their generation. They have been winning gold medals at the highest level for years. They are both entitled to the occasional lapse, but ironically their first major defeats have been simultaneous. If Cram and Thompson had won as I am convinced they will in the future, the British team's performance would have been loudly applauded.

So this year both my celebrations and those of British athletics are more muted. But, for me, the season is not yet over. Last year after Stuttgart I did not want to race. I had won the biggest race of my life and found it difficult to muster any enthusiasm for my final two races of the year. This year I feel different. I have been injured for much of the summer and I want a few more competitive opportunities before I go on holiday at the end of the track season. I intend to run another 5000m, a race in Lausanne and the Westminster street mile. After that, three weeks of complete rest, relaxation and gluttony.

September 12. An athlete's peak fitness is unfortunately a finite resource. It is like a bank account. All winter, whilst the athlete is training, deposits are being made into the account. Races are the athlete's withdrawals. The aim of training is to build up sufficient resources so that when the major events happen the account is at its maximum. An event like the World Championships is when athletes make their biggest withdrawals of the year. Not surprisingly, most athletes' accounts are now depleted and this is reflected in the general post-World Championship performances.

Last night's Grand Prix final in Brussels illustrated how tired most athletes were. The exceptions were athletes who had been disappointed with their performances or had not competed in Rome. Tonie Campbell, the American 110m hurdler who missed out on Rome because of the savage USA trials system – automatic selection for the first three, tough luck if you fell over – beat the World Champion Greg Foster. Campbell had something to prove and was fresh, Foster did not and was tired. For the supposed highlight of the Grand Prix season, standards were pathetic. In the 5000m the winning time was not as fast as the World Championship qualification mark. So why do athletes run in these meetings? The answer is that although athletic bank accounts are low athletes are all prepared to scrape together the final dregs of fitness to boost real bank accounts.

Tomorrow I am running in my final 5000m of the season at Crystal Palace. I would like to win and run a respectable time to round the season off. If my performance in Rome had been more satisfying I would not feel this urge to run. My motivation is therefore partially athletic but also partially financial. The subvention money from Sunday's race will boost my trust fund for the forthcoming winter. If next year a situation arises when I need some money to go abroad and train, or to cover medical bills, I shall be able to rely upon these end of season earnings. I will not have to race half fit or injured in order to pay 'athletic' bills.

A few years ago George and I decided that athletic considerations would always take precedence over financial considerations in planning my racing strategy. The challenge to today's athlete is to use the current commercial opportunities available in the sport to enhance performance rather than to bankrupt fitness. I have turned down dozens of lucrative races in order to concentrate exclusively upon my preparations for the most important events. Many times this year it has been much more important to keep depositing training sessions than to withdraw through races. Athletes must find their individual balance between training and racing. The recent danger facing the sport has been that athletes would ignore the traditionally important events and chase the dollars, resulting in an overall decline in standards. The classic example of this is the USA road racing circuit. Most USA distance athletes have over-competed in lucrative 10kms and half marathons. In Rome, the only American to win a medal at a distance event was Jim Spivey with a bronze in the 1500m.

Fortunately many British athletes have remained primarily athletically not financially motivated. In Britain standards are continuing to improve assisted by the money that is now available in the sport.

September 13: 5000m, Crystal Palace. Today the weary athletics circus gave its final London performance of 1987. The small crowd indicated that it is not only the competitors who are exhausted. This year Crystal Palace has hosted the Peugeot-Talbot Games, the AAA (Amateur Athletics Association) Championships, the IAC Classic, the Dairy Crest event and finally the McVities meeting. Five international athletics meetings at Crystal Palace in one summer are too many for athletes and spectators alike.

It is only a week since Rome, but jogging around the warm-up area before this afternoon's 5000m I felt like an actor preparing for a performance in a half empty provincial theatre just after he has left Broadway.

At the World Championships there was a sense of occasion. Everyone from spectators through to officials and athletes knew that this was the pinnacle of the athletics year. The event was sufficient motivation to performance. Even though my own effort was lacklustre, I was better prepared both physically and mentally in Rome than for any race since the previous year's European Championship 5000m. After such an occasion there is inevitably a period of anti-climax. I had hoped that I could partially compensate for my dissatisfaction with the result in Rome by a reasonable race this weekend. But this afternoon post-World Championship depression was clearly evident. My physical condition was the same as in Rome a week earlier, but my mental condition was not. I felt as little enthusiasm for the

McVities 5000m as I do for my second run of the day on a wet Saturday afternoon in February. I was lacking in interest and inspiration. An athlete needs to feel nervous before a race. This pre-race anticipation is an important aspect of competition. The aim is to arrive at the start line sufficiently 'on edge' to produce your best performance. In Rome the problem was to keep the adrenalin under control. At Crystal Palace I found it difficult to summon any pre-race nerves.

But, at this afternoon's meeting there were athletes who had not run in the World Championships and who were hungry for success. Some were recovering from injury or had not been selected for Rome, whilst others had trained hard throughout the summer and were now in peak condition and ready to challenge their more illustrious rivals.

Mid-way through the 5000m I realised that there was someone on my shoulder who was better prepared for the confrontation than me. Gary Staines is a talented young London runner who spent much of last year training in Australia. He returned to England in July, thinner and fitter than ever before. He beat me over two miles at Gateshead when I was recovering from injury and then finished second behind me in the AAA Championship 5000m running 13.30 to my 13.25. Unfortunately the World Championship team had been virtually decided. Gary Staines watched Rome on the television and continued to train.

I took the lead early in this afternoon's race, trying to exorcise the memory of the previous week's decisive indecision. Staines followed me and the two of us gradually extended our lead. On the basis of our previous encounters I should have beaten Staines comfortably but his motivation was greater than mine. As we circled the track all the thoughts that athletes should never think buzzed through my mind. 'This race is unimportant, I've won a medal in Rome, I'm tired, it doesn't matter if Staines beats me, who really cares? Once this is over my season is virtually finished, I'll let him win, I'm not bothered . . .'

Staines overtook me with about 1000m left. I let him pass

and then reversing our roles dogged his footsteps. At the bell I went into the lead and gradually drew away over the final 400m. My time was 13.17, the fastest 5000m at Crystal Palace for six years, whilst Gary Staines ran 13.20, improving his personal best by ten seconds.

It was a relief to win. Tomorrow I travel to Lausanne for a 2000m race.

September 14. Lausanne is rife with rumours. It is impossible to walk through the hotel without overhearing the latest gossip about the meeting. The event 'HQ' is situated in the hotel lobby adjacent to the coffee shop. There is a notice board displaying the start times and lists of the competitors in all the events. Tracksuited athletes discuss pace-makers and winter training plans, whilst agitated managers wait impatiently for the latest press releases and argue about airplane tickets.

These are some of the rumours circulating in this fertile environment. Ben Johnson is to receive $30,000 for running in the 100m. Carl Lewis wants to race in the 100m also, but Johnson does not want a repeat of their epic clash in Rome. Johnson is insisting on running a separate 60m leaving Lewis to run the 100m. But the story is that Johnson still wants his full appearance fee for the 60m. Billy Konchellah, the World Champion at 800m, does not want Tom McKean in his race. McKean, furious with his dramatic failure in the Rome final (he finished last), has already beaten Konchellah at Crystal Palace. Konchellah wants McKean to run in the 800m 'B' race. John Bicourt, who is organising this race for McKean, insists that Tom competes in the 'A' race against Konchellah. Eventually it is agreed with the meeting promoters that Konchellah will race McKean, but Lewis and Johnson will be in separate races. In my 2000m race, Steve Scott, who is dissatisfied with his current form, will act as pace-maker. The 2000m is five laps of the track and Scott is intending to pace-make to the mile mark (four laps). What sort of pace will he set? The rumours circulate wildly. Some say 3.58, others 3.54 and quicker. My personal best for 2000m is 5.02, equating to a mile time of 4 minutes. It is the end of the season, and I cannot believe that the eventual time will be much quicker than 5 minutes, so I discount the 3.58 and quicker figures.

A final rumour: Ben Johnson has apparently spent $10,000 on a watch.

September 15: 2000m, Lausanne. Unlike Crystal Palace, the Lausanne stadium was packed. In Switzerland, athletics is the major summer sport and the crowd is always vociferous. Firstly they voiced their disapproval for Ben Johnson when he ran in the 60m. Johnson was loudly booed before and after his inevitable victory. There was no prize ceremony for the 60m. By contrast Carl Lewis received the loudest ovation of the evening when he ran and won the 100m. Tom McKean outsprinted Konchellah in the 800m, and I suffered for ignoring the 2000m pace-making rumours.

As Steve Scott shot off I drifted lackadaisically to the back of the field. I was confident that nobody would run fast and that my patience would be rewarded. After a couple of laps I was still near the rear and the pace was not slowing. I started to speed up and so did everyone else. I had not run that fast all year, and it was exhilarating. The crowd were rhythmically clapping in time with the runners. They were seeing a world-class race. Steve Scott dropped out after four laps. The mile split was 3.54 for the leaders, 3.56 for me. It was a frantic last 400m with Peter Elliott and Jim Spivey alternating in the lead as I desperately tried to catch them.

Spivey won in 4.52.5, Elliott second in 4.52.8, I was third in 4.53.06. The times were astonishing. Spivey had broken the American record whilst only Steve Cram amongst British athletes had run a faster time than Peter Elliott and myself. Peter Elliott's performance will shock the world's 1500m runners. Elliott, the Rome 800m silver medallist, has shown his stamina and potential at a longer distance. He is an exceptional 800m runner but is vulnerable over two laps when the pace is slow. However, his 800m speed will make him a highly effective finisher at 1500m. He will now have to decide whether to concentrate his training for next year's Olympics on his established event, the 800m, or where his potential indicates, the 1500m. If Peter Elliott trains without injury for the next twelve months he has the ability and tenacity to challenge anyone in the Olympic 1500m final.

And as for me – my first personal best of the summer, an improvement of nine seconds over 2000m – I should not complain, but I wish I had started quicker and taken the pre-race rumours more seriously.

September 20: Road Mile, London. The City of Westminster street mile sponsored by Peugeot-Talbot takes place on a Sunday afternoon in late September. It is part of a 'family day out' organised by the City of Westminster. There are a series of road races around a one mile loop course for runners of all ages and abilities. Then there is an international women's mile race followed by the international men's mile race. Later in the afternoon is a cycle race for professional riders. The two street miles and the bicycle race are covered by television.

At the press conference I attended earlier this week Cliff Temple, journalist and athletics coach, asked a question of Andy Norman, the director of the British Athletics Promotions Unit. Some friends of Temple had decided not to attend Sunday's street mile because last year spectators could not see very much of the runners as they raced around the streets of Whitehall. This year, the course was the same and once again spectators would only see the competitors briefly on the one mile lap. Cliff Temple asked if, bearing this in mind, it would be correct to say that Sunday's event existed primarily for television. Andy Norman's reply was that it is important for athletics to be part of an occasion. Sunday would be a day out for the family and the street mile would be one aspect of an afternoon's entertainment.

'Street miles' are the runners' equivalent of tennis players' exhibition matches or golfers' pro-ams. In serious athletic terms they are meaningless. Street miles are 'promotions', not genuine athletics. This does not mean that the athletes do not try their best to win. The race itself is competitive but the result is unimportant. The race exists as a promotion. Cliff Temple's point about television is correct. Without television and sponsorship an event like the Peugeot-Talbot Westminster mile would not take place. The street mile concept is popular because it satisfies the criteria for marketing athletics in the 1980s. The television producers like the idea because two one mile races, plus interviews, plus shots of the City of Westminster makes a neat 30 minute programme. The sponsors like the idea because they will receive 30 minutes of publicity on TV and coverage in the newspapers. The City of Westminster like the idea because spectators will watch the races and there will be extensive media interest. The athletes like the idea because we are well paid. Street miles are popular with everyone but they should not be confused with track athletics.

This afternoon the whole marketing/promotions exercise passed off without any problems. It was a glorious sunny late September day. There were large crowds of spectators and participants. Races had been in progress most of the morning and many of the runners had stayed to watch the international street miles. Adults who had competed earlier in the day were enjoying picnics with their families. There was a cheerful, relaxed and healthy atmosphere around the course. Youngsters rushed around collecting autographs of the stars. One of the benefits of an event like the Westminster street miles is that the international 'stars' mingle with the public. Peter Elliott and John Walker, while jogging around the course, were regularly accosted by autograph hunters and well-wishers. They and all the other runners were prepared to oblige all requests for pictures, smiles and signatures. There are very few sporting occasions left where there is such direct contact between the leading participants and the fans. I bumped into Dave Moorcroft who was posing for some pictures with a team of runners who had just completed their event. Dave is one of the most popular athletes amongst both his peers and the running public. Everyone admires his ability, integrity, but above all his tenacity in overcoming a succession of dreadful injuries. He is the ideal personality to appear at the Westminster street miles and was, not surprisingly, surrounded by enthusiastic runners asking advice and wishing him well. In this congenial atmosphere it was once again difficult to prepare mentally for competition.

The race itself was a personal disappointment. I finished eighth, or it could have been ninth. I lost count as I performed a 'dying swan' act in the last 100m. In trying to remedy my slow start at Lausanne earlier in the week, I was determined to stay with the leaders from the start. I managed to maintain my position for about three quarters of the race, but as we turned the final bend from Northumberland Avenue into Whitehall I could sense the wave of faster and stronger 1500m runners about to engulf me. Peter Elliott won the race in a course record of 3.53.6, an exceptional time and further proof of his abilities at the longer distance. I ran somewhere between 3.56 and 3.57 which is not too bad for a lumbering carthorse of a 5000m expert.

I did overhear some complaints of spectators who hardly saw the runners during the race, but overall the promotion was a success, not only because of the competition but also because of the rapport between participants and spectators. Unlike his parents, little Freddie will not mind if he has not seen much of the race when he can go home with the autographs of Peter Elliott, John Walker and Dave Moorcroft.

Kerin and I left Westminster with some friends as a Peugeot-Talbot car with the two winners, Peter Elliott and Kirsty Wade, was whizzing around the course, lights flashing. The cyclists were preparing for their appearance later in the afternoon. My season is over at last.

3

Inside Running

October 13: The Athlete's Life. Fat and unfit, the countdown for Seoul starts today. After my end of season break I have now resumed training. We returned to Loughborough last weekend and I have just been out on a tentative jog around the University campus, my first run for three weeks.

At the end of every track season I take a minimum of two weeks' complete break from the sport. During that time we go on holiday, relax, eat whatever we want and I completely forget about the sport that dominates my life. This year we walked in the Lake District. It was peaceful, quiet and invigorating. Our usually disciplined diet was ignored. I consumed large amounts of the foods I always crave: chocolate, cheese and ice-cream. This year I have managed once again to put on about twelve pounds in the space of a month.

It is important to completely relax at the end of every track season. The training demands of the sport are so intense that unless I had some period of time when I can escape, I could not maintain the dedication that is necessary to succeed in athletics.

For eleven months of the year I am training intensively. Most days of the week I train twice. Occasionally I will have a rest day. The training is hard and never-ending. Training also dictates how you spend the rest of your life. If you are running seven or eight miles every morning, followed by another training session in the evening, you are demanding a considerable commitment of time and energy. Brendan Foster, in his biography, explained the situation of the demands of training perfectly:

> 'For, if we are talking about any athlete who wants to be an international, then I would say that you have to accept that their life will be planned around their training and not the other way round. The regularity and the quantity of it is so important that it has to take precedence if you are ambitious.'

The implication from this is that if you are committed to becoming a top international runner your life revolves around running. That does not mean you cannot work, cannot go on holiday or cannot go out for a couple of drinks. You can indulge in all these pursuits but only if they fit in around your training. Even our one holiday away from athletics has been dictated by the demands of training. The timing of the break has to coincide with the two weeks of the year in early October when training is not so important.

Today, the prospect of several months' routine, steady and progressive hard training does not appear very enticing. I feel like a cross-Channel swimmer who has gingerly tested the sea with his foot, and finds the water cold and uninviting. I do not want to resume the spartan regime of training, but I know that I have already accepted the challenge and have to plunge in sooner or later.

October 16: My daily plod has gradually extended from 30 to 45 minutes. Within a few weeks, a 45 minute run will become my routine morning activity. It will be an everyday feature of life slotted in between opening the post and breakfast. Currently, running for 45 minutes requires a significant physical effort but soon I shall be training twice every day, and the morning run will be the easy session.

Just as in Brendan Foster's time, the demands of training are great. But I and many other athletes have an advantage over our predecessors. In recent years a new generation of athletes has emerged. They or rather we are self-employed, often under the title of 'Sports Consultant'. We are, in fact, full-time athletes dependent upon our running successes to finance our houses, cars and general living expenses. But we are still amateurs according to the rule book. Our lifestyle is possible because of the way athletics has changed over the last ten years.

Interlude: Towards A Professional Sport? In 1977 Brendan Foster was at his peak; Daley Thompson a promising young decathlete; Steve Ovett an outspoken, brilliantly talented 800m runner (fifth place in the 1976 Olympic final); and a youngster called Sebastian Coe had surprised the athletics world by winning the European Indoor 800m. For the record, the 1977 intermediate boys' English Schools 1500m at Hendon was won by a tall lad from the north-east, S. Cram, with a J. Buckner knocked out in the qualifying round in a time of 4.07.9, for fourth place.

The World Championships had not been invented and competitive opportunities for international athletes were limited to the AAA Championships, a series of boring international matches, and the occasional European meeting outside the major games. But during the 1970s changes were afoot. The International Athletes Club organised a meeting at the end of every summer sponsored by Coca-Cola. The 'Coke', as the event became generally known, was the most popular meeting in the British athletic calendar.

Brendan Foster wrote about the 1974 Coke meeting in his biography: '. . . traffic was jammed for miles around. An estimated 18,000 spectators watched the athletics that night, far more than the stadium held comfortably and a long fence on the back straight collapsed under the weight of people climbing on to it to try to get a sight of the competition . . . that evening was the first of the great "atmosphere" meetings, which must have been what it was like at White City stadium in the early fifties . . . suddenly athletics was a booming sport again . . .'

The 'Coke' heralded the invitation meeting where athletes from all over the world were invited to compete. Gradually invitation meetings would improve and replace the regular two and three sided international matches that were of limited interest to the general public. I can recall watching my first international meeting at Crystal Palace during this period. It was the UK versus Finland, a two day meeting. The stadium was virtually empty, the races slow and dull. The highlight of the two days' competition was when my coach, Jeff Millar, who was an official, accidentally walked through the freshly raked long-jump pit.

The Coke meeting, Brendan Foster's own events at Gateshead Stadium, and the Southern Counties promotions at Crystal Palace supplanted the dull pattern of British athletic fixtures. As cricket was revived by one-day knockout competitions so athletics was revived by the invitation meeting. Spectators, sponsors and television were much more interested in seeing world record attempts with pace-makers than some unpronounceable Russian throwing twice as far as British athletes in the discus.

Whilst these changes were taking place in the organisation of athletic meetings, the performances of British athletes also began to improve. In the 1976 Olympics in Montreal, Foster had won Britain's only athletics medal, a bronze in the 10,000m, but before the next Olympics in Moscow, British athletics was to undergo a remarkable transformation primarily as a result of two runners – Sebastian Coe and Steve Ovett. In 1978, Steve Ovett proved himself the best 1500m runner in the world. He followed up his 1977 World Cup victory with a gold medal in the European Championships and then with a marvellous victory over Henry Rono in a two miles at Crystal Palace. The two miles was the highlight of that year's Coke meeting. Rono had rewritten the distance record book that summer, and had tried desperately to break away from Ovett throughout the final stages of the dramatic race, but Ovett hung on and sprinted away over the last 100m to the delight of the crowd.

The following year, the mantle of the world's greatest runner was snatched from Steve Ovett and placed upon the shoulders of Sebastian Coe. In the space of forty-one days, Seb Coe broke world records at 800m, 1500m, and one mile, stunning the athletics world and creating one of the greatest sporting rivalries. Coe versus Ovett did not take place until the 1980 Olympic Games when Ovett won the 800m and Coe the 1500m. Unfortunately their two confrontations in Moscow were the only occasions that these two great runners raced each other at the peak of their prowess. But during the years 1979–81 when they were both regularly setting world records, once in different events at the same meeting, athletics dominated the summer sports pages.

I gained my first junior international vest at Meadowbank in 1980. It was the day of the Moscow Olympics 800m final and the competitors for the Junior Boys' 1500m, the final track event of the afternoon, were left in no doubt as to where the officials would rather be. 'Hurry up,' I was told, 'it's Coe versus Ovett in under half an hour.' My race (I was second) was the final event of the meeting and was followed by the inevitable parade and speeches. All the athletes and officials were assembled impatiently on the track. I cannot remember whether the dignitary addressing the ranks of athletes actually managed to finish his speech or not, but as the time for the great race drew near we all began to edge towards the exit. Suddenly the trickle of athletes leaving the arena became a flood as all the competitors and officials rushed for the television room. Only the band was left behind to conclude the ceremony. I do not know if the various dignitaries managed to view the Moscow 800m, but they certainly would not have found any vacant seats in our television room.

The Coe–Ovett story and the opportunity to watch exciting competition in Britain transformed athletics in this country. There were increased opportunities to race and the standards improved. Daley Thompson and Allan Wells also won gold medals in Moscow. Steve Cram emerged from being a talented junior to a potential world beater. The sport with its healthy, trouble-free and friendly image attracted more and more interest.

At the time of the next Olympics in 1984, the BBC's exclusive television contract to cover domestic fixtures expired. Instead of the usual renewal, ITV bid against the BBC. The contract was effectively auctioned to the highest bidder. ITV offered £10.5 million over five years. Athletics had become a wealthy sport. There was another auction at about the same time to determine which marketing company should be responsible for 'selling' the sport and attracting sponsors to athletics. Alan Pascoe Associates, the company headed by Alan Pascoe, the former 400m hurdler, won this particular auction. APA had to guarantee the sport a minimum of £750,000 a year for five years. After three years the company had surpassed their total five year guarantee.

In the 1986–87 tax year television income received by the AAA was £2,100,000, and sponsorship income was £1,716,053. One of the tasks facing the AAA since 1984 has been to satisfy the demands of television and the sport's sponsors. Alan Pascoe Associates and the AAA have between them had to provide the usual requirements of sponsors such as advertising hoardings, television visibility, press coverage, tickets to the meetings and hospitality. A small example of this task has been the intrusion of a sponsor's marquee onto some grass near Crystal Palace stadium that has traditionally been used by the athletes for warming-up. Whenever there is a big meeting at Crystal Palace this marquee appears, to provide hospitality for whoever is sponsoring that evening's event. As it is summer, a quaint lattice fence encloses a drinks area in front of the marquee. Sponsors and their clients drink champagne and watch the athletics on TV monitors whilst we athletes, our usual warm-up area invaded, jog around the discarded bottles behind the marquee. Such minor inconveniences are worth tolerating when one considers the benefits athletes have received from the influx of money into the sport.

In order to satisfy the demands of television, the AAA had to ensure that Steve Cram, Seb Coe, Steve Ovett, Zola Budd plus any other Olympic medallists and athletes who rank in the world top fifty of their event, participate in the televised British meetings. Therefore large amounts of the newly created athletics wealth have been spent on 'athletes' subventions'. Thus the legacy of the invitation meeting and the Coe–Ovett years has been the British Athletic Promotions Unit (headed by Andy Norman), subventions, and finally trust funds.

The British Athletics Promotions Unit (BAPU) was set up by the AAA to ensure that sufficient British and international stars attended the events covered by ITV. In the last tax year subventions expenditure of the AAA was £1,264,244, including £411,744 carried over from last year. International athletes do not come cheap.

It is these subvention payments that permit athletes like myself to pursue our chosen careers as full-time sportspeople. But, in order to maintain the amateur status of athletes with all this money floating around, another development in the continually changing structure of British athletics has been necessary. When it became obvious that athletes were benefiting financially from the increasing commercialism the IAAF introduced 'athletic funds'. According to the IAAF rule book (Rule 17, paragraph 2), 'the funds must be held, controlled and administered by a Member Federation. The Member must establish regulations for the administration of the funds, which must comply with the IAAF rules . . .' Therefore the British Amateur Athletics Board (BAAB) looks after any financial rewards British athletes receive from the sport.

Any subventions that an athlete receives are placed in an athletic fund managed by the BAAB. The athlete can draw upon this fund to cover a variety of expenses such as 'sports equipment and clothing, insurance to cover illness, costs of medical and physiotherapy treatment, the services of a coach as well as accommodation, food, transport, education and professional training' (BAAB pamphlet: *Money and Athletes*). If an athlete has more than £5000 deposited in the fund he or she has the option of establishing a Trust Fund. When a Trust Fund is established the BAAB appoint two trustees and the athlete one, thereby observing the amateur rules of the sport. The sport maintains control of the money until the athlete retires. But there are a variety of investments that the Trustees of the fund can make on behalf of the athlete such as pension plans. The athlete can also have a mortgage based upon his or her fund. Income tax is payable upon the fund and athletes have to be registered for VAT like any other small business.

There are other regulations concerning the administration of the funds, such as the BAAB deducting a percentage of commercial contracts, but the essential point is that athletes can remain amateurs whilst earning money from the sport. Only some of the money can be used by the athlete whilst he or she is competing, but sufficient amounts may be available to enable an athlete not to seek work or draw unemployment benefit. I can have a mortgage, draw general living expenses, and buy a car from my athletic earnings (a legitimate purchase from the fund), yet I can compete in an amateur sport that bears little relation to amateur athletics of even ten years ago.

I have given a broad summary of some of the recent changes in athletics. These changes are far from complete and as I write there are further political developments in British athletics. I have not outlined the intricate relationships between the AAA and the BAAB nor the anomaly that exists between the governing body, the BAAB, with its debts, and the AAA, a constituent member, with its large profits.

Regardless of these continual internal wranglings in athletics my career has blossomed at exactly the right moment to take advantage of the opportunities currently available. In 1985, during the first year of the ITV contract, I began to perform better than ever before. The first race that ITV covered was the AAA Kodak 10k road race at Battersea Park in early April. The favourite was Steve Jones, who was competing in the London marathon the following weekend. I had just returned from a successful visit to the USA and I outsprinted Jones over the last kilometre to win.

Afterwards, I was quite happy to wait for a quarter of an hour on a chilly afternoon without a tracksuit, for the obligatory post-race interview, as the technical hitches were overcome. Unfortunately, though, my actual performance was of less interest than that of ITV. But for the next ITV road race, an International Athletes Club promotion in Cardiff, I was offered a subvention of £1500. It was my market value, based on my previous 10k victory at Battersea Park. At that point in my athletic career I was still naive about the financial opportunities available in the sport. £1500 seemed a large sum of money for running a single 10k road race. But once I considered how I had persevered in athletics for so many years without any financial reward, such a payment was justifiable. My subvention fee was also insignificant when viewed against the sums earned by my more illustrious competitors.

Later that spring I had a meeting with Andy Norman, the director of BAPU, who offered me, based upon my world ranking, £500 for each of eight British track meetings that summer. I could earn £4000 in one summer, more than I had earned from competing in my entire career.

I sat down with my coach, George, and discussed the proposals. We decided that although the financial inducement was attractive I should be selective about where I competed and avoid the perennial trap that so many athletes fall into – overcompeting. Together we organised my racing schedule for the summer of 1985 and looked forward to the athletic rewards first, the financial rewards second.

A week before my first subvention meeting I tore the ligaments above my left ankle whilst on a training run, and only raced once more in 1985. Such are the tides of fortune in sport!

Subsequently I have avoided the potholes of the woods around Loughborough and my running career has fared better. Victory in the 1986 European 5000m guaranteed me a substantially improved subvention for 1987. I realised my performances in 1986 had elevated me several categories in the eyes of meeting promoters and sponsors, but I was stunned for several days when a figure of £7000 per domestic fixture was revealed. I was like the characters in the Tom and Jerry cartoons whose eyes light up with '$' signs. £7000 was the subvention available to all the British European Champions, apart from those like Steve Cram and Fatima Whitbread who were paid significantly more. Was such a payment justified? It was much more than I had ever received before, and in excess of what, at the time, I would have expected. On the other hand, I was the second best 5000m runner in the world. Also, any career in sport is both short-lived and insecure. The £7000 subvention was my reward for the past, and insurance for the future.

Before the summer George and I once again carefully discussed my plans. My running requirements have always been given priority over financial inducement and this year was no exception. Temporarily, I may have been blinded by the prospect of a large subvention, but when the season arrived, I concentrated upon reaching the World Championships in peak condition regardless of my bank balance. I did run in some of the £7000 meetings, but declined the opportunity to earn the subvention as often as I accepted it.

Not surprisingly, it has been the subvention payments that have attracted as much attention as performances since 1985. The political and financial machinations of the sport have provided excellent copy, especially during the winter months when a controversy over how much athletes are paid makes a more interesting story than who won the National Cross-Country Championships.

In 1988, it appears that the athletics/money story will provide its usual quota of news items. There are already indications that the 1987 subventions were too much and there will be 'substantial cutbacks' in 1988. A familiar sounding phrase, and one that we athletes are going to hear much more often in 1988 than 1987.

October 24: Back to Training. After the hectic events of the summer track season, normality is returning to the Buckner household. My aim at this time of year is to re-establish the running routine and keep that pair of precious limbs moving as frequently as possible. Every morning I stretch and exercise for about three-quarters of an hour before embarking on a prolonged plod of between seven and eight miles around the University campus. Later in the day I repeat the exercise, occasionally with more vigour than in the morning.

Unfortunately athletics training does not remain this simple for long. Once I am running regularly twice a day, all sorts of complications appear in the training regime. On Monday evenings there is a weights and sprint drills session. Tuesday and Thursday evenings are track or road workouts. Wednesday evenings a circuit session in the gymnasium, and Saturday mornings the activity that ruins the entire weekend, hill runs.

Although I am a full-time athlete I do not train harder than many other equally committed but less fortunate runners. My training schedule is identical to many full-time students and employees living in and around Loughborough. But because I am a career athlete I can spend longer ensuring that I can train better. So whereas most runners have developed a routine of rising early and training before work, I have the time to complete a more leisurely morning workout. I can eat, stretch and exercise before I run in the morning. My morning run usually starts after 9am, by which time most runners are at lectures or work. Likewise, with my afternoon training session I do not have to wait until 6.30pm, the usual time for Tuesday and Thursday workouts, if it does not suit my own plans.

All this training came as a shock to my wife Kerin during the first years of our marriage. Before we met she took little interest in sport. We were students at the time and running was very much a hobby to be fitted in around work and the pleasant social whirl of University life. Gradually my relationship both with Kerin and with running became more serious. When we were married I was on the fringe of international athletics. Kerin has had to endure all the tensions and drama of living with a committed athlete. To her credit she has accepted the demands of the sport even when this means personal inconvenience. It would be impossible for me to run at the highest level without a supportive and understanding wife.

Another advantage of running full-time is that if I am injured I can arrange appointments at the physiotherapist's immediately, and when necessary, on a daily basis. If training is especially hard I can rest during the day. Basically I am able to organise my life around running rather than squeezing running in around a career. The danger is the temptation to over-train. As I have extra time available I could introduce more training sessions in the continual quest for improvement. In my opinion, though, it is more important to recover adequately between training sessions. The activity of twice a day training is very demanding. I have the opportunity to relax during the day and this should enable me to train at a much higher quality. Once I stopped working I noticed that my morning runs became quicker. Previously the first fifteen minutes of any pre-9am run were completed in a semi-somnolent state. Now, I run much more quickly and smoothly at a later hour.

But the opportunity to be a full-time athlete is not without its problems. In most careers outside sport, the salary awarded to an individual will be directly related to their standing, and the amount of time invested in that career. If you work hard and regularly, the chances are that your salary will be commensurate with your efforts. Most people's career path follows a logical and gradual progression, with increasing financial rewards. Not so in athletics. My training may be improving and my life is inevitably more organised around athletics, but that is no guarantee of increased success. Anyone who relies upon sport for their career is taking an immense risk. All sports are full of ghastly stories of injury and disaster. It is feasible that I could lay all the foundations for outstanding performance, with years of dedicated toil, only to have the fruits of success snatched away by the injustice of a torn hamstring muscle. I could be in the form of my life only to twist an ankle jogging in the woods around Loughborough, as happened to me in the summer of 1985. If an athlete is unable to compete, there will be no subvention money and large physiotherapy bills. Suddenly an athlete can make a big breakthrough and the financial rewards are immense. Just as quickly, injury can strike and the athlete is left with nothing for all the months of sweat and tears. A career in athletics, as in many other sports, can contain immense excitements and opportunity as well as the depths of despair.

Today's full-time athletes have more opportunity than our amateur predecessors, but the pressures inevitably have become greater. I have chosen this career but must also accept the risks associated with that decision. Besides the shadow of illness or injury that continually lurks in the back of most athletes' minds, there will also come a time when performances deteriorate through the ageing process. What happens when I am in my early thirties with very limited work experience and few job prospects? The future beyond sport is very uncertain. Once the old legs pack in, it will be difficult to resume an alternative career. My college friends are now mostly established in some form of regular employment, but not me. Ideally I would find a part-time job. My perfect job description would be as follows: 'Hours of work 10am to 3pm, no physical exercise required, as much time off as necessary, summer hours dependent upon competition programme, good prospects and a substantial rise whenever injured.' Somehow I do not think I am going to find that elusive job.

These concerns are enforced whenever I am injured. Then all the fears about my future become especially acute. My thoughts follow a depressing pattern: 'I'm injured so that means limited income, when will I be fit again? What happens if I never recover from this injury? Perhaps I'd better start looking for a proper job . . .' Before long I am searching the newspapers and writing out my CV. So far (touch wood) my injury frustrations have not led to any genuine job applications.

When I recover fitness all these concerns evaporate. There is no career that could provide me with the same tension, excitement and satisfaction as athletics, except perhaps batting number three for Somerset and England. Unfortunately I have long given up any hope of achieving that particular ambition.

The one activity that enables me to survive injury without resorting to the job centre is that I, like many international athletes, receive assistance from a sports shoe and clothing manufacturer. The athlete will act as a consultant to a particular company perhaps providing information and advice on shoe development. In return the company will supply the athlete with free kit and possibly some sponsorship. I have such an agreement with a shoe and clothing manufacturer. In the USA where money is subject to general debate, the magazine *Runner's World* has published lists of how much leading athletes earn. But in Britain the whole area of shoe contracts has not been publicly analysed.

My work involves me in various promotional activities for the company. These are usually trade shows, exhibitions and runners' clinics. I have found it enjoyable and interesting work. I hope the experience will help when I am forced to hang up my spikes. Without the support of an equipment manufacturer I would be forced to race much more often than I would choose. I can afford instead to concentrate on the major championships. The most important aspect of my consultancy is that the company do not interfere with any of my training and racing commitments. It is fully understood that my priorities are on the track. My promotional involvement has been limited to off-season activities, leaving me free during the summer.

The lifestyle I lead is becoming closer to that of the professional sportsperson than at any period in athletics history. I am one of a new breed of sportspeople benefiting from changes in the rules. I can pursue a full-time career in athletics yet remain a participant in an amateur sport.

4

The Winter Work Begins

October 27. 'The greatest fallacy of the lot, however, is people's tendency to say "it must be great to be fit!" You never feel fit when you are training hard, so in all honesty there is not a great recommendation in international running to keep you sprightly, wide awake and active all day in the same way that there is for recreational running and jogging.'

Another quote from Brendan Foster's book, neatly summing up my current physical state. It was a book that inspired me during my teenage years. Little did I realise at the time how much truth there was in his advice about training. My recent experience confirms his comments: international runners never feel fit and healthy. I am permanently tired from training and never want to engage in any physical pursuit other than my sport. Runners are the world's worst gardeners, decorators and shoppers. The only time when I feel healthy is when I am out training. There have been many occasions when drained and exhausted I have staggered out of the front door only for a complete transformation to occur. Suddenly my body wakes up and I am full of strength and enthusiasm. I bounce along refreshed, enjoying my daily dose of running. Partners and spouses of international runners should be given a warning:

your companion is hopelessly addicted to running and this will be a continual source of amazement and frustration to you.

This commitment to training is one reason why there is such a good comradeship between runners. At the end of every race there is rarely animosity between competitors. We respect each other because we all realise how hard our rivals have trained. I know as I am training on the frosty mornings in Loughborough that Tim Hutchings will be running around Wimbledon Common, Pierre Délèze training in Switzerland and the Castro twins running together in Portugal. All over the world my potential adversaries in Seoul will be clocking up the miles, struggling with injuries and trying to achieve their overriding ambition of athletics success. That kind of dedication inevitably leads to respect and perhaps that is why, beyond the fierce desire to win that exists at the moment, there will be a time in five or ten years when we retired athletes may feel closer to each other in some respects, than to many friends and companions whom we see on a more regular basis.

November 2: The Coach – George Gandy. In September 1980 I started a three year BSc degree in geography at Loughborough University. I had decided to attend Loughborough University because of its excellent sporting reputation and the influence of the athletics coach, George Gandy. During my first year at the University I managed to avoid the athletics track as much as possible, embarking instead upon some of the hedonistic pleasures available to undergraduates. Fortunately, I managed to prevent myself succumbing permanently to the various vices that would have threatened my development into an international athlete. At the start of my second year at Loughborough I approached George Gandy and asked him to coach me.

Six years of coaching later, Loughborough has become my home. I originally imagined myself spending the three years whilst I was attending the University concentrating on my running and then leaving to find a career in the big wide world. Instead I have married and settled in this East Midlands market town and have no desire to leave as long as I am an active athlete. It is George Gandy's influence and advice that made Loughborough an attractive environment for running.

George is a biomechanics lecturer at the University. He was described in *Running Free*, Sebastian Coe's book, as 'a tall, dark, sardonic humorist, a man whose rolling glances from behind heavy rimmed glasses, occasionally gave him the air of a Balkan spy in a Bond thriller'. After that description, any further comment is impossible.

Besides lecturing, George is the coach and driving force behind the University athletic and cross-country squads. He has been the man responsible for making these Loughborough teams the 'Liverpool' of student sport. In recent years there have been innumerable student sports victories making Loughborough the most respected, and in some quarters the most reviled, athletic University in the country. Additionally, George has coached a variety of international athletes including Graham Williamson, a 3.50 miler, and Chris McGeorge, World Student Games 1500m champion in 1985.

During the six years that he has coached me my running has continually improved. When George began advising me my personal bests were 1500m – 3.41.7; 1 mile – 4.02; 3000m – 8.20; and 5000m – nothing. This autumn they are 1500m – 3.35.2; 1 mile – 3.51.5; 3000m – 7.40.4; and 5000m – 13.10. I hope I can improve as much over the next six years.

During the initial years of our relationship it was George's presence beside the track that was most important. My knowledge of training methods was limited and his experience showed me what specific training was necessary for me to improve as a runner. But as my performances have progressed, training sessions have become second nature. I have learned how to train effectively and what work is necessary to produce successful results on the track. The job of the coach has changed beyond the traditional image of holding a stopwatch and shouting encouragement.

It is no longer essential that George attends all my training sessions. His presence is always useful but his role has broadened, encompassing all aspects of my running career. Once a month we discuss long-term strategy as well as immediate training requirements. These monthly conferences have more in common with business meetings than with shouting out 400m splits, but the plans we develop are, we hope, the key to my continued success in athletics.

We had our first 'winter meeting' a few days ago. The objective of the next eleven months does not have to be mentioned. It is so obvious, the Olympic 5000m. We had a prolonged post-mortem on last summer. Good progress has been made, with satisfactory but not outstanding results. We analysed the current position – training resumed reluctantly but without any problems. Next the main item on the agenda, winter strategy. This year unlike the previous two winters when Kerin and I have travelled to the USA, we intend to brave the British weather and stay in Loughborough. I want to continue with my Monday weights workout and Wednesday evening circuit session until April. In previous years whenever we go abroad these extra activities are quickly forgotten under the pretence of lack of facilities. If I winter in Loughborough I can train around my favourite haunts and there will be no excuse to miss circuits and weights. We will have to keep our fingers crossed about the weather and be prepared to fly south like migrating birds, should the snow arrive in sufficient quantities to make running around the streets of Loughborough a hazardous activity.

Finally, George and I discussed races. Last year I raced on average once a month over the winter. Both George and I feel it is essential to avoid over competing outside the track season. Athletics, like tennis, cricket and golf, is a global sport. It is no longer confined to the summer months and there are opportunities for the top competitors to travel abroad and race in exotic locations most months of the year. In Europe there are road races and cross-country races most winter weekends. During January and February the show-business style USA indoor circuit is in operation. February is also the month for a series of lucrative road races in Florida. There are increasing opportunities to race in Japan, and finally how can any international distance runner resist the opportunity to race over 10k in Bali, on April 3, with a first prize of $30,000?

Unfortunately I shall not (to Kerin's disappointment!) be pursuing any of the above. This winter I shall once again race sparingly. If you are serious about competing on the track, winter races should be used to assess fitness rather than to achieve results. Many athletes are exhausted by July from their winter globe trotting activities. We shall be using the occasional race as an indicator of how my training is progressing. Races can therefore be stepping stones towards my ultimate objective.

At this stage it is possible to sketch in a few tentative plans bearing in mind that they may be scrapped through illness or injury as has happened before. Such pessimism is an ever-present element in George's and my discussions. I will not race before Christmas but on December 27 there is an 8k road race in Switzerland. I came second in the Zurich Silvesterlauf last year and enjoyed the experience of racing around the city streets spurred on by a large vociferous crowd, even if they were all encouraging the eventual winner, local athlete Pierre Délèze. Also a race over Christmas will prevent too much festive indulgence.

Last year I ran the Midland road relays in March and the Kodak AAA 10k road race in April. I would like to compete in both again in 1988. These events will leave me looking for a couple of outings in January and February to complete my winter plans.

Looking further ahead to the summer, the big problem will be gaining selection for the British Olympic team. Rumours are circulating amongst the athletic fraternity that the BAAB are intending to scrap pre-selection. The policy of pre-selection has proved very successful throughout the 1980s but following media criticism of the British team's performance in Rome there is pressure to change the selection procedure. As usual, the athletes will hear nothing but rumours, until the oracle, or rather the selection committee, announces its decision. There is a BAAB meeting in December when the policy will be determined. In the meantime, George and I shall express our opinions to those few members of the selection committee who we hope may listen to the views of a humble athlete and his coach.

The first athlete/coach discussion of the winter ended with exhortations from the latter that it was about time I put in my first, long overdue appearance at the Wednesday evening circuit session. The athlete reluctantly agreed and promised that tomorrow night he would arrive at the gymnasium ready once again to display his inept rope-climbing abilities.

November 7. The twice per day training regime is re-established and slowly my winter's training is gaining momentum. From now on I shall be regularly attending the weights and circuit sessions. Within the next couple of weeks I might venture back on to the track.

I am reluctant to attend the Tuesday night track sessions before I have achieved a reasonable level of fitness, as the workouts can become competitive. Every year a crop of talented runners begin courses at the University. These youngsters throw themselves enthusiastically into all the athletic club training sessions. Eager to prove their ability, sedate workouts become races and the poor oldtimers like me recovering from my post-season binge are blown away by the exuberance of youth. The annual danger facing newcomers to the Loughborough athletics scene is to become fit by December and injured by March. The art of surviving winter training is patient progression.

I may moan about all the hard work necessary in athletics, but it is a lifestyle I would never change through choice. The training is hard, but the enjoyment of running on a clear crisp autumnal morning easily compensates for the physical effort required. It was my childhood dream to pursue a career in sport and I am fortunate so far at least to be achieving that aim.

It is only since my victory in the European Championships in 1986 that I have been able to accept running as a legitimate career. Until that momentous 5000m I regarded my running as an extended adolescence, an opportunity to earn some money for what I would willingly do for free. I assumed that sooner or later I would knuckle down to the serious business of earning a living and running would return to its place as my obsessive diversion from the real world.

My victory in Stuttgart changed all that. I am now gratefully reconciled to a career in athletics. I can now accept that my once part-time hobby is currently a lucrative profession. But in accepting running as a career there has been a subtle change in my mental approach to the sport. Training is my work, racing my pay day, injuries an occupational hazard. My lifestyle has become even more oriented around running. Sometimes this seems an unhealthy development.

November 21. Saturday morning – hill session. During winter the two are inextricably linked. At 10.30am I jog over to Thorpe Hill and wait impatiently for the rest of the training group to arrive. They are always late and I am always eager to complete the session so that I can enjoy the rest of the weekend. We jog down the hill, turn round and endeavour to sprint back up it. The session is ten or twelve repetitions of this demanding activity. The first Thorpe Hill session I ever attempted was after a particularly robust party on Friday night. I turned up tired and hungry, dreading the forthcoming session. For the first repetition I was hanging on to the back of the group, but on the second, a transformation occurred, I felt tremendous. I stormed up the steep incline as if it did not exist. I completed all twelve repetitions like a fleeing gazelle. Nobody could keep up with me. Unfortunately my subsequent performances on Thorpe Hill have never matched that initial workout. Perhaps it is because I now train harder during the week or perhaps I should return to late night parties on Friday nights.

November 25: Life on the Fringe. Last night I received a rude reminder of my current level of fitness. I attended the Tuesday night track session, six repetitions of one mile with a 100m jog in between each run. I was dropped off the pace after the third repetition and struggled to complete the session. Although it is always disheartening to be comprehensively destroyed in a training session, I am, underneath my immediate dissatisfaction, quite pleased with my running. It is impossible to maintain a high level of fitness throughout the year. There have to be peaks and troughs in an athlete's performance. The best time of year to be unfit is now, when the track season is several months away. Hopefully in programming my low period for the autumn I shall find it easier to reach my peak at the Olympics.

Currently there are some fit athletes in Loughborough. Amongst those who thrashed me last night was Adrian Royle, a talented road runner who came to live here a couple of years ago. He ran some outstanding performances in the USA in the 1980s. Since then he has struggled through a depressing catalogue of injuries and illness. At last he is beginning to reach full fitness. He could surprise the running world this year.

Adrian is one amongst many who are attempting to emerge into the athletics limelight. He has tasted the fruits of success and is fighting hard to regain his former status. Searching for the elusive breakthrough into the big time is a frustrating experience for any athlete. I spent some years as one of the nearly-made-it gang who existed in the twilight zone of international athletics. This is a world of small shoe contracts, difficult decisions concerning employment and scratching around for the performances necessary for elevation into the first division of athletics. 'Twilight zone' athletes have the same demands of training and competition but their results are not quite good enough to provide the subvention monies and sponsorship necessary to finance life as a full-time athlete. Middle-distance runners whose personal best is about 3.56 for the mile, sprinters who finish seventh in Grand Prix meetings and virtually all field event athletes provide examples of this existence.

For some, the twilight existence can be a frustrating apprenticeship to an athletic career. For others it can result in the premature retirement of an outstanding talent. Patience, luck and fortitude are all required if the athlete is to emerge into the spotlight. The athlete will face many difficult decisions. The hardest usually concerns employment. Most twilight zone athletes are looking for that elusive part-time desk job.

My first minor escape from the twilight zone occurred in 1982. I had just completed my second year at Loughborough University so had not yet confronted the daunting prospect of employment. I had been waiting for an opportunity to compete in a fast race. My problem was familiar to many promising young athletes – I needed a fast time to ensure race invitations, but I would never record a fast time unless I was invited to an important race. It was a Catch 22 situation. Then in July, George informed me that he had managed to secure an invitation to run in a mile race in Cork, although I would have to pay my own airfare. The quality of the competition would be outstanding – Maree, Walker, Cram, Wessinghage. I had never broken four minutes for the mile and this would be my big chance, but first I had to find £130 for the airfare. A penniless student, my father bailed me out, and I was off to Cork. The race was perfect. The pace was fast and regular. I simply followed a group of the world's leading milers the entire four laps of the track. I finished eighth but my time was 3.53. I had broken the elusive four minute barrier by seven seconds. At the time it was the biggest margin by which anyone had broken the four minute barrier for the first time. The Cork mile was a turning point in my athletics career. Since that day I have never had any problems in obtaining race invitations.

My performance in Cork provided me with the incentive to try and pursue an athletics career. But, suppose my father had not been able to pay my airfare. How much longer would it have taken me to achieve the much needed breakthrough? After Cork I did suffer setbacks and problems – a hip stress fracture in 1983, a long quest for part-time employment later that same year – but I never again doubted my running ability. Four years after Cork I completed my progression from talented junior through the twilight zone to European Champion.

Now in the autumn of 1987 I am one of the fortunate athletes. I compete in a popular event at a time when the sport is at its zenith. There are dozens of promising athletes throughout the country in a similar position to mine before Cork. They are seeking satisfactory jobs that give them time to train and compete. They are trying desperately to gain an invitation to the major meetings and they are not sure whether to commit themselves to an athletics career.

I sometimes wonder if more could not be done to help aspiring youngsters in the sport. Perhaps one of the companies that sponsor the athletic invitation meetings could start a scheme of part-time employment for talented athletes. The company would give the athletes time to train and compete abroad, whilst at the same time providing useful work experience for the future. These part-time jobs would be an immense service to British athletics. This could be a more sophisticated form of sponsorship than staging yet another international fixture in an already overcrowded season.

When I left University I naively wrote to most of the companies sponsoring athletics, wondering if there might be the chance of such a job for me. I did not receive a single encouraging reply. Older and wiser I would not attempt such a rash route these days (fortunately it is no longer necessary). I now realise that what matters to most sports sponsors, is how many times a company's name appears on the television and in the newspapers, not how many young athletes can be helped in their careers.

December 16: The Olympic Selection Debate. A few weeks ago, after my discussion with George, and as rumours were rife throughout the athletics world concerning the likely selection policy for the British Olympic team, I sent the following letter to *Athletics Weekly*:

> Dear Sir,
>
> How is a selection policy judged? This time next year we will all be discussing the Seoul Olympics and looking at how well or badly the British team performed.
>
> The verdict on the Seoul performance will depend on how many medals the team wins. Any Olympic selection policy

must therefore be aimed towards producing the best results in South Korea.

If, for example, the British team won no medals in track and field, after adopting the first past the post system of selection, nobody will applaud the selectors on their adoption of a simple and fair policy.

No, the verdict on the British selectors and their policy will depend upon the numbers of medals won in Seoul. Consequently the selectors must decide which policy to use to produce the best results.

The selectors' options vary between two extremes. One would be to use the USA first past the post system: one trial date, everyone competes, tough if you fall over, first three gain automatic selection. At least everyone has the opportunity to make the team – very fair, but it does not produce the best results. The USA are perhaps the only country in the world with the athletics resources to survive such a system. There is so much strength in depth in USA sprinting that the team can afford to be without Calvin Smith in the 100m and Tonie Campbell in the 100m hurdles.

But look at the conspicuous lack of success amongst the USA distance athletes in Rome and Los Angeles.

The other extreme would be massive pre-selection with only a handful of places left to be filled next summer. This would give little opportunity for currently unestablished athletes to qualify for the British team.

The selectors must opt for something between the two. A policy that ensures the best results whilst giving opportunity to everyone.

Unfortunately that is impossible, but there is no harm in trying.

The current front runner appears to be the first two from the AAA/WAAA Championships plus A. N. Other, with no pre-selection. In my opinion this policy is too close to the USA system and will not ensure the best results in Seoul. Pre-selection has proved a successful policy throughout the 1980s. Unfortunately, in the post World Championship debate, athletic pundits have ignored the achievements of Moscow, Los Angeles and Stuttgart where pre-selection was a contributory factor to British success.

I was pre-selected for the 1987 World Championship team. During July I missed three to four weeks' training with a hamstring injury. If I had not been pre-selected for Rome I could have been forced to resume training before the injury had healed in an effort to qualify for the World Championships. Fortunately I recovered, ran in the AAA without excessive pressure and then gained a medal in Rome. If the proposed policy for 1988 had been in operation this year I might not have made the British team for the World Championships.

The advantage of pre-selection is that it enables athletes to prepare exclusively for a major championship without the additional pressure of qualifying. But it is controversial. The danger facing the British selectors for the 1988 Olympic team is that they will ignore the achievement of previous European Championships and Olympics and base their policy upon the results in Rome, where some pre-selected athletes did not perform to expectations.

My suggestion for a selection policy is as follows:

(1) Pre-selection for all medal winners in the 1987 World Championships, provided they prove their fitness prior to the Olympic Games.

(2) The opportunity for all gold medallists in Stuttgart to gain selection by showing good form prior to the AAA/WAAA Championships in 1988.

(3) (i) In events where there are still three places available at the time of the AAA/WAAA in 1988 following 1 and 2, the first two at the AAA/WAAA would be selected, the third place being allocated according to the selectors' judgement.

(ii) In events where there are only two places available following 1 and 2, the winner of the AAA/WAAA would be selected, the third place being allocated by the selectors.

(iii) In events where there are only two places available

following 1 and 2, the first place would be decided by the selectors taking into consideration the AAA/WAAA results.
(4) I'd pick Daley Thompson automatically for the decathlon.

This is a complicated policy, loaded with controversy. What happens in the men's 800m? Peter Elliott and Seb Coe can gain selection leaving only one place for Steve Cram and Tom McKean. What about the 100m hurdles with Ridgeon and Jackson pre-selected? However, any genuine selection policy will cause controversy.

The role of the selector is to make the hard decisions based upon his or her knowledge and expertise. Anyway, it is not the controversy that is important, it is the results in Seoul.

Yours sincerely,
Jack Buckner

Last night at the beginning of the BBC Sports Review of the Year, several officials arrived late after their meeting to decide the selection policy. Athletes and officials mingled later at the reception. It quickly transpired that the following policy had been decided – no pre-selection, the first two past the post in the AAA Championships in early August will automatically be selected for Seoul, the third spot in the British team will be chosen by 'selection'.

The reason I and other leading athletes are opposed to this policy is because it will directly affect our preparation for the Seoul Olympics. The Olympics take place at the end of September. This is very late in the year for athletics. I have explained previously the importance of an athlete attaining a peak at the Olympics. Because the standard of British athletics is so high athletes will be forced to peak for the trials in early August and then peak again seven weeks later. It will be difficult for anyone who produces their best performance in the trials to repeat it in Seoul. The other problem with the selection policy is that as far as I am aware there are no let-out clauses. So if one of our top athletes falls over or is injured at the time of the trials – bye bye Olympics. For example, in the 800m, Peter Elliott could rely on a fast early season run to secure the third selection place. Tom McKean might be injured in early August and therefore unable to run the trials. According to the current policy only one of these potential medallists would go to Seoul.

As I indicated in my letter, the selectors have ignored the successes of the 1980s and concentrated instead upon the events of Rome. If Steve Cram and Daley Thompson had won I am sure the selectors would never have abandoned pre-selection.

Tonight's decision will affect my plans for next summer. I was hoping to prepare for the Games without reaching full fitness until the Olympics. I did not want to race intensively early in the season, preferring to wait until nearer the Games. The 5000m is likely to be one of the hardest races in the AAA Championships. Assuming I qualify for the British team, I shall then have the problem of maintaining form until the Olympics themselves.

There is a final twist to the selection saga. The AAA and WAAA Championships is now going to become the most crucial event of the summer outside the Olympics. The three days of the joint Championships at Birmingham will have widespread media coverage. Even if many of the competitors are unhappy with the selection policy, ITV and the sponsors Kodak will be delighted.

December 17. Yesterday a large consignment of kit arrived from my sponsors. I have been pestering them for the last couple of months to replace my increasingly threadbare supplies of running clothing. At this time of year the weather and my high mileage means that the household washing machine and tumble drier are in constant use. All the splashing around campus and pounding of Loughborough streets have taken their toll upon my grey sweatsuits. Grey is probably the most suitable colour for running clothing. It is inconspicuous and washes easily. Grey also matches the weather.

But everything changed yesterday. The parcel I received revealed an assortment of brightly coloured clothing that has never before graced the running routes of Loughborough. No more inoffensive, dull grey jogging suits. In future I shall be ploughing through the mud in pastel shades of yellow and peach. Bright red, blue, white, and green colours will shock the Loughborough running community. Last night I ventured down to circuits in a bright new jogsuit. The assembled athletes in their dingy tracksuits and faded T-shirts were horrified. 'Shouldn't you be doing aerobics?' was one of the more polite suggestions.

Unfortunately, the majority of athletes are not really fashion conscious. The great fitness fashion boom has passed us by. We all turn up to the club house in our mud splattered comfortable old wetsuits. We are tough, seasoned athletes, not trendy keep-fit fanatics. My flashy colours and innovative designs are going to cause something of a stir amongst my training partners. Somehow all these bright colours do not correspond with the image of the archetypal distance runner. Sprinters can get away with loud, figure-hugging tights because they are fast and flash. Coaches can wear tracksuits with Great Britain emblazoned on the back because it gives them prestige. Determined stoical distance runners should wear drab unpretentious outfits that reflect their dedication, not pastel co-ordinating jogsuits. Perhaps it is just that runners are ten years behind the trend. In 1997 when grey jogsuits and faded T-shirts become fashionable, all the runners will be wearing hot pink.

December 22. I keep a training diary. Every run is methodically recorded together with an appropriate comment. The diary has become an obsession. A few years ago I made the fatal mistake of noting my weekly mileage. In the top left hand corner of the page a number is entered, 70 or 75–80. My weekly mileage has over recent years assumed an unnecessary importance in my training. Until I started recording my mileage, it did not concern me. Now I have to run at least 70 miles per week in order to satisfy my diary's demands. It gives me untold pleasure to flick through the weeks and see a succession of weeks over 70 miles. I glance through the months and imagine all the endurance gained, all the extra strength and all the additional fitness. My training diary is kept with a religious fervour. It is concrete evidence of a lifetime's running. All my strategies and experience are recorded within the pages of the diary. I would rather lose all my medals than my training diaries.

There are two entries that I am loath to write in the diary: 'Rest day' and 'injury'. A rest day can ruin the entire week's detail. My neat rows of '30–35 minutes steady' and '45 minutes – feeling tired' are ruined by the two stark words rest day. My weekly mileage figure, the sacrosanct 70, can be jeopardised by rest day. An injury is even worse. Entire weeks can be devastated as the ugly word is scrawled day after day. The whole pattern of the diary is broken, weekly mileage becomes meaningless, the structure of my training diary is threatened.

I have made serious efforts to reduce the stranglehold my diary can place upon my running. I tried unsuccessfully to stop including the weekly mileage figures. For a few weeks I managed to leave the space reserved for mileage blank, but withdrawal symptoms rapidly set in and the 70 or 75–80 was quickly restored to its rightful position. Recently I have managed to realise that a rest day does in fact benefit my running even though it interrupts the diary's relentless thirst for training information. Gradually my training requirements have gained the advantage over the diary's requirements. I can now view the occasional week of 60 as productive rest.

As the quantity of my winter's training has increased and the weeks have passed, so the volume of diary entries has grown. The last couple of months make satisfying reading. Several weeks 'over 80', plenty of 'weights' and 'circuits' entries. Admittedly, there was a '40' in November when I caught a cold, but since then the pattern has been unbroken: 85, 70, 85–90, 80–85, 85 – good solid stuff. The entries reflect my improving fitness. A few weeks ago I was struggling on the Tuesday night track sessions. The diary entries were accompanied by comments like: Tuesday November 24, 'worked very hard, struggled after the first three reps, feel unfit, heavy, uninspired and sluggish, back to the grind, shattered afterwards'. But by December 17 a more promising picture emerges: 'good effort after a hard week's training, felt comfortable and strong, best session of the winter so far'.

The winter has started solidly. Nothing spectacular, no outstanding fitness, just regular steady progress towards next year. Christmas and New Year should be only slight hiccups in the continual flow of diary entries. On December 27 I shall be running in an 8k road race in Zurich. Last year I came second to Pierre Délèze. It was the result the Swiss organisers wanted. The European 5000m Champion from Britain beaten by the local superstar. The crowd were delighted. As we raced the final lap through the packed city centre the chanting and ringing of cow-bells reminded me of the downhill skiing. 'Allez Pierre' on every street corner. No 'Allez Jacques'. Appropriately, Délèze won an enormous cow-bell. This Christmas I do not think I am as fit as I was in 1986. Still the Zurich race is not that important. Whatever happens it will be a useful indication of my current state of fitness. I am aiming for a medal next October, not a cow-bell to ring in the New Year.

5

Clocking up the Miles

December 27: Road 8k, Zurich. Heathrow was crowded with skiers on Boxing Day. I had not realised that the day after Christmas was so popular with holidaymakers. George and I joined the throng heading for Switzerland. The skiers were disappointed with the weather, I was not. Zurich was warm and dry, with no snow visible except on the peaks of the surrounding mountains. Last year the race, called the Silvesterlauf, had been run in sub-zero conditions. This year the city was bathed in warm sunshine.

The course is three laps of a circuit through the city centre. The lap can be divided into two sections – one a straight stretch along the river bank, the other a twisting route around shop fronts and cobbled streets. As spectators pack most of the route there is an exciting atmosphere for the runners racing through the crowd, along narrow streets, beneath grand old buildings.

In Zurich the local favourites are Pierre Délèze and Markus Ryffel. These two Swiss athletes enjoy a popularity in their native country far greater than any British athlete does in the UK. In Switzerland athletics is the main summer sport so Ryffel and Délèze are, apart from the skiers, the most celebrated sportsmen in the country.

In last year's race, fresh from my European Championship victory, I had ignored any tactics and led from the start. Confident and cocky, I was outsprinted by Délèze. This year with a sore calf and a lack of racing since this summer I began more cautiously. I followed the leading group for the first lap and during our second circuit of the city centre gradually closed on the leaders. Ryffel and the Austrian athlete, Hartmann, were alternating in front. Their combined efforts reduced the leading group to six runners. As we began the final lap, Ryffel continued his surging, but I sensed an air of desperation in his attempts to reduce the pursuing pack of athletes.

We crossed the river for a final time. I followed another of Ryffel's bursts and continued the acceleration, running hard along the straight stretch of river bank. I felt fresh and strong. These are the moments that every athlete trains for: a warm afternoon, a competitive race, a large, loud crowd and that exhilarating sensation of gradually extending a lead over your rivals. I knew I had won the race before I completed the final kilometre through the cobbled streets. I was able to coast the final section, prolonging the enjoyment of victory. Baccoche from Morocco was second, with Scotland's Nat Muir third, his best performance since an Achilles tendon problem wrecked his summer season.

Afterwards, like Délèze the previous year, I was awarded an enormous cow-bell. It was slung around my neck and the following day my picture appeared in the papers, flowers in one hand and head bowed down under the weight of the cumbersome bell. When I phoned Kerin later that day, I did not have to tell her I had won the race. The loud clanging down the telephone line was sufficient evidence of my result.

The cow-bell now resides in splendour in the Buckner home. We have not decided what we are going to do with it, although it was a major topic of family discussion over the Christmas–New Year period. Various suggestions have been made. A doorstop is the most practical: hanging the cow-bell on the front door would not be a sensible idea.

December 29. My performance in Zurich has provided a boost to training. I seem to have done nothing but grumble about running throughout the autumn. I did find it harder than usual to resume training in October and initially progress was slow, but now I am back in the groove and ready to face the rest of the winter.

I always enjoy running during the week after a good race. There is a spring in my stride as I look forward to improving fitness and new levels of performance. I was surprised at the ease of my victory in Zurich. My time was a new course record, and although I won by only four seconds I had relaxed over the last kilometre. The Zurich Silvesterlauf was also my first race for three months, whereas most of the other runners had competed more regularly since the summer. If I can win my first race of the winter campaign all the indicators are positive for next year.

Enough self-congratulation. Kerin and I are off to Pembrokeshire tomorrow for a New Year's house party. Our family group of brothers, sisters and respective partners have rented a cottage near Haverfordwest. Prolonged New Year celebrations and bracing cliff walks are the plan for the next week. Limited steady running will be permitted, but nothing too serious.

January 5, 1988. Since my last entry a week ago I have not run a step. The winds on the exposed Welsh coast were gale force rather than bracing. As soon as we arrived in Pembrokeshire I caught a heavy cold. I do not think the wind dropped below Force 5 all week. Fortunately the farmhouse where we stayed possessed a large open fire and every evening we thawed out in front of it after our daily battering by the elements. I spent most of the week muffled in layers of clothing, a scarf and balaclava. We returned to Loughborough this morning. I ought to be feeling better after a complete week's rest from running. Usually my colds only last a couple of days. A week off is ridiculous (and more than the diary can stand). I shall try a thirty minute jog tomorrow morning.

January 6. I started running again today. There was considerable debate between Kerin and myself about the importance of rest and complete recovery before resuming training after illness. I maintain that I am fit enough to ease back into my training schedule, Kerin disagrees. I went for a thirty minute splash around waterlogged Loughborough. Verdict: felt OK. My usual problem, impatience to resume training, must be kept under control. But in my favour I am sure that the psychological effect of starting training again helps me believe I am better, and thereby dispels any lingering germs.

January 8. One of my plans for the winter was to visit Seoul. I wanted to experience the time change and visit the proposed British pre-Olympic training camp in Japan as well as Seoul itself. I have never flown to the Far East before, and if I ran a race approximately a week after my arrival I could see how I had recovered from the flight. Last October this seemed a good idea. I approached Alan Pascoe Associates who contacted *The Times* and Minet, an insurance company who are sponsoring British athletes in their Olympic preparations. It was arranged that I would write some articles for *The Times*, appear in Minet sweatshirts for pictures and my trip would be paid for. I was only awaiting the final arrangements for the race in Japan.

Information at the Japanese end has taken some time to arrive. Meanwhile I have spoken to various reliable sources who have visited the Far East and have found out most of the relevant information I hoped to obtain on my trip. I have also lost about two weeks' proper training because of my cold. Suddenly a trip to South Korea in February, and the further interruption to training this would involve, does not appear so sensible. The problem is that I have now involved APA, *The Times*, Minet and a friend in the USA who organises some of my overseas races. All like the idea and want it to progress. Now I must inform everyone of my changed mind. My original excuse was lack of information about the race in Japan and that problem has now been resolved.

It is a classic dilemma facing a committed athlete. In favour of the trip are good publicity exposure, writing articles for *The Times* and the opportunity to widen my horizons beyond the running track. Against the trip is my training. It is the confrontation of my running versus the promotional activities associated with running. It is my personal objectives against the assistance I have received from others in arranging a project I initiated. In deciding not to go, I shall be letting people down who may be reluctant to help me in the future.

But I do not really have much choice. Athletics is a selfish sport, and this is one of those decisions that any serious athlete occasionally has to make. Sometimes it is a case of not attending functions, other times not helping in the home. Dedicated athletes are always letting down others for the sake of their sport. I am not looking forward to the telephone calls I shall have to make in the next few days. I shall feel awkward and clumsy about my behaviour. But my training as usual has to come first.

January 10. Once again I have messed up my return to training after illness. I have been making the same mistake ever since I started running. I always start running too soon after an injury or a cold. This time I rested for an entire week, but it was not long enough. Kerin told me that I had not recovered sufficiently but as usual being a stubborn athlete (with a diary obsession) I ignored her advice. I should know that it is better to rest for an extra couple of days than to return to training too soon. I ran for four days at the end of last week, feeling heavy and sluggish. My cold has returned worse than ever. If I had been sensible I might have avoided further illness. I am resigned to several more days' inactivity. It serves me right!

At least these problems have confirmed my decision not to visit the Far East. Today I informed all the interested parties about my decision. The phone calls were not as bad as I expected. APA were most understanding and appreciated where my priorities lay. They are used to athletes being awkward. In the delicate balance of sport and promotional activities, it helps that APA, the company responsible for marketing British athletics, is headed by Alan Pascoe, a former international hurdler, who knows what life is like as a sportsperson.

January 14: The Drugs Debate. In the summer of 1984 I shared a room with David Jenkins. It was at the same Cork city sports where two years previously I had made my first big breakthrough in athletics with a 3.53 mile time.

David Jenkins was reaching the end of his long career as one of Britain's most successful sprinters. He had a reputation as an amiable but neurotic athlete and even relatively inexperienced runners like myself had heard stories about 'Jenks'. Apparently he was so nervous before his races that he could not pin his number onto his vest. Once, unable to sleep the night before a race, it is rumoured that he did a track session in the early hours of the morning.

He was pacing around the room of the Cork hotel when I walked in. Jenkins was full of good natured advice. I lay down on my bed as he continued to wander, folding tracksuits, commenting on the sport, hanging up clothes, checking the windows. He seemed unable to keep still for more than a few seconds. He pulled a bathroom bag out of his holdall and unzipped it. The bag was full of bottles of pills. 'Vitamins,' Jenkins exclaimed. 'They're good for you. Have some.' He started opening various bottles and throwing tablets onto my bed accompanied by comments such as 'vitamin C keeps you strong, vitamin D good for your bones'. By the time he had completed his monologue on vitamins there was a pile of about twenty different tablets on my bed. 'No thanks' I said, and made some comment about trying to eat a healthy diet.

Three years later and Jenkins is accused of masterminding an anabolic steroids ring that holds 70 per cent of an estimated $100 million illegal drugs market in the United States. The charges encompass such offences as conspiracy to smuggle and distribute steroids, illegal importation of anabolic steroids and other prescription drugs, and numerous counts of aiding and abetting these actions. It makes me wonder whether the vitamin tablets that were thrown onto my bed in Cork were all as innocuous as I thought at the time.

Since the summer season, the main preoccupation of the British athletics press has been drugs. Whilst I was competing in Rome I had no idea of the impact Carl Lewis's drug accusations were having on the athletics world. When I returned from Rome with a bronze medal and the only question reporters asked me was 'What are your opinions on drugs?', I began to feel irritated. Throughout my athletics career I have never had any direct contact with drugs unless, in the current drug-obsessed climate, that episode with David Jenkins is considered to be one. I had returned from Rome as one of the few British medal winners and the press were not remotely interested in my performance. All through the first half of the winter the situation has been the same. A reporter rings up: 'What do you think about the latest drugs scandal?' Never a question about my training or athletic ambitions.

The problem is that nobody knows how widespread the use of drugs is in athletics. For example the articles that have fuelled the current controversy have been a series in *The Times* by Pat Butcher and Peter Nichols. The second of the three articles included 'evidence' from Dave Abrahams, a former high jumper. He alleged that on the plane back to England from the 1982 Commonwealth Games in Brisbane '. . . most of the English team were talking about drugs. I'd say 80 per cent of them were, or had been on them.' I know the majority of the English athletes who attended the 1982 Commonwealth Games. It is complete and utter nonsense that 80 per cent of them were on drugs. I would find it difficult to believe that even 10 per cent of them were on drugs.

The danger in the athletics world is that anyone can accuse another athlete (especially if he has been beaten by him) of drug taking. Cliff Temple summed up the situation perfectly in a recent article in the *Sunday Times*:

> 'For when any group of athletes get together in hotel and airport lounges, or on long journeys, the conversation

> inevitably revolves around a limited number of recurrent topics: injuries, money, training and now drugs. You can picture the scene. "Well of course you know why Fred didn't compete in Prague don't you." Nudge, nudge. Wry smiles. Knowing looks. Actually, no real idea. Do they mean drugs? I'd never have guessed he was on them.'

In Stuttgart at the 1986 European Championships everyone was talking about the Italians and blood doping. Alberto Cova, the world's leading 10,000m runner, had apparently admitted in an Italian newspaper that he had been blood doped. (Blood doping is the term used for the removal of a pint of your blood and its subsequent replacement after a period of training, during which time the body has already replaced the amount of blood removed. The increased red blood cell count from this simple operation boosts the oxygen carrying capacity of the blood so that the muscles are supplied with more oxygen and can work harder.) The Italian team had finished 1st, 2nd, and 3rd in the men's 10,000m. Throughout the village stories were circulating about how the Italian Athletic Federation condoned blood doping and even made it compulsory in certain events. Once again these were rumours. Perhaps some were true, but the point remains that rumours can be based on very flimsy evidence. Furthermore, if you, as an athlete, spend the vital days before a major championship worrying about how unbeatable your rivals will be because of some artificial aid it will upset your performance. Even if the Italians were blood doped, I beat them all in the 5000m, and the one fact I do know is that I was not blood doped, and I have never and will never touch anything even vaguely connected with drugs.

Even though I think that many of the current drugs stories are exaggerated, it is important to ensure that we in Britain do all we can to detect any drug takers and ban them from our sport. In this context, if newspaper articles lead to more effective testing procedures their authors are to be applauded. There is some evidence in *The Times* articles of past irregularities by the BAAB in connection with their drug testing operations. Hopefully the appearance of these facts in print will lead to a more rigorous system being enforced in future. Apparently a Sports Council committee is shortly to be set up to examine how more effective measures can be introduced to catch offenders and prevent the further use of drugs. The committee will be independent of the BAAB and therefore beyond reproach.

Part of the problem is that we in Britain are showing the initiative to tackle the drugs problem, but the IAAF is reluctant to enforce the stricter regulations that Britain will shortly introduce. I find it highly offensive that Marti Vainio, a Finnish distance runner who was positively tested at the 1984 Olympics, was only banned for two years. Vainio, the silver medallist in the Los Angeles 10,000m, had been taking steroids at the time when a pint of blood was removed from his body for blood doping purposes. When the blood was re-injected shortly before the Olympics, the steroid present in the blood was detectable, even though he was no longer taking steroids when the test was carried out. (Ironically he was beaten in the Games by Cova, who has subsequently admitted that he was blood doped also!) Vainio's positive test resulted in a life ban. However the IAAF have a strange idea of what 'life' means, because two years later he was reinstated for 'good behaviour' in time for the European Championships.

I am on the International Athletes Club Committee. The IAC is an independent organisation. When an athlete represents Great Britain he or she is invited to join. Virtually all British international athletes are members of the club. At the next IAC committee meeting I am going to make some suggestions about drugs. If the athletes are seen to be opposed to drug taking this will increase the impetus for change in the existing regulations. If, furthermore, the vast majority of British athletes show themselves prepared to be tested at any time, anywhere, by an independent organisation it will help to dispel some of the more preposterous rumours that are in current circulation.

Unfortunately, the drugs problem will not disappear overnight, but if participants in the sport show a willingness to tackle the problem, progress can be made in the fight.

January 19. It has been fairly obvious from my miserable ramblings of the last couple of weeks that I have not been well. This is the time of year when I, like all other dedicated athletes, should be relentlessly pounding out the miles, ignoring the bleak winter weather. Instead I have been wrapped up indoors, blowing my nose and struggling to walk up the stairs. A couple of days ago Kerin and I decided we had had enough. She is suffering with a stomach bug and is fed up with my pathetic condition. We decided to do something drastic. We resorted to sunshine.

I arranged a flight, booked an apartment and forty-eight hours later we are sitting on our balcony in Santiago 3, Playa de las Americas, Tenerife, the Canary Islands. The hope is that a week's sunshine will destroy my cold, recharge our batteries and I shall return home, eager and ready to resume training. We shall relax and recuperate in the warmth. I shall train, gently and occasionally. That anyway is the rationale behind our sudden decision to flee Loughborough. We are having a sunshine break to recover from the after-effects of our New Year break in Pembrokeshire.

January 20: Tenerife. Today I ventured out onto the streets of Playa de las Americas. The first five minutes of running dressed in a pair of shorts and a T-shirt were delightful. Unless you run regularly it is hard to appreciate the simple pleasure athletes can feel when the sun comes out. After months of trudging through wind and rain in layers of clothing, to run in the barest minimum of kit with the sun on your back is a boost to any athlete.

Unfortunately today, the sun has not been out for long enough. The weather conditions are pleasant, like an overcast English summer afternoon, but when the sun does not shine in Playa de las Americas its main virtue is lost. There are other attractions in this rapidly expanding resort but we are not interested in cheap alcohol, discos and building sites. Our accommodation is in a vast white-washed Lego complex that is being erected alongside the sea front in competition with several other 'de-luxe' apartment hotels. Below us the electricians and carpenters are completing the ornate bandstand and 'Jungle-Jim' style bar, whilst the sun-worshippers wait patiently beside the pool.

Once the initial novelty of running unimpeded by cumbersome clothing wore off, I realised why athletes do not come here to train. There are two possible running routes around Playa de las Americas. One is along the sea front, the other along the road. Along the sea front progress is impeded by the thousands of promenading tourists, along the road it is the constant flow of taxis and coaches that threatens life and limb. On balance though the road traffic movements are slightly more predictable than the pedestrians. Also there is less chance of interrupting holiday snapshots on the road. But I should not be complaining. I am here to recuperate, not to train seriously. As long as the cacophony of bulldozers and electric drills does not become unbearable we are quite happy here on our balcony waiting for the sun to emerge from behind the thinning cloud.

January 22. Despite my scathing comments about Playa de las Americas I am quite prepared to admit that I am enjoying myself. This is the first 'sunbathing' holiday we have taken for years. The last couple of days the weather has been glorious. We are both recovering from our various ailments and already I am regaining enthusiasm for running.

Playa de las Americas is a resort on the southern slopes of Mount Teide, an extinct volcano that dominates the island of Tenerife. The dark landscape has been determined by the volcano, whose eroded ash has, in places, formed black beaches. It is only in this century that the Canaries have been exploited by man. The tourist boom has reached these islands, whose most popular natural asset is the sunshine, and sun-starved northern Europeans now flock south every winter. Resorts litter the southern shores of Tenerife. Snow-capped Mount Teide looks down upon row after row of tower-block hotels. Every year buildings creep further up the flanks of the mountain.

From my various runs around the area I would conservatively estimate that there are at least forty hotel and apartment developments currently in progress around Playa de las Americas. There are large hoardings along the roads displaying luxurious villas in verdant surroundings. These developments all have evocative names such as Acapulco, Windsor Park, Park Lane, and Orlando. The imagery is either of sunshine paradises or upmarket unattainable Britain. Behind the hoardings are empty building sites. The luxury accommodation is still a developer's dream. Next year though, Acapulco will be finished and the advertisements will be for Acapulco 2. All this development has completely altered the economy of the Canaries. The various leaflets and maps of Tenerife picture the inhabitants wearing 'traditional' costume working in the fields. Really they are serving behind the bar of the Princess Di English-style pub, working in the discos and renting out sun-loungers around the swimming pools.

January 27. We have returned from Tenerife to the chilly wastes of Britain. Refreshed and healthy I am ready to resume the burden of training. As I prepare to flaunt my sun-tanned body at circuits I notice my hot-pink sweatsuit. Yes, I now feel ready to wear it in public. I shall risk the ridicule and parade my flashy clothes that complement my bronzed appearance. I shall be elevated to the first rank of athletic posers. Unfortunately I do not possess any gold chains or hair on my chest to complete the image.

Whilst we were on holiday in Tenerife a number of problems have emerged at home. Top of the list is money. I have been receiving regular bank statements with all the figures in red. The problem is I have ample sums in my trust fund but no money in my bank account. This situation has arisen because of the late payment of subventions I received for my races during the summer. Although I ran the races in June the subventions were not deposited in my trust fund by the AAAs until December. Since June I have had plenty of legitimate athletic expenses but have not been able to use my subventions to pay for them. Consequently my bank account has become overdrawn and I am still waiting for the trustees of the fund – remember two are appointed by the BAAB to preserve my amateur status – to release sufficient amounts to cover my substantial overdraft. First the trustees wanted a breakdown of my expenses; now they require receipts. The trustees are quite entitled to check the validity of my claims but unfortunately my receipts are with my accountant, so payment has been further delayed. I organised our recuperative holiday in Tenerife assuming that the cost of it, along with other outstanding expenses, would be covered by the time I returned.

I am confident that the problem will be resolved eventually, but like all financial matters the solution will take at least a week longer than you anticipate. In the meantime I must not let my cashflow situation concern me. I never feel comfortable when my bank balance is under pressure, but it is important that I learn to cope with the frustrations of remaining an 'amateur' athlete.

Essentially, although the money problems are annoying, I am more worried about the stress my concern places upon my training. As I expect you have realised by now, I am devoted to and obsessed by my sport. No aspect of my life can be considered, nor difficulties encountered, without evaluating their influence on my running.

February 5: The IAC Drugs Initiative. Last week I attended an International Athletes Club committee meeting. The IAC is an attempt at an athletes' trade union. Membership is limited to British international athletes. The IAC performs a variety of functions to assist its members. There is a medical and physiotherapy scheme to help injured athletes, and financial assistance is given for warm-weather training camps in the spring. These initiatives are funded by the track and cross-country meetings that the club organises.

The IAC has also been in the forefront of the anti-drugs campaign, and at the meeting I raised this issue once again. I argued that the time was now ripe for the athletes to take an initiative and speak out against drugs. I realise that any initiative by British athletes will be of limited effect internationally, but if most or all British athletes could sign an anti-drugs statement expressing their willingness to accept stricter testing procedures, this would be a small step forward. The BAAB have instigated a random drugs test policy and their declaration that all athletes had to sign did include some of the points I wished to make, but my idea was to provide a further impetus. After the meeting I drafted the following letters to send to all British international athletes. The first is the cover letter and the second the actual declaration that athletes are supposed to sign and return to myself or the IAC.

Dear Athlete,

I feel that drug abuse in athletics will continue to cast a shadow over our sport for several years to come. Administrators and journalists have all voiced their opinions in recent months. Unless we, the athletes, are prepared to take the initiative and show our abhorrence of drug taking the problem may never be satisfactorily resolved.

We can start to help overcome the drugs threat by giving our support to random independent testing anytime and anywhere without notice.

Drugs are not going to disappear from our sport overnight, but if all British athletes can sign the enclosed declaration we will be starting to tackle the problem. This initiative is supported by the IAC Committee but is one coming from athletes currently active at international level and is not confined to IAC members.

If you want to help rid athletics of drugs please sign and return the enclosed letter as soon as possible.

We intend to publish a list of all athletes who have signed the letter in the second week of March.

Yours sincerely,
Jack Buckner

I the undersigned will support any initiatives to help rid athletics of drug taking which I abhor.

I am prepared to be tested for drugs anytime and anywhere without notice. I fully support a random drug testing policy and would like to see random testing introduced throughout the world.

I would like all drug testing to be conducted independently so that the system is beyond reproach. I abhor the use of blood doping and support all initiatives to have this practice detected. If an effective medical test is developed to detect blood doping, I will support its immediate introduction throughout athletics.

Signed: ....

Dated:...

I wanted to broaden the initiative beyond the IAC because the club represents a political stance on one or two issues that has alienated certain of our top athletes. This is particularly the case on selection policy where the IAC supports the first past the post system. (I spoke against this policy when it was raised by the committee.) The letter therefore includes the clause about not being confined to IAC members. It was also signed by me, not the IAC committee, and was not sent on IAC headed paper.

I hope that we will receive a good response. If it is obvious that the vast majority of British athletes support this initiative the pressure on the authorities to improve and enforce testing procedures will be greater. The next and far greater problem is for effective international legislation to be introduced.

January 12. Fed up with the weather and with battling against strong winds, I ran my usual ten mile road run on the treadmill yesterday. One of the advantages of living in Loughborough is the excellent sports science department at the University. Occasionally during the winter I use their treadmill facility. It is amazing what information a computer can provide. For the duration of my ten mile run I could see not only how fast I was moving in miles per hour, but also the time taken to complete each mile and how much of the run I had completed. If I had been rigged up to some of the technical apparatus the laboratory possesses, information on heart rate and oxygen uptake would have been easily obtained. But I did not want to be encumbered with a nose clip and mouth piece so settled just for the mileage statistics.

I ran ten miles quicker than ever before – 46 minutes, 33 seconds, to be precise. I should emphasise that it is easier to run fast on the treadmill than on the roads. There is no wind resistance or any inclines, so the runner can relax and run at a fast steady pace.

The treadmill run is my first respectable performance since I have recovered from my January health problems. I do not intend to race for several weeks and shall concentrate on building my fitness base for the summer.

6

Portugal and Problems

February 21: A Long Run. One of the few universal features in a runner's training regime is the long run. The long run is a tradition passed from generation to generation of athletes. Every Sunday morning, groups of athletes throughout the country embark upon this weekly ritual. I do not know how this strange habit emerged or why it usually takes place on Sunday morning. Perhaps the long run began as a group recovery exercise, a comradely excursion into the countryside after the previous day's race. Perhaps on the other hand it was a repentance from Saturday night excesses. Regardless of its origins, the Sunday long run is ingrained as deeply into runners' lore as calluses are into their feet. The Americans have caught onto the idea as well, although dissatisfied with our terminology refer to it as LSD – Long Slow Distance.

My feelings regarding this weekly exercise invariably depend on the weather and the time of year. An hour and a half ramble through the Leicestershire countryside on a bright spring morning when the bluebells are in flower is an invigorating experience. But, at this time of year trudging through thick mud and staggering up Beacon Hill into driving rain is not a pleasant way to spend Sunday mornings.

Frequently I am accompanied on this run by Bill Foster. Bill has lived in Loughborough for the last couple of years, but I first met him at school. He has run below 3.45 for 1500m and has formidable stamina. Although I can outpace him on the track he cruises with far less effort than me on long runs. Between us we resolve the problems of the world on our weekly excursions.

Usually I find the first hour of the run comfortable. The pace of a long run is slower than my daily training sessions so I am more relaxed, despite the demanding climbs of the Charnwood hills. Depending on underfoot conditions and personal motivation I am near the top of the Beacon after about an hour's running. As long as the weather conditions are not too inclement I am still experiencing positive emotions at this stage of the exercise, especially if the impressive views around the Beacon are clearly visible.

Between sixty and ninety minutes my enthusiasm begins to wane. Limbs tire, muscles ache, the incessant pounding jars the body. I start feeling envious and resentful of the vast majority of the population, sitting down to a leisurely breakfast with the Sunday newspaper.

After ninety minutes serious fatigue commences. Perpetual movement has dulled both mind and body. I have lost all interest in the surrounding scenery. Life has become reduced to the basics. All I want is a hot bath, food and water. I cease my friendly 'good mornings' to passers-by and instead swear under my breath every time a car drives past without pulling out.

Fortunately the end is in sight. My long run rarely lasts more than an hour and three quarters. Later, reclining in the luxury of a warm bath with a cup of tea and the colour supplement perched precariously on the nearby toilet seat, I philosophise about the morning's stoical activity.

The long run has not only helped my fitness, it has benefited my soul. I return from the long run with no interest or ambition in life beyond the essentials – food, water, and shelter. Every week the long run teaches me to be grateful for my ability to satisfy these simple requirements. After the run I appreciate how fortunate I am to have good health, fitness and a comfortable home. It will take me the rest of the day to lose this virtuous view of our complex world, but unfortunately by the time of my next run on Monday morning all noble thoughts will have evaporated, I shall be dreaming of gold medals again.

The long run is an escape from the problems and stresses of modern life. Anyone wishing to regain perspective should try it, instead of lying in bed on Sunday morning.

March 6: Road Race, 10k, Nottingham. Last Wednesday evening, exhausted from another relentless circuit session, I persuaded George to let me race this weekend. A race would temporarily alleviate the rigours of training and would be a rough guide as to how all the hard work was progressing.

This morning, whilst most sensible folk were preparing for Sunday lunch, I was waiting in an impatient throng of masochistic runners for the start of the Kodak 10k around the damp streets of Nottingham. The race started promptly and the opening hectic kilometres passed without incident. Midway through the race, as a leading pack of some fifteen runners snaked around a twisting undulating circuit, I began to doubt the wisdom of my suggestion four days previously. The course through the city centre was tough and the weather miserable, but more importantly I was uncomfortable with the persistent pace in the leading group.

On the final of the three laps, I decided to increase the speed despite my apparent tiredness. I hoped my effort might ignite the spark of inspiration dampened by 7k of toil on this wet morning. I did manage to establish a small lead, but glancing at the reflections in shop windows, I could see my break had not been decisive. With a kilometre left, my motivation was rapidly doused as one, two and then several runners overtook a fading European Champion. I eventually finished seventh hardly bothering to compete over the closing metres.

One of the hardest challenges in sport is to lose gracefully, whether it is the Olympic final or a 10k road race in

Nottingham. Defeat should never be accepted, but it has to be tolerated reluctantly. My instant reaction to losing is a desire to escape the venue, talk to nobody and sulk like a small child deprived of his favourite cream cake. But, such a petulant display would be inappropriate. Instead the emotions of bitterness and indignation have to be masked by compulsory handshakes and offers of congratulation to the victor.

To me, this race was unimportant. The reasons for my poor result sprang quickly from my lips upon request, '. . . only decided to race a few days ago . . . haven't eased down . . . been training hard . . . haven't raced since December . . . obviously I'm concentrating on the summer.' These assertions are all true, but still the ignominy of seventh place in a 10k road race causes inner frustration.

The TV reporter who briefly leaves the shelter of the Council House to meet the 'gallant' loser has to be confronted with a fixed smile. When the reporter, clad in his dry, warm jacket, enquires of the drenched despondent runner, 'How much of a set-back is this?' from beneath his umbrella, I cannot reply with the irritation I feel. Instead I shrug my shoulders and mouth the appropriate platitudes.

Subduing my true feelings, I managed to chatter away in the crowd of weary runners, recovering from our exertions in Nottingham's Market Square. Overall, the race was another successful Kodak/APA promotion. The Kodak series illustrates the benefits of sponsorship to the sport of road running. Before these races existed, opportunities to compete in well-organised events with good prizes and a quality entry were limited. In today's event half the British World Cross-Country Team had the ideal preparation for the forthcoming World Championships in New Zealand. At the same time, aspiring marathoners could tune-up for the London. The sponsorship attracts a class field (first prize £750 subvention, and the inevitable Kodak camera) and therefore ensures competitive opportunities for emerging talent.

The race was not confined to elite runners and the thousands of club athletes who pounded the streets were rewarded with a fierce but friendly morning's sport. T-shirts for the first 200 finishers and various other 'freebies' help explain further the popularity of the Kodak series. My only criticism of a well-organised event was on the final lap, when the leaders were forced to zig-zag through lapped joggers. A suggestion to alleviate this problem would be to run two separate races, one for the 'elite' runners, the other for less serious athletes. The disadvantages of two races would be extra administration and the disappointment of club runners not having the opportunity to compete against the country's leading road racers.

The race was won by Michael Chorlton, a promising young Yorkshire athlete, who like many others before him, has fought back from a prolonged period of injury. He was justifiably delighted with his victory and is looking forward to the summer. The quality of British distance running continues to amaze. The course in Nottingham was difficult and the weather conditions awful, but the standard of performance was impressive for a regional race. International athletes like myself will never have an easy ride in the fierce domestic environment of British road racing.

After performing the various social activities with a suitably correct appearance, I left and returned home to drop my false smile. Later in the evening we went to the cinema; anything to forget the race.

March 7. I have managed to swallow the irritation of yesterday's defeat and can now view the situation more rationally. I overreacted to the result yesterday. I realise my emotions were not justified. After so long in the sport I am still a bad loser.

But there are reasons for my seventh place. I have trained very hard and did not ease up for the race. The runners who beat me have raced extensively over the winter. However promisingly training is progressing, there is no substitute for competition to improve results. Nevertheless, I would have liked to have performed better.

I must forget this minor interruption to what has so far been a relatively smooth winter of consistent work. There is no point in any alteration of plans because of one upset. I am intending to run in the Midland Road Relay at the end of March and a 5k road race around Newcastle city centre on April 6. In between these two competitions will be my sixth annual training trip to Portugal. If my results have not improved significantly over the next month, then I shall be more concerned.

March 15: Running Blues. Since my disappointing performance in Nottingham, I have lost much of my enthusiasm for training. Every year there are periods when I become disenchanted with the tediousness of running. The constant repetition of the same boring activity can become depressing. Usually these feelings follow poor performances, so it is not surprising that the Nottingham race and the miserable weather have reduced my current motivation to a low level. Running has become like a dose of unpleasant medicine administered twice daily.

The cure for these running 'blues' might be the annual training trip to Portugal in a couple of weeks' time. The Tenerife week was my January training tonic, I hope Portugal will have the same effect in early April. I complained to George after a dismal session around the waterlogged University campus last Saturday. He told me I was becoming soft. Perhaps he is correct. This winter is the first since 1984 when I have not escaped to the warmth of the USA for several weeks. My tolerance of rain, wind and cold must have decreased. Instead of running beneath the palm trees of California, I have trudged in seemingly never-ending circles around the familiar Loughborough training routes. All this mileage would seem more worthwhile if I could see the benefit. If my level of fitness was improving and my training times were quicker I would stop complaining. But, because I am training so hard and because I am concentrating on peak fitness in September I shall not gain from the hard work until the summer. In the meantime I must ignore my training malaise and continue to pound out the miles. During the course of every running year there will be times of doubt and frustration. I have experienced these symptoms before and must keep going until the blues disappear.

March 16: The IAC Drugs Initiative. Tomorrow I am attending a press conference concerning the anti-drugs letter sent to all British international athletes a few weeks ago. An excellent response has been received. Over half the three hundred athletes who were sent the declaration replied within a fortnight. It is a firm indication of the strong anti-drugs sentiment that exists amongst British athletes. During the last week I have been speaking and corresponding with those athletes who did not initially return their forms. The IAC office has also pursued any elusive athletes, some of whom have been training in exotic locations abroad. Between us, we have communicated with virtually all the three hundred British athletes. The overwhelming majority have signed the declaration and this will be announced to the media tomorrow. I hope this initiative will be a positive step in the fight against drugs in the sport.

Certainly, this declaration should help improve the tarnished image of athletics as we, the competitors, are inviting unprecedented testing procedures to be implemented. However, to be effective, these measures should be introduced throughout the world. It is the problem of achieving effective international action that concerns many of those who have signed the declaration, and in the occasional instance it has been the excuse not to sign. Their argument is as follows: 'What is the point in us introducing these measures? The rest of the world won't take the slightest notice. It's a waste of time and money when there is so much flagrant drug taking in Eastern bloc countries.' I disagree with this school of thought and maintain it is important for the future of the sport that we do everything possible to combat the drugs menace. I also hope that the athletes' voice is listened to in the IAAF corridors of power.

My fear for tomorrow's press conference is that some journalists will be more interested in the minority who have not signed the letter, than the majority who have. The two notable non-signatories are Steve Ovett and Linford Christie. Ovett has written me a letter, from which I shall quote should the necessity arise. He comments 'whilst I agree with you both morally and on an emotional level, I cannot accept your method. Various reports . . . have only just been received whilst others are still in action. I therefore think it best that we wait for the outcome of such findings before taking any further steps which within themselves could indirectly shed bad light on our sport.' I sympathise, but disagree with Ovett's opinions. I fail to see how a strong anti-drugs statement can be seen in anything other than a positive light, especially when such a statement reflects the mood of most British athletes.

But, I have no intention of criticising Ovett and will try hard to deflect attention from his name as I want the press to headline a strong 'British Athletes against Drugs' message not 'Buckner slams Ovett'. Ovett has expressed his opinions on the issue whereas Christie would not. He told me he was fed up with hearing about drugs and had aired his feelings on the subject elsewhere. Fair enough, but a pity he could not help the collective effort.

March 17. This morning I ran at 6.15am in order to catch the 8.00 am train to London. I ran for 35 minutes and only woke up after 20 minutes' plodding. The tranquillity of Loughborough at that early hour partially compensated for the shock to my system. What was surprising was the visibility of several sets of runners' footprints in the early morning dew. Somewhere in Loughborough there are runners who were training around the University campus before 6.15am. I am torn between admiration and disbelief for these enthusiastic runners. I hope I never have to train regularly at that unearthly hour.

The 'Drugs Press Conference' passed off without too many difficulties. I was slightly disappointed with the small number of reporters in attendance (between ten and fifteen), but Dave Bedford, the IAC Chairman, assured me this was a respectable turnout. (Perhaps he was trying to boost morale.) The massed ranks of the fourth estate received a copy of the letter and a list of the athletes who had signed. This was, eventually, 254 out of

260 British internationals. Of the remaining six, four we had been unable to contact, leaving only Ovett and Christie who had actually refused. By anybody's standards we have received an excellent response.

I gave my well-rehearsed monologue: '. . . positive step forward against drugs . . . strength of feeling amongst British athletes . . . improve the tarnished image of the sport . . .', all uncontroversial straightforward stuff. The questions from the press were fended by Tim Hutchings, Judy Oakes and myself. We were careful to avoid any negative comment: 'Steve and Linford perfectly entitled to their own point of view . . . respect their opinions . . .', and continued to emphasise how we, current international athletes, are opposed to drugs. When the questioning was directed towards areas beyond the athletes' declaration we steered our answers back to the basic text. We managed to avoid becoming bogged down in the complexities such as, what tests can be used to detect blood doping? Were we tacitly admitting the problem of drugs in athletics? Who should pay for the enforcement of the testing? These are all valid areas of questioning, but beyond the scope of the signed letter. I stressed that the main contribution athletes can make to tackling the drugs problem has been achieved by the declaration. We have agreed to random independent testing anytime, anywhere.

Tomorrow, I shall buy most of the newspapers and read how the conference is reported. After that I shall forget the issue and concentrate on training. I may appear callous, but I feel I have contributed positively to the problem and any more involvement in the drugs issue will divert me from my main objective. Therefore, despite today's excitements, I have no excuse to miss tonight's road run – the best way to ruin Thursday evening.

March 18. 'WHY WE'LL SHUN DRUGS PLEDGE', the headline from that reputable publication, the *Sun*. 'Sunsport starts with the row splitting athletics.' The *Sun* could interpret a friendly chat with my Grandmother as a 'family feud', so when 254 out of 260 athletes support a clearly stated position the paper has no ethical or mathematical problem in describing a 97 per cent endorsement as 'the row splitting athletics'.

The other newspapers reflected yesterday's events more accurately. The most comprehensive coverage was provided by *The Times* who, following their pre-Christmas exclusives, have more interest than the other newspapers in the drugs story. *The Times* article supported our position. 'Initiative is one of the most welcome ways of attacking the problem.' Pat Butcher's article also commented about Ovett's and Christie's position: 'It would be unwise to read too much into their refusals. Ovett has always been averse to publicity, other than that which he engenders himself; and Christie has taken over the Ovett mantle in his distrust of the Press and allied enterprises.'

But, the most interesting piece of athletics information was a snippet in the *Independent*: 'The British Amateur Athletic Board admitted yesterday that they are re-considering the selection system (for the Olympic Games) after strong criticism by many senior athletes.' I wonder what is going on behind the scenes at the BAAB? And who is complaining to whom? Who would have guessed that athletics could be so filled with intrigue? Our sport will be as bad as cricket before long.

March 22. Another press conference in London, this time for the Newcastle City Centre 5k on April 6. I, along with most of the leading British middle-distance runners, will be racing along the Newcastle quayside that Wednesday evening.

I was at the press conference with Steve Cram. We are the 'headlined runners' as the Americans would say, although both Crammie and I stressed that there are many others, notably Passey, Rowland and Davies-Hale, who have had a more extensive and successful winter campaign than ourselves. We downplayed our respective chances and stressed our aims are for the Olympics so that we do not want to be in top form in early April.

This led chronologically to our respective summer plans and before long the press conference became a statement against the BAAB Olympic selection policy. Crammie opposes the first-two-past-the-post system as vehemently as I do, so there was some pretty strong stuff said about the selectors. Whether our comments will make any difference is hard to tell, but the surreptitious remark in last week's *Independent* is a possible indication of some division in the selectors' ranks. Continued criticism of the policy by leading athletes might deepen any rift and increase the pressure on the selectors to reconsider their controversial decision.

Returning to the Newcastle 5k, I am hoping for a much better performance than my last outing in the Nottingham 10k. I would like a run-out before the Newcastle race, but unfortunately the only alternative, the Midland Road Relay, takes place when I am in Portugal. 'Gandy's gang' leaves for Portugal on the 27th and I return separately on Tuesday 5th. Ten days in the sunshine of the Algarve will hopefully assist my fitness and enable me to relax after my recent off-track activities.

March 26. During my teenage years I dreamed of life as a sportsman. My visions were usually of cricketing achievements, scoring centuries against the West Indies, hooking Holding and Roberts for six at Lord's. As my cricketing career declined rapidly after my fourteenth birthday these dreams were replaced by thoughts of Olympic victories and World Records. For years I imagined glory in the 1500m sprinting past rivals down the home straight. I still dream, but recognising the limitations of my fast-twitch fibres I currently content myself with images of glory in the Seoul 5000m with a flagging Aouita decisively beaten.

Dreaming of glory is, I am sure, a fairly common practice amongst many youngsters aspiring to a life in sport. I am fortunate that I have reached my mid-twenties with my dreams intact. I have yet to suffer the rude awakening of declining ability or fulfilled potential. It will happen sooner or later, but until the sad day arrives I shall continue to desire better results and faster times.

Part of the appeal of sport is that it offers a feasible opportunity to achieve such common dreams. The road to an

Olympic gold medal, a Wimbledon title, or an Open golf championship is essentially the same. The qualities necessary for the journey are determination, single-mindedness, devotion and, of course, luck and ability. These characteristics must accompany any individual on the well-trodden path of sporting self-improvement. In a complicated world this challenge is simple and attractive. It is a pure, almost idealistic quest in life that many would envy. The image of the determined athlete, the loneliness of the long distance runner, is an appealing but accurate myth. Free from the influence of others, divorced from the complexities of co-operation and compromise, the sportsperson pursues this solitary ambition.

I am currently pursuing my ambition – the Seoul 1988 Olympic Games. It is a challenge that is perceived as noble and healthy. But there is a less endearing aspect to this continual search for personal physical excellence. The sportsperson, eyes fixed on the road ahead, can become blinkered and lose sight of his surroundings. It is easy for the quest to develop into an obsession as the sportsperson is frequently isolated from the real world. This is especially true in athletics when training and competition encourage complete selfishness. On the track the athlete is alone, relying only upon his or her own ability and strength.

W. R. Loader talks about the athlete's attitude to sport in his book the *Testament of a Runner*. 'Running is the athlete's business. He conducts it with no partners. Friends, clubmates, coach, these do not count as partners. The runner would happily push them all under a train if he thought mass slaughter would expedite his winning an Olympic title.'

I have no intention of such a drastic training method, but Loader's half serious comment illustrates how a runner can become obsessed with sport. The harder you train, the more successful you become and the easier it is to lose a sense of proportion and absorb yourself entirely in the world of sporting self-improvement. Success causes the circle of interest regarding your achievements to extend beyond family to friends, the media and eventually fans. All reinforce, through their interest and attentions, the importance of sport in an individual's life. 'Congratulations – great race' – is an innocuous, pleasant and appreciated comment, but repeated endlessly manages to boost the ego still further. Cliff Temple, writing in the *Sunday Times* about athletes, comments 'It is a lonely sport at the top. International athletes can be selfish, introverted, suspicious, insecure and quick to put others down.'

Temple's article was about drugs but his remarks are applicable to any aspect of top level sport. It is success in sport that has caused those unfortunate characteristics to develop. The qualities necessary to reach international standard can all too easily become the vices that distort sportspeople as individuals. Presumably these problems have confronted sportspeople ever since the Ancient Olympics began but the status of contemporary sports heroes and heroines receives an additional boost from television. Every great sporting occasion is beamed into our living rooms and the waving victor salutes not only the crowd but millions of TV viewers. Sportstars are amongst the idols of our age.

So, engrossed in sport and surrounded by admirers, no wonder the behaviour of the leading participants has deteriorated. When an individual's life is completely devoted to sport, is it surprising that tennis players and cricketers argue with umpires?

Success in sport has caused my life to be centred on running. This has affected my character. It is hard to prevent the qualities necessary to win on the track from spilling over into my personal life. On the track I must be single-minded, determined and not give a thought to the performance of others. These characteristics are best confined to the track, but as running dominates my experiences it is difficult to divide my personality.

Running is my method of expression. So long as I remain a competitive athlete I can allow this powerful addiction to persist. My problem will be in adjusting to the real world once my running career is over. It may not be easy.

March 28. Last month *Athletics Today* interviewed Kerin for a series on athletes' spouses. The April edition of the magazine has appeared on the newsstands with our picture on the front cover. Unfortunately the title of the article is 'Why Karin and Jack keep a low profile'. I have never met this Karin. Kerin's name has been misspelt throughout the interview. This is very irritating especially as the author had checked the spelling with us twice before publication.

It is unusual to read about Kerin, sorry Karin, in an athletics publication. Kerin has always supported and encouraged my running career but prefers to stay out of the limelight. Most of the interview is concerned with our relationship or rather her handling of me. Due attention is given to her commitment to my welfare but rather less to her as an individual. I would not quibble with the description of the devoted wife and mature relationship, but would point out there are sometimes conflicts between us regarding running. Running is a lifestyle and my devotion to it inevitably encompasses Kerin. She is less free to pursue her own interests because I insist on placing running first. Most of the time she tolerates this, but I realise it must be irritating when, for example, long standing plans have to be cancelled to accommodate a sudden running development.

I am off to Portugal in a couple of days without Kerin. She has been on our Portugal training trip in the past and would prefer to save her holiday until the two of us can go away together without the third partner in our relationship dominating the scene.

March 30. On the Algarve. Acoteais – the largest sporting complex in Portugal – the sign alongside the beach cafe proclaims, but despite the vast numbers of Swedes, Germans and British who pack this popular warm weather training camp, the beach cafe will not open until the Easter weekend.

The Bank adjacent to Acoteais is also closed for winter and the beach transport, a tractor pulling a trailer, is not yet operational. Instead, prospective sun-worshippers must walk the mile from the complex to the beach, hardly an onerous task for fit young athletes, but an inconvenience nonetheless. As I sit alongside the patio of my apartment I can see a steady procession of scantily clad visitors, sometimes carrying booming cassette players, dodging the traffic as they make their daily pilgrimage to the sea in search of the perfect sun-tan.

The Scandinavians are the most dedicated to this occupation. In the evenings bronzed Norse gods and their accompanying ladies parade themselves around the track. They look supreme athletes with their elegant stretching exercises and sophisticated warm-up routines. Unfortunately, or so we cynics maintain, the Scandinavians never seem to progress beyond these initial activities. They are never out of breath and their training appears confined to endless prancing, displaying their magnificent physiques. By contrast, we anaemic looking specimens are struggling through repetition sessions and collapsing exhausted on the grass. There is no doubt who looks the better group of athletes, just as there is no doubt who is the more successful group of athletes.

This is my sixth visit to Acoteais. I first came here as a rebellious youngster resisting the yoke of regular training. Over the years I have graduated to the 'old man' of the training group – mature, dedicated and possibly slightly unapproachable. This attitude of aloofness is not intentional but develops because I no longer want to sit in a crowd around the swimming pool with the ever-present threat of immersion in the cold water from some joker or other. Many of our party are at that stage of development when throwing someone in the pool is as compulsory as the disco. Like most spirited youngsters, I have had my fair share of late nights and pool throwing, but perhaps I can be forgiven for not wanting to indulge in these pastimes any more.

Instead I am here to concentrate on running, and just as importantly relaxation between training sessions. I am quite content to while away ten days reading and running, filling the spare hours with siestas and lounging on the patio as the gentle breeze wafts the scent of blossom through the pine trees.

Unfortunately my idyllic reverie is interrupted at Acoteais as in Tenerife by the noise of progress. The crash of falling pine trees and the grunting of bulldozers disturb the peaceful atmosphere. The beach road that six years ago was the preserve of pedestrians and the occasional taxi or car now trundles with lorries transporting building supplies.

What first attracted athletes to Acoteais were the facilities and climate. Pleasant spring sunshine is almost guaranteed from mid-March. The complex possesses a synthetic track, the pine woods for steady running and the cross-country course, a two kilometre grass circuit maintained like a golf course and ideal for training. This ideal combination has led to a rapid growth in the popularity of Acoteais as a spring training venue. The manager told me that all 700 beds in the complex are currently occupied and that over this Easter period he could fill a camp three times as large. I have my own gauge of the growing number of visitors to this part of the Algarve. The local supermarkets stock fresh bread rolls from Albufeira and Faro every morning. These are much in demand at Acoteais and competition has become fierce. In previous years the supermarkets contained bread rolls until after the mid-afternoon siesta, but this year all supplies disappear by about 11am.

The trade in bread rolls is just one spin-off of the tourist boom on the Algarve. All areas of the local economy are flourishing. The growth in tourism and the success of Acoteais have caused land prices to rocket. Large areas have been sold to developers who are understandably quick to capitalise on their newly acquired assets. It is the result of this process that is currently disturbing my siesta. The bulldozers are clearing land between Acoteais and the sea. The owners have sold to a company who are building a five-star hotel, golf course and some apartments. Additionally, the camp management has plans for its own hotel.

The last person to complain about the disappearance of the Algarve under luxury hotels, apartments and 'fun-filled water parks' should be the foreign tourist whose presence in the country is responsible for the development in the first place, and who probably comes from a nation that succumbed to haphazard construction hundreds of years ago, so I spoke to the manager about the past, present and future of the Algarve.

Cliff Richard was the key. In the late 1960s he bought a villa in Albufeira, drank and fished with the locals, and apparently lived an idyllic existence. The Beatles visited Albufeira in 1968. The visits of these pop superstars, according to the manager of Acoteais, created 'the myth of Albufeira'. The town had a name and an image as the hideaway retreat of the famous. The next step was the building of the obligatory five-star hotels attracting an up-market clientele. This led to land speculation, more building and ultimately mass tourism. Twenty years after Cliff and the Beatles, Albufeira is the most popular and over-developed resort on the Algarve.

The manager admitted that Albufeira and Quarteira were now a mess, but he was quick to add that they (the local government, hotel managers and everyone concerned about the Algarve's future) had learnt from the mistakes of these resorts. Albufeira, with its high-rise blocks and poor infrastructure, was an example of what to avoid in the future. The town currently attracts the rowdy teenage holiday crowd. Roads are poor and there is concern about the low standards of some accommodation.

The Portuguese are not going to allow the mistakes of the early tourist developments to be repeated elsewhere on the Algarve. The manager spoke of 'universal standards', 'improved facilities', 'a four-storey maximum building limit' and 'a lower density of inhabitants'. The aim is to emphasise quality development, attracting a more 'sophisticated tourist'.

I wonder what the Algarve will look like in another twenty years?

April 2. Training continues to be steady and unspectacular even in the sunshine. This morning I completed the most demanding track session of our annual Portuguese jaunt. My times were slightly disappointing and not as impressive as last year's efforts on the Acoteais track. Overall my current mediocre performance is unimportant, but on warm-weather training trips it is easy to exaggerate small deficiencies into major problems. When ten days are spent in a pleasant environment with good weather and no diversions from running, there is a tendency to take training too seriously. Sessions that you do not even think about at home become bench-marks to check your progress. Fortunately I have had sufficient disappointments in the past to become too disheartened by my current poor form.

I have averaged 80 miles per week for nearly three months. By any standards I have completed an impressive block of training that will prove crucial in the summer even though I am not gaining the benefits of this hard work at the moment. If I rested for a couple of weeks and sharpened up with some track work I would be in outstanding physical condition, but currently I cannot afford the luxury of two weeks' relaxation.

Instead I must keep ploughing away with the occasional respite until training becomes less intense in late June. I have one such respite in the relentless drive towards Seoul in preparation for next week's Newcastle 5000m. Four days of easy running will I hope be sufficient break to produce a respectable performance against the outstanding competitors who will assemble on the banks of the Tyne next Wednesday. Unfortunately, although four days' easy running is a welcome pause in the training regime, it will not guarantee complete recovery. There will be runners in Newcastle much better prepared than me for the confrontation and I must remember this if my performance reflects the Nottingham 10k rather than the Zurich 8k.

April 7: Road Race, 5k, Newcastle. This was awful. This was my worst performance for years. Starting in the middle of the pack I gradually edged towards the leaders and then slowly slipped further and further behind, losing confidence and motivation with every leaden stride. Fourteenth out of twenty-five. My time 14.05 a joke, a training plod. My best 10 kilometre road time is 28.03. 14.05 for 5000m is 28.10 for 10 kilometres. I am supposed to be fit. I realise I have had little respite from hard training to prepare for this race, but I should not run this badly. After three months' consistent training I am performing worse than when I raced in Zurich after Christmas.

At the reception after the Newcastle 5k (in the race a rejuvenated Mike McLeod sprinted away from Dave Lewis to win) I spoke with several of the athletes whom I most admire, all of whom have suffered far greater set-backs than my current form. Brendan Foster, Dave Moorcroft and Steve Cram, all offered the same advice, the same advice I would give anyone else in my position, but like all advice, far easier to give than to take oneself. 'Don't worry, be patient, the Olympics aren't until October, better to run badly now and save your best performances until it matters most' was the tone of their comments. George endorsed this viewpoint over the telephone. We discussed in detail my recent training and both agreed that I have completed a demanding training phase and cannot expect to compete at my best with so few races.

But, despite all the evidence that excuses my dismal performance, I still worry. A trace of doubt has crept into my mind. How can I expect to compete against the Kenyans and Aouita when I cannot even break 14 minutes for a 5000m road race? Ngugi has just raced in Bali, where in hot humid conditions he ran the second fastest road 10 kilometres ever. He would have beaten me by 20 seconds in Newcastle and then continued at the same speed for another five kilometres.

I should try and copy Steve Cram's attitude to the sport. He is always so laid-back – or rather appears to be laid-back. I do not know if his casual approach is genuine or not, but I am sure it helps him maintain a perspective on his results whether good or bad. If I want to overcome my current difficulties I must cease this unnecessary concern. What am I complaining about? The Olympics are over five months away. I have raced three times this winter and I have a solid fitness base that will prove essential when the serious competing begins.

Regardless of my feeble performance on the quayside of the city, I always enjoy running in Newcastle. The great North-eastern athletic tradition has generated an informed running public who appreciate the sport. Jogging around the streets before the race there are shouts of encouragement for every athlete and afterwards, despite my fourteenth place, I was thanked for 'coming up here' by several spectators. There is a far greater comradeship between the Geordie public and their runners than in any other area of the country, or so it seems to an outsider. This affinity appears to be reciprocated by the runners, so that there are close links between the local athletic clubs and the North-east community.

Crammie and Big Bren identify with the area that nurtured them. It was Brendan Foster's company that organised the Newcastle 5k, so it was not surprising that a local sponsor was forthcoming. At the post-race reception this strong regional identity was in evidence along with the quickfire Geordie wit. I find it hard to compete with the dry North-east humour at the best of times, but after finishing fourteenth I had no chance.

April 12. After my Newcastle disaster I have taken a few days off running. Uninspired and disinterested I decided to forget training until I regained my motivation. Last weekend was Chris McGeorge's wedding. Chris and his wife Sonia are both international athletes who form part of the training group in Loughborough. Free from the necessity to run, I celebrated the occasion to the full. Unfortunately, even rest does little to dispel the doubts. I resumed running this morning and then made the mistake of weighing myself. I am at least eight pounds heavier than I should be. Usually I manage to lose a few pounds in Portugal and at this time of year I aim to approach my racing weight of nine stone four pounds. Normally I would laugh off such a minor concern, realising that a couple of weeks' running and culinary discipline will restore my body to its trim condition. But in my current paranoid state, any slight problem is grossly exaggerated. Perhaps I should embark on a crash diet? What about limiting my calorie intake? Such suggestions might be suitable for non-athletes, but when you are training twice per day any drastic measures will rapidly affect training performance.

I have decided to cut down on fats, although on our careful, healthy vegetarian diet it is hard to find much fat to eliminate. We do not eat any biscuits, cakes, sweets or processed sugar. Cheese and oils will only be used in small quantities. Alcohol is definitely out. Plenty of fresh vegetables, rice, pulses, bread and pasta are the order of the day.

7

Track Chat

April 19: Zola Budd. A long time ago I thought athletics involved turning up for races and a daily training run. At the moment the actual process of running takes far less thought and effort than all the problems that surround this simple activity. There is the drugs controversy, the selection controversy and controversy over money, but above all else there is Zola Budd.

Before I continue I should like to state that my personal contacts with her have always been excellent. Whenever I have met her she has been polite and friendly, if a little shy, hardly surprising after all the difficulties she experienced at an early age. But unfortunately Zola Budd, the athlete, cannot be divorced from Zola Budd, the political problem.

Budd arrived in Britain in 1984. She was persuaded to leave South Africa by the *Daily Mail*. Neil Wilson, a journalist formerly with that paper, currently writing for the *Independent*, explains how Budd came to leave South Africa:

> '. . . the *Daily Mail* sent two journalists – one of them myself – to persuade her that the paper had the influence to smooth her way to running as a Briton if only she would throw in her lot with them. There was also the little matter of

> £100,000 to make her decision easier . . . Budd, let us remember, was the creation of a newspaper editor's imagination. Had she not been white, so child-like and run bare-foot she would have been running still on the veldt.'

Budd was quickly granted a British passport and competed in the 1984 Olympic Games, where to make her story all the more sensational she entangled with the favourite in the Women's 3000m, Mary Decker (now Mary Slaney). The latter was left sprawling on the track as Budd, accompanied by the boos of the Los Angeles crowd, finished fifth, an excellent performance by a youngster but widely perceived as failure in the hyped atmosphere surrounding her every move.

Her life as a British citizen could hardly have begun more traumatically and it is hardly surprising that she regularly wanted to return to South Africa. Neil Wilson again:

> 'Twice in her first week in Britain she had to be talked out of taking the next plane "home". With hindsight, perhaps, the most unfortunate piece of advice she was given at that time was to "give it another three weeks and all the fuss will have died down", but that first act set the scene for the pantomime that followed.'

Over the next few years she received advice from a succession of interested parties: two South African businessmen, BAAB officials and currently a 'senior newspaper executive'. Her running performances under the guidance of her South African coach improved dramatically in 1985 culminating in a Women's 5000m world record at Crystal Palace and two World cross-country titles. But, although a British citizen, she still retained strong links with South Africa through her Afrikaans advisers and her continual visits to her native country. She made no anti-apartheid statement, wanting to steer clear of politics. This was an understandable attitude for any young runner, but one hardly likely to endear her either to the black countries of Africa, or the various anti-apartheid organisations who inevitably used her as a focus for their protests.

There were protests against her participation in the 1986 Commonwealth Games, eventually causing her suspension under some 'minimum residential qualification'. (Ironically, the games were boycotted because of the British government's reluctance to impose sanctions against South Africa.) Earlier in 1988 there was a threatened disruption of the World Cross-Country Championship in New Zealand over her proposed participation. This time the world governing body, the IAAF, took action. They banned her temporarily for 'taking part' in a meeting in South Africa last year. She missed the World Cross-Country Championship and last weekend her case came before the IAAF council.

Her case hinged on the interpretation of 'taking part'. Any athlete who 'takes part' in an athletics meeting in South Africa can be banned for breaking the Gleneagles agreement on the boycott of any sporting links with South Africa. Zola Budd did not run in this particular meeting at Brakspan in South Africa, but she did apparently spectate as well as, it is alleged, presenting prizes and running alongside the competitors. Does that constitute 'taking part'? It appears flimsy evidence, but to attend such an event was hardly a shrewd move by someone whose every move is subject to public scrutiny. If a leading Conservative politician attended a left-wing Labour meeting and merely sat at the back without saying a word, there would still be public repercussions.

At the meeting last Saturday, the IAAF examined the report of Budd 'taking part' in the meeting in South Africa. However if the IAAF had decided to ban her, based on the evidence they had received, she could have responded by taking them to court. This could have led to lengthy, expensive legal proceedings, possibly bad publicity, and a case they were by no means likely to win on such slight evidence. On the other hand if they refused to take any action and she remained eligible for the Olympics there was the threat of another boycott by the African nations.

The IAAF were in an awkward position and they resorted to a classical manoeuvre. They passed the buck. They transferred their responsibility to the BAAB, urging the board to suspend Budd for at least one year. This ploy received widespread criticism. The *Independent* commented in a leader on Monday morning;

> '. . . there is something about the activities of the federation (the IAAF), whose worthies happily accommodate themselves to sudden and unseemly political pressures from regimes whose respect for civil liberties and democratic values leaves much to be desired. For the federation to note in its ruling that Miss Budd was "at the very best . . . in breach of the spirit of the rules" (reference to her attending the meeting in South Africa) was to employ weasel words. Either the runner had broken the rules or she had not. Moreover, to suggest that the British Amateur Athletic Board "ought to consider" suspending her for at least twelve months was downright cowardice.'

It is now the BAAB who face the latest awkward decision. Do the board at next Sunday's meeting succumb to IAAF pressure or not? If they do Budd might take legal action against the board, but if they do not there is the threat of the IAAF suspending the BAAB, therefore leaving the British team unable to compete abroad and most importantly banned from the Olympics.

The IAAF action has implicated every British international athlete in the affair. It is the BAAB council who have to decide whether to support Budd or not, but the opinions of most Olympic hopefuls are being canvassed by our representative on the council (the athletes are represented by the grand total of two out of twenty-three on the BAAB), and of course the press.

'Do you support Zola? Would you sacrifice your place in the Olympics for her?' have been the never-ending questions all week. Really, any athlete's answer is academic as the final decision is not in our hands. My stock reply is 'I have tremendous sympathy for her. I feel she has suffered over the years from misguided advice, but at the same time must take some responsibility for her own actions. If she had behaved impeccably, renounced all links with South Africa and made every effort to become a British citizen I would feel more inclined to support her. But there are very few things I would sacrifice an Olympic place for, should I gain one. An Olympic place can be a once in a lifetime opportunity and I would not be prepared to give one up for Zola Budd.'

This is usually shortened by journalists to 'no'. Again I emphasise that I bear Budd no personal malice. She is suffering from the political expediency that in 1984 provided her with a British passport so conveniently, and her own continued links with the country of her birth. Ernest Obeng, a world class sprinter, who lives here in Loughborough working on a postgraduate thesis, applied four years ago for a British passport and is still waiting. Budd waited ten days.

Nobody seems to know what the BAAB will decide on Sunday. They are under pressure from all sides. One hundred Conservative MPs have signed a motion urging the board to oppose her suspension. A similar number of Labour MPs are calling for the opposite. Britain's participation in the Olympics could hang upon one individual. There are hundreds of us training so hard for so long, striving just to make the team, and it is all threatened by Zola Budd.

April 22. More off-track developments. I am now sponsored by a different equipment manufacturer. In future, my kit will be provided by Adidas. I know some of the employees at the company and am looking forward to wearing their products. Adidas will not supply me with too many hot-pink track-suits. So far I am impressed with the trainers and running spikes.

April 25. The BAAB have appointed a committee to examine Budd's alleged participation in the meeting at Brakspan. This committee will report back in late May and then the BAAB will decide whether to support or refuse the IAAF request to ban Zola. Therefore the issue will not be resolved for a few more weeks. In the meantime we runners can concentrate on our training, and everyone else can return to the other preoccupations of athletics like drugs and money.

With hindsight, if Budd had served a period of residential qualification in the UK like South African cricketers, even though that would have meant missing the Los Angeles Olympics, all the current problems might have been averted.

Returning to the IAAF, new evidence has recently emerged regarding the long jump controversy at the Rome World Championships. You may recall that the Italian athlete, Evangelisti, was awarded a bronze medal with an over-measured jump and I wondered if this was a legitimate mistake or an opportunity for abuse. It now transpires, following an investigation, that there was a plot hatched by Italian officials in advance of the competition. Evangelisti's sixth jump was deliberately measured wrongly.

The only individual who emerges with any credit from this blatant cheating is Evangelisti himself. He was unaware of the plot and offered to return his medal months ago. The IAAF have decided to rule out the athlete's sixth jump and award the bronze medal to fourth-place Larry Myricks, but their apparent lack of action against the Italian Athletic Federation contrasts vividly with their protestations over Budd. It is surprising that at the moment such obvious deception is not being dealt with much more severely.

Leaving the problems of international athletics for a moment and returning to the problems facing one runner and his preparations for Seoul, I am slowly (as ever) improving. I have tackled training with surprising optimism since my instantly forgettable race in Newcastle a few weeks ago. I am still not as fit as I was at this stage last year, but perhaps that is no disadvantage in the long term. Hopefully, even if my initial track performances this summer are not as fast as usual, I shall be reaching peak condition at the correct time of year. In the short term my final road race outing of a disappointing winter is next weekend. I am running in an eight kilometre city centre race in Lucerne, Switzerland. After that race I shall not compete until the track season begins.

Apil 30: Road Race, 8k, Lucerne. There could hardly be a more pleasant location for a road race than through the cobbled streets of the ancient town of Lucerne. The town, a popular tourist attraction alongside the lake, is reminiscent of the pictures on those brightly covered Swiss chocolates that most visitors bring home as presents. Lucerne has wooden bridges across the river, steamers on the lake, and exclusive watch shops in narrow streets overhung by timbered houses. The race course encompasses many of the sights on a short lap through the town centre, ideal for spectators and joggers but not much fun for serious athletes who find the tight corners an interruption to the rhythm of the race.

I had a good look at the course as I wandered through the crowds of Saturday afternoon shoppers on my way to the Mayor's pre-race reception. I dislike attending any function before a race but all the leading athletes were compulsory guests at the reception even though none of us touched the ornate buffet or drank any of the high quality plonk. Instead we stood around chatting aimlessly and eagerly waited to be dismissed. First, however, were the speeches. Unfortunately I managed to be pushed to the front as the assembled dignitaries edged to the rear of the room when the Mayor stepped forward. It is always difficult to look interested in speeches when you would rather be elsewhere, but on this occasion not only was I uncomfortably positioned in front of the speaker, I could not understand a word. The Mayor addressed us at length in German. I stood stationary with a considered expression on my face rendered meaningless by my immobile features when the rest of the audience burst into laughter. Standing at length listening to foreign speeches is not a recommended form of pre-race preparation and as soon as the Mayor was applauded there was a rush to the door by all the competitors. As I was escaping from under the Mayor's nose, I heard a slight gasp of shock as the room rapidly emptied but I dared not look back.

The race itself was straightforward. My old adversary Pierre Délèze, or Pierrot as the Swiss affectionately call him, stormed off from the start like a man possessed. He set a vicious pace and before long the two of us had opened up a large lead. Spurred on by the chanting crowd Déléze charged around the streets of Lucerne. I stayed with him for seven of the ten laps before gradually losing contact. Déléze won, I finished second, fourteen seconds behind but faster than the previous course record, and Peter Wirz was third forty-five seconds behind me.

Déléze had just become a father and I asked whether this had made him so aggressive. I had thought that becoming a parent might reduce your motivation as you realise there is more to life than running, but Pierre appeared more motivated than ever. He told me that fortunately his three month old daughter slept soundly and he was delighted with parenthood. His running was progressing without any problems and he was optimistic about the summer. Pierre is one of my closest adversaries. We have raced each other many times, most notably when I pipped him for the bronze medal in Rome, but our rivalry, although intense, is friendly. His performance in Lucerne indicates he is fitter than I am at the moment and he will start the summer in excellent condition. My result was nevertheless a significant improvement on my other races this year. Unlike Pierre, I shall have to rely on training not parenthood to boost my results.

May 7: Subventions. More off-track drama. The Zola Budd saga is on temporary hold and it is back to money matters. Early May is the time of year when the British Athletics Promotions Unit (BAPU) announce the subvention payments British athletes will receive for competing at televised events in Britain this summer. Last year BAPU significantly over spent, and for 1988 its budget has been cut by £300,000. We (we being all British athletes who receive subventions) realised that cut-backs were inevitable and have awaited the BAPU proposals with bated breath. The 1988 subvention scheme has just been announced and reactions have been mixed.

I have suffered more than most. My 1987 performances ranked me second in the world and I won a bronze medal in the World Championships. I was one of the successes of last summer. I was one of the few top athletes not to receive a Minet grant of £5000 towards my winter training and I have supported BAAB promotions loyally over the years, frequently without payment. I was quite prepared to accept a cutback in my subventions but expected I would suffer less than other athletes who had not achieved such good results as myself in 1987. My subventions have been cut by 60 per cent, whilst the overall budget has been reduced by 40 per cent – and I had an excellent year in 1987. The most annoying aspect of the proposals is not the money reductions, but the conditions the athletes must accept in agreement.

Once the athlete agrees to run in any of the meetings he or she cannot race abroad two days before or four days after each of the five meetings. If an athlete refuses to compete in one of the five meetings on such grounds, his or her total subvention money for the year will be halved. In Olympic year it is essential to have complete control over your own racing programme and BAPU's proposals are interfering with that vital aspect of Olympic preparation.

Once again, we are back to the good old conflict of promotion versus Olympic preparation, the problem of balancing the demands of television, the public, the sponsors and the athletes. It is the conflict that has been present throughout this diary and it is the dilemma that every international athlete must face – to chase the money or to concentrate on the major championships? As I have stated many times before, I think it is important to put athletic considerations ahead of financial ones. In the past it has been possible to achieve the right balance in a racing programme that enables the former without too severe effect on the latter. This year the choice has been made starker than previously. I know where my objectives lie and have written to BAPU to inform them that their proposals do not coincide with my athletic plans for 1988. What this means is that unless a compromise is reached, I shall not be racing in any of the British televised events this summer apart from the AAA Championships (the Olympic trials meeting where no subventions will be paid, as an automatic place in the British team is a sufficient inducement to participation – the selection policy coincidentally saving the BAAB money).

Instead, George and I shall prepare a racing programme suited to the main objective. I am looking forward to concentrating more on running and less on these peripheral off-track dramas. I have never known a winter and spring like this year. Hardly a week passes without some new scandal or controversy emerging.

I wanted to write an athletic diary not a soap opera tale of politics and intrigue. Sport should still, despite all the impediments of our current age, be about the simple virtues of sacrifice, determination and competition. Sport should not be swamped by the demands of commerce and politics. Perhaps I am only beginning to appreciate the effects of a sport's transition from amateur to professional. Perhaps once we accept the lure of Mammon we should not complain if we risk the true nature of our sport. Athletics has become so complicated. It is still a marvellous sport and by all accounts considerably 'cleaner' than many other sports, but we are currently bogged down in a mire of conflict and controversy. My wish for the forthcoming summer is that once the real action starts, once we witness some exciting athletics, the sideshow dramas will be returned to the periphery and we can concentrate on the genuine purpose of the sport. In the meantime my intention is to drastically reduce all discussion of non-athletic matters.

May 10. Back to the millstone. Eighty miles per week in the last month. Lots more in prospect throughout May and June. A couple of half decent track sessions, no news on my racing plans. Zola Budd has decided to take a long break from the sport. She will receive sympathy from many athletes (including me) for the pressure and problems she has faced. At the same time I hope that a lasting solution can be found by the IAAF and BAAB.

May 13. Track repetition runs, or reps as they are known in athletic circles, are a standard and much hated element in most athletes' training. Reps are a specific number of runs over a set distance with a timed recovery between each run. For example, twelve 400m with a one minute rest or ten 300m with a thirty second rest. Reps run at a pace close to or slightly quicker than that encountered in race conditions are ideal preparation for track competition. I have been churning out reps regularly for over ten years, but they have not become any easier.

The trick to running track reps is to learn accurate and economical pace judgement so that if you are running several 400m reps your times are not 61, 57, 62, 59 but 60, 60, 60, 60. I find that once I have found a groove, I can produce a string of times varying by at most one second. Reps sessions are best conducted in a small group of runners so that the lead and responsibility for the rep can be shared. Sharing the lead during reps is a constant source of grumbling amongst runners. In every group there is always someone reluctant to perform his share of front running, content to loiter at the back of the group and conserve his strength for the final rep, hoping to sprint past and 'win' the training session. Such behaviour is considered very bad form. Over the years at Loughborough there have been some real experts at this trick. Athletes who have remained invisible for the entire training session discover a burst of energy on the last rep. Interestingly they never seem to perform as well in races as on the last lap in training.

From the start of a reps workout I become absorbed by fractions and percentages. If I am running twelve repetitions and have completed two, I never think two down ten to go, but rather only one more until I am a quarter through the session. Likewise three out of twelve is a quarter, or one more until a third, or only just over a quarter until half-way. Six out of twelve is never half-way, it is one more until over half-way and only two until two-thirds completed. These complicated and trivial mathematical games take up so much time that before long I have reached ten and after double figures I am so near the end I forget about my mental calculations.

My absorption with numbers is, I suppose, an attempt to

ignore the pain I am feeling as I lap around the track. I read somewhere that the best athletes embrace rather than ignore pain. My own experience is less romantic. I certainly do not embrace the pain. I think the effect of pain – that tightening of the muscles and the increasing tension throughout the body – is to cause the mind to wander so the challenge becomes one of concentration. The aim is to override the pain by concentrating on relaxation whilst maintaining and perhaps increasing speed, to keep movement under control even though your body is screaming with the effort.

Some nights, the reps workout becomes an exercise in concentration from the opening lap. Occasionally as I approach a high level of fitness I can afford to let my mind wander as I relax at speed, confident in my ability to produce lap after lap controlled and fast. Last night was the first occasion this year I had such a training session. The track seemed to shrink and I could predict the 400m times before George shouted them out. My confidence has been boosted and I am beginning to look forward at last to the races ahead.

May 18: Summer Plans. The summer now has a definite shape. George and I met the director of BAPU, Andy Norman, and reached an agreement over my racing plans. I was worried that I would be forced into compromising my summer racing programme to meet the demands of BAPU. George and I were prepared for me to race abroad rather than accept a rigid programme of races in this country. A satisfactory compromise was achieved by me agreeing to run most 1500m and 3000m races in the televised British meetings, leaving me free to run 5000m abroad. I am quite happy to accept a reduction in my subvention payments for running over shorter distances, and my greater pulling power over 5000m is tacitly acknowledged by Andy Norman. He does not expect me to run the distance in Britain for a much reduced subvention that does not reflect my market value.

We managed to agree on a programme that should, fitness permitting, provide the right balance of 1500m, 3000m and

5000m prior to my hopeful participation in the Olympics. I want to try and run a fast 5000m in early July as an insurance policy before the trials in early August. A fast time will help my case for the third 'selection' place in the British team. Ideally I should like to obtain the third place (remember the first two from the AAA Championships in early August are automatically in the team) before the trials and therefore avoid the pressure and potential dangers of running the 5000m in the AAA Championships. I therefore intend to run a low key 3000m in the annual Loughborough versus AAA fixture on June 12, followed by two 1500m races on June 24 and 27. These races are in the BAPU televised package – England versus USA at Birmingham on the 24th and the Belfast Games on the 27th – and will provide good speed work before my first high point of the summer, a 5000m in Oslo on July 2. Oslo is where I want to try and run a fast time for the event I hope to contest in Seoul.

After Oslo, I shall compete in the occasional 1500m and 3000m before the AAA Championships where, if I can rely on my Oslo performance and undisputed world ranking of the last two years (in 1986 and 1987 I was ranked second to Aouita over 5000m, well ahead of any other British runner), I shall run the 1500m for more speed work. If my favoured plans are disrupted by poor results or injury I shall have to race the AAA 5000m on August 7, which could become one of the most important 'pressure' races of my career if my Olympic hopes rely upon the outcome. Thus, the aim of an Oslo insurance policy!

After the AAA, assuming I am selected for the Olympic team, George and I shall review the final six weeks before the Games, looking for another 5000m and a few more shorter distance races to keep the leg speed ticking over. In a nutshell, those are my plans leading up to the Olympics. The twin aims are first to gain selection as painlessly as possible, and secondly to be in condition to run better than ever before in Seoul.

1. Winning the 1986 European Championship 5000m, Stuttgart

2. World Championship 5000m final, Rome 1987

3. Me and Kerin

4. Clocking up the miles

5. Training in Bradgate Park

6. Competing for position
with Gary Stains (23),
2 miles, Crystal Palace

7. Seoul Olympic 5000m semi-final. Leading a group including Castro (861), Ondieki (667), and Maree. In the distance Kunze, Baumann and Thiebaut. All caught me on the last lap.

8. Olympic 5000m final, Seoul. John Doherty, Sydney Maree and me.

8

Injury Trouble

May 20. Typical – no sooner have I worked out my plans for the summer and run a couple of decent training sessions than I injure myself. I was beginning to regain confidence after a low key winter and now I am reduced to inactivity. This week my right hip has been gradually developing soreness. I have had problems with my hip before. In 1983 I ignored a painful injury in the same hip and ended up with a stress fracture that prevented me from running for three months. I should have been more careful when I felt the first twinges of discomfort a few days ago. If I had listened to the complaining gripes from my right leg and rested I could have avoided the injury. Instead I ignored the pain, convinced it was a figment of my imagination. I kept on running. Last night my leg was throbbing when I walked around the house and this morning I dared not even attempt to run.

Instead I visited the physiotherapist, Glynnis Boon, in Nottingham. She has treated my injuries at regular intervals over the years and quickly diagnosed the problem, an inflamed bursa. This was precisely the injury I had in 1983 that through negligence developed into a stress fracture. If the injury persists for even half as long as in 1983, my Olympic plans will be in ruins. Hopefully, having learnt from experience, swift and intensive treatment will contain and eliminate the inflammation before too much time disappears. But, as the physio explained, bursitis can persist for several weeks even with regular treatment. She called up the specialist Dr Mike Hutson who conveniently works downstairs. They both conferred and decided the best course of action was to give me a cortisone injection. A cortisone injection would reduce the inflammation. It should be followed by forty-eight hours' rest and then physiotherapy treatment every day next week. I might be running within a fortnight.

After my gloomy thoughts of a complete destruction of the summer I willingly settled for (hopefully) a mere fortnight of complete running inactivity, so the injection was duly administered. It was not as painful as I expected. I must allow the injection to settle and return after the weekend for physiotherapy. No exercise is permitted and especially no running.

May 24. Injuries are the occupational hazard of a runner's life. Training so hard, it is inevitable that at some point in the year the runner's body will protest. But, being aware of the likelihood of injury does not prevent the runner from feeling frustrated and impatient when he suffers from the consequences of continually pounding his fragile frame. Most injuries that runners develop are not accidents, like twisted ankles or broken limbs, but stress injuries from the over-use of the body. The volume of training and the constant repetition of the same physical exercise fatigues the muscles, ligaments and bones.

The problem with stress related injuries is that as their cause is directly related to the exercise the sufferer so eagerly pursues, recovery is best achieved by avoiding the source of the trouble. Therefore, in my case, no running until the hip was healed. Another difficulty with this common type of injury is that the pain develops gradually and can be ignored. If you twist an ankle playing football, the pain is immediately obvious. You must stop and rest. With stress injuries, the pain begins as mild discomfort that you usually ignore. The discomfort gradually increases, but still you refuse to acknowledge it. After all, stoical runners are trained to overcome pain. The injury persists, like toothache nagging away until at last you stop. At what point you stop depends on the individual, but with most runners it is often too late. I should have stopped a couple of days earlier.

Despite my delay the bursitis appears to be responding to treatment. I returned to the physio a couple of days after the cortisone injection, ready for some serious treatment. This comprises ice, ultrasound and the house speciality – friction massage. The first two are standard primitive and modern therapies for a wide range of injuries. The third deserves some explanation. Friction massage is used to break down inflammation. The physio finds the most tender area of the injury and then leans on it until the patient screams. The physio then presses harder. I have found this treatment does wonders for the injury, even though the personal relationship between patient and practitioner can become a little strained whilst the friction is being applied.

I am not allowed to resume running for several days, but in the meantime swimming and cycling are permitted. These two activities will not impose further stress on my hip and will hopefully enable me to maintain fitness whilst I forgo my main sporting addiction.

May 27. The visits to the physio continue and my recovery has been faster than I dared hope a week ago. My hip has regained its full range of movement. The friction massage has reduced the inflammation and I may be able to resume gentle jogging this weekend. I am delighted with the apparent speed of my healing. Perhaps I did not misjudge the injury after all. I have only lost a week's running and if I return to serious training within the next ten days, I need not alter my racing plans.

But amidst my enthusiasm there is a hint of caution. I can jog gently over the weekend and I can slowly increase my running, provided there is no reaction from the hip. Bursitis has a notorious reputation for recurring. The injury was caused by over-use and there is no guarantee that returning to running will not result in the bursa flaring up again. On the other hand I cannot discover if the injury has healed without trying to run on it. Therefore, I must take the risk and tentatively test my recovery.

June 1. Is it better or is it worse? Am I exaggerating or ignoring the pain? I started running over the weekend. Gentle jogging on Friday and Saturday, a couple of thirty minutes easy on Sunday and steady running Monday and Tuesday. The original hip injury appears to have settled down but I am now feeling discomfort in my groin on the same leg. I hope the pain I am experiencing in my groin is only stiffness as I resume regular running and not anything more serious. If the soreness disappears within the next couple of days my own diagnosis will be proved correct, but currently the pain is increasing not decreasing.

I had hoped that after my discharge from the physio last week I would be able to resume serious training this week. I should have remembered that the road to recovery is rarely smooth. I still persist in believing that after a week without running, I shall be totally cured and sufficiently healthy to restart training without any problems. I forget how hard I am pushing my body. I must be patient and if the injury recurs or develops in a different area I shall have to stop again. In the meantime, all I can do is to test myself carefully, ice the leg after every run and assess the situation day by day. If my groin has not eased within forty-eight hours I shall go back to the specialist.

Yesterday I made the mistake of reading my *Sports Injuries – a unique guide to self-diagnosis and rehabilitation* book. Like the narrator of *Three Men in a Boat* who, upon feeling unwell, reads a medical dictionary and decides he is suffering from every ailment in the book, I convinced myself that besides suffering from capsulitis (arthritis of the hip), I had also succumbed to a pull-off fracture, osteitis pubis symphysis (footballer's groin), a trochanteric bursa and possibly an adductor muscle strain. I estimate my recovery time could therefore be several years.

Actually after my run this morning I feel more positive about the future. George is a continual source of sound, practical advice. I think he is playing the experienced coach role, soothing the over-reacting paranoid athlete very well.

June 4. Back to the physio. This time it is the adductor muscle of my right leg. Nothing too serious, but another irritating interruption. I can continue to jog gently although I cannot train properly. No track training until the strain has recovered. As usual I must force myself to be patient and keep treating the injury with all the proven remedies. After over two weeks of virtual inactivity I am becoming frustrated.

June 10. Whenever I am injured there are two stories. The first is given to the press, general public and most people involved in athletics. The second is limited to my immediate circle of family, coach and physiotherapist. Currently, the first story is as follows: 'just a minor problem, will only delay training for a few days, nothing to worry about, probably a good thing in the long term.' The second story is one of greater concern and increasing irritation, tempered by the knowledge that I am doing everything possible to aid recovery.

Which story is the real truth is difficult to tell. If I can resume training within the next few days, the first story will, I hope, prove to be most accurate. If my groin injury persists for much longer I could be in serious trouble. Suppose I start running properly within a week. Then I might still race in Oslo and could still attempt a fast 5000m in advance of the AAA Championships. My plan of gaining Olympic selection and avoiding the pressure of the trials race could remain intact.

But, if I am unable to run for another two weeks I may not regain fitness before the AAA and shall be forced to compete in the AAA Championships to gain my place in the British team. In that case, I shall probably find the AAA Championships as great a pressure as the Olympics themselves, should I succeed in the former. I should not complain if I am forced to run in the trials, as I shall only be in the same boat as everyone else who has serious Olympic ambitions. The selection policy of first two in the AAA plus A. N. Other is designed to give everyone the chance to make the team, so who am I to buck the system? But, as the undisputed British number one 5000m runner of the last two years (I make it sound like a pop record), I can lay stronger claim to the A. N. Other third place than anyone else. Therefore it is not surprising that I should try to gain the third place with as little inconvenience as possible en route to Seoul. Hence, my and George's plan to run a fast time early season and run the 1500m in the AAA as speed work. This plan may shortly be abandoned, in which case there will be no alternative to running in the AAA, unless my injury persists for so long that I cannot regain fitness by early August. This would force me to miss the AAA and rely on my past record to convince the selectors to pick me for Seoul! This final alternative does not currently bear thinking about.

Such speculation is futile in my present condition. I must forget all the permutations and concentrate on recovery. But my survey of the options available helps explain why I have two stories on the state of my injury. I, like every other prospective Olympian, am engaged in the art of the selection manoeuvre, attempting to gain psychological and hopefully physical advantage over rivals for the British team. The art of the selection manoeuvre is best illustrated by the current strategies of two skilled exponents – Seb Coe and Steve Cram.

Coe and Cram are both manoeuvring for the third place in the 1500m. Both have announced their intention not to run in the 1500m trial in the AAA and both are undoubtedly looking to run a fast 1500m in advance of the AAA. Furthermore, the last strategy either will adopt is to race each other. Whoever lost would have to run the AAA. It is a game of bluff. Their hands are equally matched. Cram is a former world record holder, former world champion and European champion at 1500m, whilst Coe has likewise held the world record and is the double Olympic champion at the distance. If one of them records a very fast time, that could tip the balance in his favour. But if both of them record fast times or both are injured and cannot compete in the AAA, what happens then? The selectors have said they will stick to their policy, so who will they favour and who will win the battle of the selection manoeuvre?

It is impossible to understand the race strategies and public comments of any well known British athlete in advance of the Olympic team being selected, without appreciating that the selection manoeuvre is uppermost in all our minds. When I say my injury is 'just a niggle', I might be honest or I might be deceiving my rivals so that they do not gain a small advantage in the game. Perhaps, I do not want anyone to think that he can run a fast time in my absence and therefore force me to run the AAA.

These tactics may infuriate the athletics public who want to see genuine confrontations between our best runners, but they are understandable if the powerful motivation of the Olympics is appreciated. The aim is to gain selection with minimum pressure and disruption to Olympic plans. The greater the domestic challenge, the greater the risk of disappointment in Seoul. Therefore to improve chances in Seoul, athletes become experts in ducking questions and avoiding unnecessary confrontation, like politicians leading up to an election. The selection manoeuvre is an extension of the athlete's traditional competitiveness on the running track into the realm of the fourth estate. We are all fighting for advantage off the track as hard as we would on it.

The selection manoeuvre is not a recent development. Athletes have always indulged in such strategies, but it is particularly obvious this year because there are so many talented runners competing for so few places in the team. The selection policy is an attempt to diffuse all the weaving and dodging that has taken place in the past, but athletes have become too skilled at the game to stop now.

Anyway, as the athletes' motivation is primarily the Olympic Games, perhaps indulging in selection tactics is ultimately in the best interests of the British Olympic team. It must be preferable to ignoring the Olympics and chasing the dollars. If there were no selection manoeuvres what would happen to all the juicy speculation and gossip in the press?

June 14. Last weekend I should have run my first serious race of the summer, the annual Loughborough versus the AAA fixture. It was only the second time I have missed the meeting since 1980. I have won either the 1500m or 3000m in the event for the last four years. But on Sunday I was spectating not competing. On a bright breezy afternoon I wandered around chatting, laughing and feeling uncomfortable. I would have preferred not to attend the athletics. When I am injured I lose all interest in the sport, but on Sunday I felt an obligation to attend the only important local athletics fixture in the year.

I presented some prizes and conducted a couple of radio interviews. Everyone I spoke to was full of amiable encouragement and I replied confidently to the friendly enquiries about my state of health. I did not reveal my concern over the injury, partly because I do not want stories appearing in the press, but chiefly because I know from experience how boring it is to hear an athlete moaning about injuries. I pretended to show my enthusiasm for the athletics and I did genuinely enjoy seeing some of my training partners run well, but I still found the afternoon an ordeal.

I suppose I do not honestly enjoy athletics when I cannot compete myself. I realise that is a self-centred admission and is not a good attitude to possess, but it is my honest reaction. Perhaps in a few years when I have retired and the mere sight of an athletics track does not set my nerves tingling in anticipation I shall view the sport with more equanimity. In the future when running is no longer so important to me I hope I can watch the sport without experiencing the envy and resentment I currently feel as I watch from the sidelines, unable to jog for more than ten minutes without being aware of my injury.

June 18. Glancing through my diary for last year, it is a familiar story: '22nd June, I'm trying hard to be rational, but it is no good. Looking at the situation objectively I should regain fitness in time for the World Championships, but as always when I'm injured I worry endlessly.' Twelve months on and the situation is very similar. I am injured again and still worrying, but this time with more justification.

In 1987 I had already recorded some solid track performances by mid-June, this year I have hardly stepped on the track. Also, last year I was pre-selected for the British World Championship team whereas in 1988 there is, as I have written on dozens of occasions, no pre-selection for Seoul. Finally, I have not run for the last five weeks and am still pessimistic. Overall, my current prospects are about as slim as those of a British male tennis player winning Wimbledon. Nevertheless, in my incapacitated condition I shall spend much of the next fortnight watching that noble championship rather than the opening fixtures of the international athletics season.

My treatment is continuing, including some visits to a highly regarded osteopath whose manipulation may, I hope, do the trick. Terry Moule has had some excellent results with other athletes and his efficient treatment has already loosened up my right hip and groin. Currently my day is filled with medical appointments, either to the physio in Nottingham or Terry Moule in Milton Keynes. This is when the sporting existence can become depressing. Without running my life lacks a framework. I organise everything around running and when I am injured there is no structure to the day. I am so used to fitting meals, work, sleep and all the other aspects of living around the rigid running lifestyle that I lose motivation, purpose and discipline when running no longer binds life together. The daily trips to the physio are no replacement for the routine of training.

I can tolerate injury for a couple of weeks, but after five weeks without running at one of the most crucial periods of the year it is not surprising that I am losing patience. I cannot discipline myself to avoid my favourite calorie laden foods that I do not usually eat. I am currently half a stone overweight, but what is the point in dieting when I cannot run? The longer I am injured, the more I lose incentive to maintain a healthy diet and live a running centred lifestyle. If I remain immobile for the next few weeks I expect I shall want to escape completely and lie on a beach for the rest of the summer.

All my traditional doubts are reappearing. I am twenty-six with virtually no work experience. What can I do in the future? What happens if I never run successfully again? I imagine the next few years disappearing in a sequence of frustrating problems, culminating in unemployment as a disillusioned, bitter ex-athlete. I realise I should not take sport so seriously, after all 'it's only a game', but in accepting an athletics 'career' it is easy to lose perspective.

There is a difference between an amateur and a full-time athlete dependent upon his or her ability, and trust fund, to live. The full-time athlete adopts a more professional attitude to the sport because it provides his or her means of existence. Injury becomes all the more frustrating, therefore, because the athlete finds his or her livelihood threatened. If I was an amateur athlete in the traditional sense of the word – someone for whom sport was essentially a hobby, a diversion from the more important business of earning a living – I could afford to be more flippant about running. I would be approaching athletics with a different attitude. But, for better or for worse, running is my career and consequently I am very concerned when injury interrupts my progress.

June 23. Away gloom, doubt and despondency, there is cause for cautious optimism. I have embarked upon yet another attempt to return to training. In the last few weeks I have attempted as many comebacks as Jeffrey Archer, although so far my attempts have met with a conspicuous lack of success. I started jogging a couple of days ago and am now up to thirty minutes' easy running each morning. There is a long way to go until I can return to track training and the prospect of racing is still a distant hope, but at least I have made a start.

I do not know if I can recover fitness in time for the Olympic trials, or if I shall break down again as soon as I increase my training, or if I have any chance of selection for the Olympics, but it is wonderful to be back running.

June 30. Another week and I am still training. Nothing

spectacular and so far no evidence that I was once a genuine athlete, but at least I am progressing steadily if slowly. Regular visits to the osteopath Terry Moule have worked wonders. My approach to athletics obviously bears more resemblance to the tortoise rather than the hare. In the race for Seoul, there is no danger I shall take an early lead and it remains to be seen whether my plodding will catch up in the end.

But who cares about such future excitements? Injury has lowered my objectives and I am revelling in the simple pursuit of running. I have missed my jaunts around Loughborough, feeling the grass beneath my aching Achilles tendons and breathing the freshly M1 polluted air. Before long I even hope to escape the clutches of the medical profession.

I have only had about five weeks away from running, but it seems like years. My body seems to have forgotten how to run. In addition to my inevitably sore Achilles tendons, my hips are stiff, calves are seizing up and quadriceps are as flexible as bricks. This is all part of the grumbling return to twice per day training. My running does not feel natural any more. I have to think where I am putting my feet. Usually I simply start running and mentally switch off, leaving my body on automatic pilot. Until I have overcome my body's initial reluctance to the strain of resumed physical activity, I have to concentrate on the mechanics of running. I am hopeful of returning to automatic pilot before long.

July 7. There is an unusual aroma wafting through our house. Close inspection reveals the source of this strange odour. It is the linen basket in the bathroom that sets the nostrils twitching. If the lid is cautiously lifted all is revealed. The linen basket is filled with sweaty T-shirts, smelly socks and dirty tracksuits. The smell is a fragrance for me to savour – if not for Kerin. It is evidence of my return to running.

After all these weeks of forced inactivity I am at long last back to serious training. As my running increases, so does the volume of discarded kit and, if the washing machine is given a couple of days' rest, so does the whiff of honest toil pervade the house.

With every freshly soiled item hurled into the linen basket, my hopes rise. The more washing, the more training. The more training, the greater fitness. Today I am even contemplating a track session in spikes. If my recovery continues I shall think of racing in a couple of weeks.

Optimism in the Buckner household is directly related to the volume of washing in the linen basket.

July 12. After three weeks' running it is time for another review of the general situation. I had a conference with George yesterday to hatch our latest plans on how to take the world of athletics by storm. But first, a reappraisal of 1988 so far.

What an awful year it has been! My least successful and most infuriating year in the sport. Between the spring of 1986 and the winter of 1987–8 I enjoyed a tremendous eighteen months. Silver medal in the Commonwealth Games 5000m, gold in the Europeans, bronze in the World Championships, personal bests at every distance, several notable victories, fame and hopes of fortune. I could do no wrong.

I started this diary at the time of the World Championships and everything went smoothly until January. I won the Zurich road race comfortably in December 1987 and was satisfied with my Christmas level of fitness. But since then improvement has been erratic and insufficient to mount a serious Olympic challenge. A bout of flu ruined my New Year training and I struggled through the spring. In May my injury problem began, ruining the vital pre-season track training. I have resumed training, but my overall fitness is lacking and there is less than four weeks until the team for the Olympics is announced.

The frustrations of 1988 thus far have also affected my confidence. At one of the functions we attended last year I remember saying to George that I believed I could be capable of running 5000m in 13.20 within a month, whatever my state of fitness. I have a month to the AAA Olympic trials and 13.20 is a time that would virtually guarantee my selection. Last year I was the only British athlete to break 13.20 and this year nobody has run quicker than 13.22. But my solid confidence of last year, built on the successes of Stuttgart and Rome, has been dented by the months of injury and poor results. Doubt, the enemy of all sportspeople, has reared its ugly head.

All my doubt would be dispelled if my performances on the track improved. I am only a couple of good races away from the athlete I was last year. I believe I shall return to my high standards of the last two years sometime, but I do not know how long it will take. I am convinced that the training methods I have followed under George are correct and I am sure I am pursuing the sensible and logical route back to fitness. My fitness will return eventually so long as I continue to train progressively. I must limit my doubt and not panic.

I am training on the track tonight. It will be the first time since my injury that the stopwatch records my performance. There is no hiding from the harsh judgement of time. I am apprehensive of the result as it will reveal the extent of my recovery. This is stupid. I must relax and be patient. It is a pleasure to be running again and it does not matter if my 400m splits are not as fast as I would like. My fitness will improve and worrying will not help matters. I only hope it improves sooner rather than later.

July 13. I managed a half decent set of 400m repetitions last night. Nothing spectacular, but I might have convinced an observer that I was not a jogger trundling around the track. A few more weeks of this type of work and I could pass for a real runner again.

9

Slow Recovery

July 14: The Selection Dilemma. There are two ways to approach athletics. The first is to train until you feel you have reached a reasonable standard of fitness and then start racing. As there are so many opportunities to race these days you will have no problem finding competition. You can continue racing until you feel your performance is suffering and you need a break. The art is to know when to stop before your fitness suffers.

The alternative approach is to plan your fitness around your main objectives. You decide where you want to reach your peak performance and organise your training and racing programme accordingly. Many athletes attempt to combine the two approaches, racing according to their fitness but at the same time keeping an eye on their main objectives.

I am an advocate of the planning approach to athletics. My priority in athletics has always been to perform at my best in the events that really count – the major international championships. Experience has taught me that I do not have the ability or strength to chase around the athletic tracks of the world and then maintain my fitness for the important championships. Therefore I pick my races carefully and nurture my fitness, hoping to blossom on the right day. The planning approach is more complicated than allowing fitness to dictate your performances. An inopportune injury can decimate an entire season. But, if you set your objectives and achieve them, overcoming the problems you may face, the planning approach is ultimately more rewarding.

This year my single aim has been to reach the Olympic Games with the best chance of success. Every training session and every race has been conducted with Seoul at the back of my mind. So far this year nothing has progressed according to plan. My winter and spring form was disappointing and I have lost the entire first half of the summer season through injury. But, if I manage to reach Seoul and run to the best of my ability all these early set-backs will be forgotten.

There are indications that my form may be returning slowly. If I can train for the next ten weeks without interruption, I may still have a chance of reaching the Olympics ready to challenge for a medal. But to achieve the level of fitness necessary for Seoul, I shall require an unbroken and consistent spell of training that has so far eluded me in 1988.

The ideal plan to provide me with the best chance in Seoul would be training here in Loughborough for the rest of the summer, interspersed with a series of races to assess fitness, including at least one respectable 5000m. There is, however, one major short term problem that could potentially ruin everything – selection for the British team.

In November the BAAB selection policy was a small cloud on the horizon that could threaten me in the unlikely event of injury. Now it is a menacing presence casting a dark shadow over all my schemes. The first two in the AAA plus A. N. Other will comprise the British team in each event. My dilemma is should I run the trials or not? Can I rely on the selectors to choose me for the third place without running in Birmingham? Unless there is a dramatic improvement in my fitness it is unlikely I shall perform at my best in the AAA in just over three weeks' time. Would it be better for my selection chances to avoid the AAA and rely upon my previous record or to run a mediocre 5000m in Birmingham? Without doubt the

AAA will interfere with my preparations for Seoul, but there is not much point in concentrating on the Olympics if I am not going to be chosen for the British team.

My situation can be better understood by a resumé of the likely protagonists for the three places in the 5000m. My potential adversaries will probably come from amongst the following:

Tim Hutchings: my closest rival over the years, fourth in the 1984 Olympic Games 5000m, third in the Commonwealth Games in 1986 and third in the European Championships the same year. He is returning from injury and slowly regaining his form.

Eamon Martin: the man of the moment and probably favourite for the AAA. Injured in 1985 and 1986, but is currently running better than ever. In the Oslo meeting he ran his first ever 10,000m and smashed the British record with the fifth fastest 10,000m ever. Most pundits (including me) think he should run the 10,000m in Seoul but he continues to state his preference for the 5000m.

Gary Staines: ran well at the end of last summer. He has made the transition from 1500m to 5000m most effectively. He spent last winter in Australia and has returned to Britain in good form.

Paul Davies-Hale: has the talent, as was proved when he won the Talbot games 5000m a couple of weeks ago, but would he last the demanding Olympic programme of three races in four days?

Dave Moorcroft: the former world record holder, but has not been a serious threat for several years. Everyone (again including me) would like to see him run competitively for a final time.

There could always be a surprise but at the moment these five are my potential rivals for the British Olympic team. None of them possesses a record that can match mine over the last two years. I have been second fastest in the world over 5000m in 1986 and 1987. I am reigning European Champion at the distance, Commonwealth silver medallist and World bronze medallist. No British athlete has beaten me on the track at 5000m since the 1986 Commonwealth Games. I hope therefore the selectors would want to pick me for the third place.

But, suppose I do not run in the trials what will the selectors do? I think it will depend on the race result. Eamon Martin is very much the man in form. He should win the trials and will then have to decide whether to run the 5000m or 10,000m or both. I think to try and run both would be selfish and foolhardy. I would hope the selectors and everyone associated with Martin would try to dissuade him. Suppose for the moment he decides on the 5000m, having won the trial, with Tim Hutchings second. In that situation I think the selectors would choose me for the third place as none of the others listed above have the credentials to fill it.

The circumstance in which there could be difficulty is if Tim came third in the trials. Tim is the only athlete who has a sufficiently impressive record to lay claim to the third place if he had finished third in the AAA. I think the key to my selection if I do not compete in Birmingham is the performance of Hutchings and possibly the decision of Martin. The worst result for me would be for Hutchings to finish third. But, even if that happened I am reasonably optimistic the selectors would give me a chance to contest the third place assuming I am still making progress towards full fitness.

Fortunately I do not have to reach a decision about competing in the AAA for a couple of weeks. In the meantime I should stop this idle speculation and concentrate on training. I intend to run my first race in Derby next Wednesday (six days' time). I am not expecting an earth-shattering performance just a solid result in a fairly low-key event. Then on July 29 I shall run in the IAC Grand Prix meeting in Edinburgh, where there is an international handicap mile. A fast mile should blow away a few cobwebs and help me in my decision over the AAA.

There is no need to resolve my dilemma before the IAC mile although my intuition is not to run the AAA unless I am very confident of finishing in the first three.

July 18. Over the weekend I struggled through an especially vicious track session. Before I was injured I was beginning to withstand some of the more demanding workouts without a complete physical collapse. Six weeks of comparative inactivity and my ability to cope has been reduced dramatically.

I staggered across the finishing line after the last 600m repetition and experienced all the ghastly symptoms familiar to any exhausted athlete. My legs were lead weights that had to be dragged over the last 100m, I was gasping for air and my head was pounding. It is at this particular moment in time that I often wonder – why?

Hopefully it will only take a few more of these cruel workouts before I rediscover my track speed. As my fitness improves I shall become more accustomed to the synthetic surface of the track and I shall begin to feel slightly more relaxed and confident.

The effect of training is not only increased fitness but also quicker recovery. In a few weeks I shall find it much more difficult to completely exhaust myself in training. I shall train just as hard but because my body is better conditioned I shall recover much more rapidly. This effect explains why today's modern athlete is capable of jogging a lap of honour almost immediately after the race whereas our plimsolled predecessors would have been suffering from the final stages of exhaustion.

Advances in training mean the modern runner can run faster and more regularly than his ancestors. One of those sporting imponderables to discuss over a philosophical drink is how the great runners of the past would have fared with contemporary training knowledge, modern tracks and the opportunity to devote themselves full-time to the sport.

There are only a couple of days until my first race – a 3000m for the Midland Counties at Derby. It will be the first occasion I have run for the Midland Counties since 1980 when, for a promising junior, their fixtures provided an excellent standard of competition. Wednesday's match should include a similar mix of aspiring youngsters, quality county athletes, fringe internationals and the odd faded star trying to regain former glories.

Over the years I have fitted into every category and am currently working my way out of the last one. Roll on Wednesday!

July 21: 3000m race, Derby. Comments from my training diary on last night's race: '3000m in Derby, first in eight minutes six seconds. 4.08 first 1500m, 3.58 second 1500m. There really is a long way to go. Can I be the same athlete as in 1986 and 1987? I suppose it was my first track race and at least I won, but 8.06 is a very slow time. I was working hard over the last couple of laps. Tendons sore afterwards but no problems with hip and adductor.'

At heart I am an optimist. Before last night's race I had this silly hope that once I returned to the competitive arena the metaphorical weights that have seemed to be strapped to my legs for most of this year would fall away. Unburdened, I would glide around the track with my former efficiency. This was a forlorn hope. I won the race, but my time was slow and I struggled to maintain my fading form over the final 400m. There is no sudden recovery, no amazing return to fitness.

In some sports it is possible to suddenly rediscover your 'touch'. The best example I can remember of this is Ian Botham in the 1981 Test series against Australia. Botham's performances improved overnight as, freed from the captaincy, he dramatically saved the Headingley Test. Golfers, tennis players and footballers likewise can all make equally dramatic reversions in their standard of play. Running, particularly distance running, is different. Your form is based fundamentally on training. As your fitness improves so does your performance. You can spot athletes running into form. Their performances steadily improve and then reach a peak. I know all this, but still hope that I can make the magical transition to full fitness without the necessary period of steady conditioning.

I am making progress, even though my progress is much slower than I would wish. Last night's 3000m confirmed this. Three weeks ago I could not run a single lap of the track without experiencing discomfort and pain from my right leg. I can now run seven and a half laps at a steady pace that would be considered slow as a 3000m split time en route to an average 5000m. An eight minute pace for 3000m continued for another five laps would result in a 13.20 time for 5000m – a respectable performance, but not necessarily one to win Olympic medals. At some time in the future, through patient, consistent training I shall regain my fitness. Last night was a tiny step forward.

July 25: Review of the Summer. Another week begins, another week of training. The days are dragging as I wait for my fitness to return and as the AAA Championships and the selection of the Olympic team looms closer.

I am racing on Friday night in the IAC meeting in Edinburgh. It will be my first major track race of the summer and afterwards I shall decide whether to run the AAA or risk selection for the third place. I am running in the 'handicap' mile in Edinburgh, quite appropriate in view of my current condition. I am not sure if my handicap is to be based on my personal best – 3.51.5 – or my current form, more like 4.05! I shall find out more details in the next couple of days.

There has been a lull in the summer athletics circuit since early July. The IAC meet heralds the start of what the American agents often call the 'second half' of the European season. The 'second half' sees the culmination of the athletics Grand Prix and should indicate who are the athletes to watch in Seoul. The highlights of August and early September should be the meetings in Zurich, Brussels, Cologne and the Grand Prix final in Berlin.

The first half of this athletics summer has not produced the usual level of competition. This is because athletes the world over have been concentrating on Olympic selection and delaying their best form until later in the year. During August when most countries have selected their teams performances should be more spectacular. If the results of the US Olympic trials are a yardstick, we are in for some remarkable athletics.

The US Olympic trials took place last week. The brutal selection procedure – first three automatic selection, tough luck if you fall over – produced some incredible competition. The sprints were probably as tough as the Olympics themselves. Star of the show was Florence Griffith-Joyner with a world record in the women's 100m. Carl Lewis led home a sub ten second 100m and the men's 400m won by Butch Reynolds produced the first ever sea-level sub 44 seconds run. Second place Danny Everett also broke 44 seconds. The question to ask about the Olympic men's 400m relay is not whether the USA quartet will win, but by how much will they break the world record.

But amidst all this magnificent sprinting there were the inevitable tragedies. Greg Foster, world high-hurdle champion, ran with a broken arm and pulled up in the semi-final. In the men's 1500m Jim Spivey, possibly the only American medal contender at the distance, was outsprinted in a slow, bruising race. Both athletes will be missed in the Olympics.

The US trials was a marvellous week's athletics and there are doubtless those who would wish to see such a system implemented in the UK. First three automatic selection is the fairest method, as everyone has the opportunity to challenge for a place in the team. Everyone, regardless of their past record, starts equal. But, as I have argued elsewhere, I do not believe it produces the best results. It hinges on whether the priority is to pick a team fairly or to select the best team to win medals. I think you must try and combine both objectives with a system that allows for selection rather than merely filling in the winning names of one afternoon's sport. The USA can afford their system more than us in the UK because their athletic resources are so much greater. If Calvin Smith fell over in the 100m there would be another half a dozen sprinters all capable of winning medals in South Korea. If we adopted the USA system and Linford Christie fell over, our one sprint hopeful would be out of the Olympics.

But where the USA system is most brutal is in the middle distances. Here tactics and weather conditions can affect the outcome in a dramatic fashion. A slow, awkward race can result in an unpredictable result. This is what happened in the men's 1500m. Two of the first three finishers were complete unknowns who do not possess the qualifying time for the Games. Left behind, as well as Jim Spivey, are three sub 3.35 runners. A similar result in the notoriously windy Birmingham Alexander stadium is feasible. Seb Coe and Peter Elliott outsprinted and out of the British team could happen in the AAA.

As far as I am concerned thank goodness the third selection place exists. The way I am running at the moment it remains my best chance of competing in Seoul.

July 26. A recent diversion from the athletics world was a Central TV sports seminar in Leicester. The idea, to have a question and answer session with a panel of personalities from different sports, was simple but effective. Unfortunately on the evening in question there was an enormous thunderstorm which resulted in only a small audience attending the evening's entertainment.

Once the audience overcame its initial nervousness there were some imaginative queries. Before long there was a vigorous discussion on many aspects of modern sport. The panel encompassed a wide range of sports. There was a snooker player, Willie Thorne; a cricketer, Chris Broad; a tennis player, Ann Hobbs; a rugby fly-half, Les Cusworth; and myself, a semi-fit athlete. This diversity of sports provided a cross-section of opinions.

The best question I received was from an enthusiastic youngster in the front row. He had already asked Chris Broad how he coped with the West Indian fast bowler. He posed me an equally difficult question. 'I ran the 800m in my school sports day,' he commented. 'At the end I was a b s o l u t e l y k n a c k e r e d (roar of laughter from the audience). How do you stop yourself from being knackered at the end of a race?' What a question. I did not know what to reply other than that I had failed to find the answer in over ten years of running.

July 28: The Athletics Grand Prix and the IAC meeting. In the late 1960s it was the International Athletes Club that introduced the invitation meeting to British athletics. At the end of every summer the IAC would invite many of the world's outstanding athletes to compete in a spectacular meeting at Crystal Palace. The athletics public, bored of unexciting dual international matches – Great Britain versus Finland didn't capture the imagination anymore – welcomed the 'Coke' meeting as it became known after the soft drinks company who sponsored the event for many years.

Twenty years on and the sport has overdosed on international spectaculars. There are invitation meetings at least once a week throughout the summer months and the IAC meeting, the forerunner of this form of athletics, is fighting hard to maintain its position in the over-congested international fixture calendar. The IAC meeting's problems stem from its shaky position in the Grand Prix system.

The athletics Grand Prix was introduced a couple of years ago in an attempt to give some coherence to the chaos of world athletics. The IAAF felt that with events scattered throughout Europe every other day during the summer, an athletics Grand Prix similar to motor-racing would provide a theme. A selected number of meetings (fifteen) were given Grand Prix status and athletes scored points in them according to where they finished. These points counted towards a final. At the Grand Prix final double points were scored and prize money awarded to the overall winners in each event. This prize money was in addition to subvention payments. The awards in each event were based on the five highest positions in which the athlete finished over the course of the race series, plus the performance in the final: first, $10,000; second, $8000; third, $6000; reducing by $1000 to eighth place. Additionally there were awards for the athletes who scored the highest totals over the course of the summer (first, $25,000; second, $15,000; and third, $10,000).

Mobil sponsor the whole show. If selected a country can have a maximum of two Grand Prix meetings but no city more than one. Competition to host Grand Prix meetings is fierce. If a promoter's event has not been awarded Grand Prix status his meeting may suffer. The problems can then escalate as follows: No Grand Prix status – difficulty in attracting the best athletes – declining interest in the event – more problems in finding future sponsors – lack of interest from TV – big trouble. For example in West Germany, Berlin and Cologne are currently the two Grand Prix events. The Koblenz meeting where Steve Ovett twice broke world records, and one of the most popular venues amongst runners, has rapidly declined in standard since its loss of Grand Prix status.

In Britain, the IAAF rules were relaxed for 1986 and 1987. Our limited facilities and the dominant position of London mean that Crystal Palace is the prime location for international athletics in the country, and was therefore permitted to host two Grand Prix meetings. Sponsors, apparently, would prefer events to be located in the capital. For the last two years Britain's two Grand Prix events, the Peugeot-Talbot Games and the IAC meet, have taken place at Crystal Palace. This year the IAAF has forced the IAC meet to move. If both events were administered by the same organisation the problem would not be so difficult to resolve. But, the Peugeot-Talbot Games are organised by Andy Norman of the British Athletics Promotion Unit (BAPU). He used to be the IAC's promoter and current relations between the two organisations are about as cordial as those between the SLD and David Owen's anti-merger group.

Friday's meeting will take place in that windswept athletic outpost, Meadowbank Stadium, Edinburgh. The IAC meeting is being marginalised by the athletics establishment and a successful meeting is needed to preserve the interest of the sponsors, television and the IAAF. It is with these issues in mind that Dave Bedford and the IAC are fighting hard to produce an exciting, innovative event.

The various press reports this week indicate that the IAC's prospects for an impressive meeting on Friday night are currently very good. Scottish track fans should turn out in droves to see the local boy, Tom McKean, race the legendary Said Aouita over 1000m. The latter, my ultimate unbeatable rival in the 5000m, says he is concentrating on 1500m this summer, although he sometimes exaggerates. Regardless of his Olympic plans his clash with McKean on Scottish soil should be memorable. Amongst other attractions in 'this star-studded athletics extravaganza' – perhaps I should become a press release agent – are 'straight from his phenomenal victory in the USA Olympic trials, that demon of one-lap running, the sensational Harry Butch Reynolds'. I wonder if I could become more sensational if I changed my name to Butch Buckner.

Returning to Friday's meeting, last year the IAC introduced some innovations to spice up the evening's sport. Two have remained this year: a bicycle race on the track and the handicap mile. Twenty years after the IAC pioneered the invitation meeting, it is trying new ideas to freshen up an overused concept. Both innovations were a success last year, and the handicap mile was so popular that this year there will be a handicap 110 metres. I was second in the handicap mile in 1987. I started sixteen yards, the equivalent of two seconds, in front of the scratch runner, Steve Crabb (the scratch runner starts on the usual line, all other runners have a predetermined distance advantage), with runners spaced at intervals over the next 150 yards. A handicap race depends on accurate handicapping for its success. Last year the handicapping worked superbly. Off the final bend there were eight athletes of all abilities with a chance of victory. A string of us battled down the home straight with Crabb edging to victory in the last few yards.

This year I have been handicapped on my personal best, not current form. I am starting on scratch alongside John Walker and Dave Moorcroft. Adrian Passey has eight yards' advantage and ahead of him are a couple of other internationals and a series of Scottish athletes who, I imagine, will be encouraged by vociferous partisan support. The race is also organised as an England versus Scotland team competition. The idea is potentially a winner although I have a major reservation – I do not want to finish last. My handicap is based on an estimated finish time in the region of 3.54, ambitious to say the least. But despite my concern I am relishing the return to international competition. I realise my fitness is not yet satisfactory, but I have missed the atmosphere and excitement of athletics. I have not run in one of these kind of meetings since last September. Then, I found it difficult to rekindle my enthusiasm after the

World Championships but now, after nine months away from the track, I require exposure to the flames of competition, even if my unpreparedness results in temporary singeing.

Even if my personal prospects are unexceptional, the IAC appear to have assembled the correct ingredients to produce a memorable night. But success will require more than the right ingredients. There has to be sufficient conflict, a dash of drama and a little extra magic. In Edinburgh that last elusive element has to be a warm, windless night. If everything mixes according to plan, the IAC can produce a meeting that can survive and prosper regardless of Grand Prix status.

July 31: Handicap Mile, Edinburgh. A warm, windless night in Edinburgh! Who am I trying to kid? All day the clouds raced across the city. The castle was occasionally exposed to fleeting glimpses of sunshine before returning to its habitual grey and sombre appearance. Down at Meadowbank Stadium flags were straining on their poles and the spectators were muffled in layers of clothing. Not that the weather deterred the crowd as 13,000 braved the elements. The prime attraction was McKean versus Aouita in the 1000m.

The 1000m was run about twenty minutes before my event, the handicap mile. I jogged back from the warm-up area to catch the last lap of the big confrontation. There was no contest, the remarkable Aouita was yards clear. McKean was overtaken in the home straight by David Sharpe, but neither of them stood the remotest chance of catching Aouita. I noticed the slow final time. It would be impossible to record any respectable performance in the windy conditions.

I reported in for the mile. Tessa Sanderson was being carried away with a heavily strapped ankle. She looked in pain and was fighting back the tears. John Walker had withdrawn from the mile, leaving me on scratch with Dave Moorcroft. Adrian Passey had an eight yard handicap, but after him there was a gap until thirty-five yards. In the wind it would be very difficult for the three of us to close down such a large gap. We were led out onto the track. Our race was due off at 8.50, but the timetable was slightly delayed. This meant that the race could not be televised live on the ITV 8–9 programme. We were therefore kept waiting for the adverts to finish on Channel 4, so that we could appear live after 9pm. Jogging around for ten minutes on the track trying to keep warm whilst we waited for the commercials to finish was not the ideal preparation for a race, but then as long as we wish to receive subvention payments we must be prepared for such slight inconveniences!

Eventually TV was ready and we were off. For the first lap I followed Dave Moorcroft as we both trailed Passey. After about 500 yards I overtook Moorcroft and tried to catch Passey. It was a pedestrian race. As I had feared we three backmarkers were making only a slight impression on the yawning gap between us and the next group of athletes. The race split in half, the leading bunch and the chasing trio. On the last lap, Moorcroft and I overtook Passey and in the last 100 yards Moorcroft passed me. My final time was 4.04, Moorcroft's 4.03. Another uninspiring performance. Hamish McInnes, off fifty-five yards, won the race. He is a postgraduate student at Loughborough and was delighted with his victory. The crowd were pleased as well – a Scottish win.

Immediately I had crossed the line I was dragged off for a TV interview with Dave Moorcroft. Dave is a marvellous example of sportsmanship. He is always polite and generous about his fellow athletes whilst remaining an outstanding competitor on the track. His own career has been dogged by injury and misfortune, without which he would surely have improved on his achievements of two Commonwealth Games titles, a 5000m World record and numerous international victories. This year is his last serious attempt to recover his previous form. He is thirty-five and has an outside chance of making his fourth Olympic Games. He has struggled through another bout of injuries and this was his second comeback race.

But, in the interview he did not emphasise his own prospects. Instead he stated that I should be picked automatically for the British team. He is a rival for one of the 5000m places in the British squad, but he is prepared to support my case. Next weekend he will be racing in the 5000m Olympic trial and he privately told me that if he were in my position he would not run in the event. Furthermore, if he finished third, one place behind automatic selection, he would expect me to be picked. I only hope that when I reach the twilight years of my athletic career, I can display some of the unselfish generosity exhibited by Dave Moorcroft. If sport is supposed to set an example to the young then there is no better role model than him.

After the interview I warmed down, nursing sore Achilles tendons. All the talk was inevitably about the trials. Next weekend is in everyone's thoughts. It was impossible to avoid the topic. Will Coe run in the 1500m? What about the 800m? Will Eamon Martin go for the 5000m or 10,000m? One person who found all this speculation amusing was Enrico Dionisi, Said Aouita's Italian manager. Dionisi is one of the more flamboyant characters on the world athletic circuit with his dramatic gestures and foul smelling cigarettes. He can indulge his frequently theatrical and entertaining behaviour as he manages the world's greatest runner. He held forth to me on the crazy British selection system. 'Stupid, mad, pathetic,' he continued, and then conspiratorially confided in me that he knew that Coe was running secretly in a small meeting near Zurich that weekend. Another snippet of gossip to feed into the rumour filled cauldron of athletics.

This was my first international meeting since last summer and as I hung around the stadium, receiving treatment on my tendons, reflecting on my disappointing fitness and generally feeling sorry for myself, I realised how my standing in athletics has fallen in 1988. Journalists were wandering around talking to the Olympic hopefuls. Someone was arranging a photo-session with one of our female athletes for a colour supplement review of Britain's potential medallists. Nobody wanted to talk to the European 5000m Champion and second ranked 5000m runner in the world for the last two years. I do not think I shall be appearing in many lists of likely medal prospects. With a 4.04 mile and an 8.05 3000m to my credit this summer I am no longer perceived as a threat in Seoul – if I actually make it to the Games, that is.

In the fickle world of athletics a few months out of the action and you are quickly forgotten. I am one of yesterday's men. The athletes of the moment are as ever Said Aouita, and in Britain, Eamon Martin, Liz McColgan, Linford Christie and Colin Jackson.

Aouita is proving himself the most versatile runner of all time. Some athletes can run well over either 800m and 1500m or 5000m and 10,000m. Over their careers, a few great runners have recorded world class times from 800m to 5000m. Aouita has the world record for 1500m, 2000m and 5000m. His only 10,000m was the world's fastest in 1986. The only distance over which he has been beaten since 1985 is the 3000m steeplechase and he is thinking of running the 800m and 1500m in Seoul. Most knowledgeable pundits have so far been sceptical about Aouita's intentions over the shorter distances. As athletes age they tend to move to the longer distances, as speed is supposed to decline and stamina increase. Aouita is the exception to this and almost every other theory in running. He destroyed Tom McKean over 1000m. McKean has looked superb in all his 800m races this summer. Until this clash with Aouita he was unbeaten, and although he does not rate his ability over the longer distance highly, he must have been very impressed with the Moroccan superstar.

I chatted to Eamon Martin during the afternoon of the meeting. He is another who, like Dave Moorcroft, has suffered from injury problems. In 1984 he reached the Olympic final and then struggled with Achilles tendon trouble until 1987. Last year he competed again in international competition, but this summer he has shown outstanding form. He ran a 10,000m in the Oslo meeting, to act as an insurance should he under-perform at 5000m, and he smashed Brendan Foster's British record. He is guaranteed the third 10,000m place should he want it, but still intends to run the 5000m in the trials.

It is heartening to talk to athletes who like Martin and Moorcroft have overcome problems and returned to prove themselves. There is an unspoken respect that exists between runners. We all know how difficult it is to reach and maintain the level of fitness necessary to run at an international standard. Most of us have spent some time frustrated through injury and I expect that we have all at some point or other wondered if it is all worthwhile. Therefore, beyond the rivalry that is inevitably present, especially on occasions like these when Olympic places will shortly be decided, there is still a comradeship based on mutual experience.

I left Meadowbank with George as the reception went on into the early hours of the morning, aided by copious supplies of the sponsor's brew – Miller Lite beer. The weather had spoiled what otherwise could have been a memorable evening. Butch Reynolds had won the 400m, Colin Jackson had beaten his two domestic rivals in the hurdles, Tony Jarrett and Jon Ridgeon, and Aouita had proved his limitless versatility once again. But as with every athletics meeting there had been losers too, notably the sad sight of Tessa Sanderson limping away, out of the meeting and perhaps out of the Olympics. George and I travelled back to the hotel through the streets of the ancient city of Edinburgh. Our taxi passed along a deserted Princes Street and beneath the imposing mass of the castle. All night we had fielded questions about my fitness and my participation in the trials. We had been evasive, but both of us know that I am not fit enough to record a respectable performance next weekend.

I am glad to be back competing in international athletics, although, I am forced to admit, it is not as much fun when I am not running to my capabilities. Perhaps, though, what is important is not how successful I am, but rather using the experience to enrich life. Tonight I may have run another second class race, but I learned from the dignity of Moorcroft, from the courage of Martin, and from participating in an athletics meeting on a windy Scottish night.

10

Olympic Selection

August 1. In the first post this morning my letter was winging its way to the Chairman of the selectors, Mr Ewan Murray:

Dear Mr Murray,

I write to you as Chairman of the BAAB selection committee to inform you and your fellow committee members of my current position regarding fitness and selection for the Olympic Games.

I completed a solid winter's training and intended to open my track season in late June. Unfortunately, my preparations were interrupted by a hip/groin injury that was eventually diagnosed as a tilted pelvis. Intensive treatment over a five week period cured the injury and I am currently training hard. I competed in my first race of the summer on July 20 at Derby. I won a low-key 3000m in eight minutes five seconds – a satisfactory first outing on the track. Last Friday I ran in the handicap mile in the IAC meeting in Edinburgh. On a windy evening I recorded 4.04. Most important to me, I am racing without any recurrence of injury. However, my Edinburgh performance indicated I am not yet quite ready to race in a serious competitive 5000m.

My objective of reaching Seoul in peak condition would be best served by training throughout early August and seeking competition later in the month to aid my preparations. I have therefore decided not to compete in the AAA Championships and very much hope that the selectors will award me a place in the British 5000m squad for Seoul.

My single objective for the last twelve months has been the Olympic Games. I am confident I can return to the level of fitness I achieved in 1986 and 1987 in time for the Olympic Games in late September.

I should point out that I have won medals at every international championships in which I have competed. Furthermore I have ranked first in the UK and second in the world over 5000m in both 1986 and 1987. I have broken 13.20 on four occasions in the last two years, and no British athlete has beaten me over the distance on the eight occasions I have run 5000m on the track since the 1986 Commonwealth Games.

My coach George Gandy or myself would be willing to discuss my proposed racing programme for the rest of the summer if it would assist you in any way. I intend to compete in at least one 5000m before the Olympics to assess my fitness, and assure you I would not wish to go to Seoul without first having proved myself ready to perform again at my best.

It would be a major boost if the selectors were to include me when the main body of the team is announced immediately following the AAA Championships.

Yours sincerely,
Jack Buckner

August 2. Now that I have decided to miss the AAA I must forget about the drama surrounding the selection of the British team and concentrate on training. My main concern is not whether I am selected for Seoul, but regaining form.

In my letter to the selectors I feigned confidence. Currently I do not feel as buoyant about my prospects as I indicated in my letter. The hope is that in a few weeks my physical condition will reflect the undue optimism I displayed on paper. The team will be announced this time next week.

There could be a problem for the selectors in that Tim Hutchings is also injured and likely to miss the AAA Championships. In recent years Tim has been clearly the second British athlete at 5000m behind me. He was fourth in the last Olympics and third in both the 1986 Commonwealths and Europeans. The two of us have been friendly rivals for years, and so long as we were both fit I am sure we would perform successfully in the Olympics.

But, under the current selection policy one of us will have to miss out on the Olympics. Tim has already run a couple of 5000m this summer, both in about 13.25, only just below the Olympic qualifying mark, and is now suffering with a hamstring injury. Neither of us are in condition to run in the AAA, so we shall both be on tenterhooks until the team is announced. I suppose the only situation in which we could both be in the team is if Eamon Martin finished in the first two in the AAA and then elected to run the 10,000m. Then presumably, the selectors might choose a second athlete for the squad in preference to the third place finisher. It is all becoming, as I feared several months ago, very messy and complicated. It is also sad that Tim and I, two of Britain's top distance runners over the last few years, should be contesting for a single place in the Olympic team, unfit and off the track.

August 3. Away from the excitement of the Olympic team and onto the Loughborough University campus where the Summer University is in full swing. During July and August when the undergraduates are away the University hosts a wide variety of courses attended by more mature – in age that is – individuals. The playing fields are filled with enthusiastic summer schoolers playing and practising tennis, rugby, athletics, croquet and golf. It is heartening to see the University facilities in use during the summer months, but in recent years I have come into some confrontation with the golfers.

I do not know if it is a valid generalisation that golfers and runners do not mix. In my experience I have found that whenever golfers and runners meet, pursuing their respective activities over the same area of ground, conflict will inevitably result. My observations, based on attempting to run around the edge of golf courses from Spain to Arizona, from Worksop to Moor Park, are that golfers everywhere will not tolerate any 'joggers' on their hallowed turf. At the same time I am infuriated by any golfer taking pot shots on open fields. Why can't they stick to their precious courses?

For eleven months of the year I never meet golfers when I am running, but the Loughborough summer school golf class takes place at the bottom of the field I run around every morning. It is organised by an imposing gentleman with a Scottish accent. The golfing summer schoolers park their cars along the edge of the field. They form a line in front of the cars and proceed to practise their driving across the rest of the field under the eye of their Scottish instructor.

The route of my morning run passes directly across their improvised driving range. I have no alternative other than to run within striking distance of their swinging clubs. On the first occasion of our acquaintance two or three summers ago I raced across the target area shouting several words of warning and waving my arms dramatically. As I passed, the golfers reluctantly stopped firing. The following morning the Scotsman was prepared. As I came within range of the flashing irons he walked towards me shouting, 'danger, fore, golfers', and barred my progress. I sidestepped him and once again his students were forced to briefly cease their practise.

The next day we engaged in a more forthright discussion upon the individual's right to use this particular field. A shouting match developed. 'Laddie, golfers are practising here, go and run somewhere else,' was the gist of his argument. My reply was along the lines of 'I run here every day of the year, it is the best grass field in the area, ideal for my training and I am not prepared to change my route for any golfers.'

Ever since that little interchange of opinion, an uneasy truce has existed during the summer school season. I attempt to dodge between the golfers and their cars whilst he occasionally suspends fire whilst I dash across. But this year our relationship has been improved by this morning's unprecedented events. I was out running early before the golfers had begun their endeavours and my Scottish friend was wandering around beside his car. We eyed each other as suspiciously as ever, but then we actually exchanged pleasantries. 'Good Morning' was muttered. I see the morning's events as a possible turning point in the hitherto strained relationship between golfers and runners. Perhaps the day will come when the two sports can exist side by side without hostility. Perhaps golfers and runners are not as incompatible as I feared. Regardless, I shall be glad when they clear off back to their precious courses!

August 4. I have been trying to avoid becoming embroiled in the inevitable controversy this week over the AAA Championships. I sent my letter to the selectors and hoped that would be the end of the affair. I realised the BAAB would probably make some announcement about my withdrawal, but I was furious yesterday when I received a number of telephone calls quoting a press association statement in which I was supposed to have made a number of comments along the lines of '. . . expecting to be picked for the third place . . . requesting preferential treatment . . .'

I telephoned both the BAAB and APA to see if they knew where these 'quotes' came from and if someone had leaked the contents of my letter. Apparently only a handful of people have seen the letter and the press association item must have been based on rumour or imagination. I am torn between wanting to trace the source of the story to express my legitimate irritation and keeping quiet to avoid further hassle. I think I shall settle on the latter course. The athletics world is buzzing with rumours and innuendo regarding the AAA trials.

Tim Hutchings is suggesting a trial race to decide the selection place in the British team. He is suggesting that I race him in the Zurich meeting in a fortnight to decide who should go to Seoul. Tim is in a difficult position as he can foresee the selection position being given to me. His only chance to compete in the Games is to press for another trial race between me and him. I would be surprised if the selectors agree to his proposals as all a confrontation would reveal is who has recovered most from injury and not who is best equipped to run in Seoul. Furthermore, the purpose of the third position in the team is to help the athlete prepare for the Olympics and not to subject him or her to another trial.

The next little story to reach my ears was along the lines of '. . . who does Buckner think he is to run in the IAC meeting and then miss the AAA Championships . . . apparently he is going to run in Zurich . . . we know what he is up to, he is only interested in money . . . who does he think he is? . . . why should he behave like this and expect to be picked?'

This was the information George received via Andy Norman. I phoned Andy and informed him that if I was so interested in money I would not have opened my season with a 3000m in Derby, where I was not even paid my expenses, when I could have raced somewhere much more exotic and lucrative. Furthermore I had intended to run the AAA if my performance in Edinburgh had been of a higher standard. Regarding the Zurich race on August 17 I am intending to run there, but only if I run reasonably well in the meeting in Gateshead on August 13. I have always placed my athletics objectives first and will continue to do so, so long as I intend to run in the Olympics. If I am not picked for the team, despite my previous record, then I can do whatever I want and would certainly be under no obligation to anyone, especially the BAAB.

All this controversy merely heightens the tension I currently feel. I have enough problems trying to regain my fitness on the track and servicing my various injuries without engaging in selection squabbling. However, I am determined not to lose any sleep over the situation. The worst that can happen is for me to miss out on the Olympic Games either as a result of injury or the selection procedure. What does that matter? I have had two tremendous years in athletics and regardless of what happens this year I am still only twenty-six and will have the chance to try and come back in the future. All I face is the threat of failure in the trivial world of sport. What is wrong with sporting failure? Eamon Dunphy wrote about this in *Only a Game?* Talking about his life at Millwall, he wrote 'Sport is about accepting a challenge and accepting the risk of failure.' His comment is as relevant to me, running in the 1980s, as it was to him in the 1970s.

If I do not reach the Olympics, and if 1988 is a complete athletic disaster, I must try hard to avoid bitterness. Most sportspeople experience periods of immense frustration and disappointment. The difference between sport, my occupation, and other people's jobs, is that in sport your failure is public. If I do not make the Olympics everyone will know. I hope most of my friends and acquaintances will be sympathetic but as well as dealing with my own disappointment I shall be continually reminded of what has happened. But why should I complain when I have received so much public acclaim in the past?

The weeks ahead are going to be difficult and exciting. They hold the possibility both of joy and misery. They will determine whether my year is a success or failure.

August 8: Waiting for News. Monday morning, 10.45am. The British Olympic athletics team is announced to the public at noon. The majority of the team was decided at the weekend's AAA Championships, the first two automatically gaining selection, but there is the third selected place, so a small number of athletes are waiting apprehensively. I have heard nothing. I wonder if I shall receive the news from a phone call, a newspaper reporter or from the radio. It would be most pleasant to hear from the selectors so I could have a little time to reflect on their decision rather than receiving the information from a journalist.

The trials themselves were a weekend of tremendous athletic competition in blazing sunshine. They were a classic three days full of terrific competition, great performances and plenty of drama. In most events the established stars finished in the first two. Linford Christie won the 100m and 200m. In the women's events there was a double hurdles victory for Sally Gunnell. Colin Jackson recorded another impressive hurdles win and Kriss Akabusi broke 45 seconds for the 400m flat, but still intends to compete in the 400m hurdles in Seoul. All the above are potential medallists in the Games.

As for the middle distance events, pride of place must go to Steve Cram. He shot past Tom McKean in the home straight in the 800m. Crammie ran as fluently as I have ever seen him. McKean is a fast finisher but Cram powered away from him in the last 60 metres. He is intending to run both the 800m and 1500m in Seoul (he will be given the third place in the 1500m) and on current form could threaten anyone including Aouita in both events. The men's 1500m provided the drama of the weekend. In the heats on Saturday evening Seb Coe did not qualify for Sunday's final. After all the controversy and speculation surrounding Seb's participation, you had to feel admiration for him, but at the same time if he could not qualify for the AAA final the selectors cannot either change their policy or select him at that distance.

The 1500m final was won by Peter Elliott from Steve Crabb. It was a slow, tactical race with Crabb taking the lead 500m from the finish and winding the pace up from the bell. Crabb and Elliott quickly opened daylight between themselves and the chasing group. Elliott was the stronger, covering the last 400m in under 52 seconds. Both runners have shown impressive form over the summer and deserved their selection. Peter Elliott has like Cram expressed a wish to double in Seoul. He ran a fast 800m a couple of weeks ago and won the silver medal in last summer's World Championships. Will the selectors grant Elliott his wish or give Coe another chance at the 800m?

In the 10,000m Steve Binns won from Mike McLeod. And finally to the 5000m. I sat in front of the TV screen feeling frustrated and faintly apprehensive. I had chosen not to compete, a decision I still believe was correct, and watched the race slowly unfold. In the heat and with so much depending on the race the dawdling pace was unsurprising. It was an eleven and a half lap jog followed by a final lap sprint, no genuine test of 5000m ability. As expected, Eamon Martin won, with Gary Staines second. Eamon Martin is expressing a wish to run both the 10,000m and 5000m in Seoul. This will pose a problem for the selectors. If Martin had decided to run only the 10,000m, the distance at which he broke the British record in July, the selectors could choose both Tim and me in addition to Staines. (As the race was so slow, I think it unlikely that Paul Davies-Hale would receive or expect consideration for the third place in the team.) But Martin is the man in form and can make his own decisions from the most powerful position. He has to be selected for the 10,000m and has won the 5000m trial so can call the tune.

Assuming Martin runs both events, the selectors have three options. They are: to pick me for the third place, to pick Tim Hutchings for the third place, or to leave the third place open and see what happens in the next few weeks, perhaps forcing Tim and me to race each other. It is 11.30, half an hour until their decision is known. I think it unlikely the selectors would choose Hutchings in preference to me, although he has been lobbying hard all week.

So I imagine the choice will be limited to selecting me and leaving the place open. I hope for the former. Surprisingly, I am currently remarkably calm about the whole affair. My priority is to recover fitness. Even if I am in the team I shall have to prove to myself I am capable of performing adequately in the Olympics, and so far this year there has been scant evidence of that. Selection would temporarily relieve the pressure, but at some point I would have to run significantly better than I have yet in 1988.

11.45 and no news. I have just phoned the BAAB. They do not know anything. There is a press conference at noon, and all will be revealed then. I wonder if I can hear the announcement on the radio or TV. The secretary at the BAAB said 'usually they try and tell everyone, but you know what it is like . . .' For the first time I am becoming nervous. George does not seem to be around. I am going to switch the TV on and tune the radio.

No information on the noon TV or radio news. The TV showed pictures of the selectors in conference and the radio stated an announcement would be made early this afternoon. I think it is going to be one of those days, rather like at school when you waited for the exam results to be posted. I do not want to spend the day in a state of prolonged anticipation, but I suppose I have no option.

2pm. I have an appointment with Terry Moule at 3pm and am travelling down the M1 with Kerin. We are listening to the radio. The latest news is that the team will be announced in ten minutes, with details on the next sports desk at 3pm.

3pm. I am on the treatment table having my lower back hoicked around when there is a knock on the door. Kerin, who has been waiting in the car listening to the radio, rushes into the room. She is smiling and I realise, before she speaks, I am in the team.

August 9: Thoughts on the British Team. Yesterday's news has removed a burden from the next few weeks. It is a tremendous relief to know that after all my recent problems I am in the Olympic team. One hurdle is out of the way, but unfortunately there are still several more before I depart for Seoul. The main priority is still to regain fitness. I may be selected, but I do not want to attend the Olympics unless I am ready to run to my potential. By early September when, injuries permitting, I hope to have completed a couple of 5000m races I shall have a realistic impression of my chances.

I suppose I need not have worried so much about the discretionary place. It would have been a major surprise if anyone other than me had been chosen for the final 5000m place. But, as the rumours circulated I inevitably felt more apprehensive than I should have done. Eventually, although I am loath to admit it, the selection policy worked out almost according to plan (with one notable exception). In the majority of events all the fancied athletes gained selection either in

Birmingham or by committee. The possible disaster over the women's javelin was averted when only Sharon Gibson gained the qualifying distance, thus allowing the selectors to choose both Whitbread and Sanderson. Nobody fell over in any of the sprint events and even the steeplechasers finished without any embarrassing pile-ups.

The one big controversy has emerged over the 800m. Following Seb Coe's disappointing run in the 1500m heats there was no chance he could be picked to compete over that distance in the Olympics. The final place belonged to Steve Cram whilst the performances of Crabb and Elliott guaranteed the other two berths. But, in the 800m Coe would probably have been granted the discretionary place if Peter Elliott had not requested to double in Seoul. The selectors were forced to choose between Coe, the World record holder at the distance and Britain's greatest 800m runner ever, and Elliott, the World Championship silver medallist who has already run a very fast time this summer. The selectors eventually chose Elliott, the man in form, ahead of Coe. Inevitably the Coe–Elliott story has dominated the newspapers. It must have been a very difficult decision to make, but perhaps it is better the selectors should decide now rather than prolong the agony.

On a more trivial level my selection has a family side effect. This weekend is my brother Tom's wedding in Portsmouth. I was supposed to be Best Man, but as it became apparent I would not be breezing into the Olympic team I withdrew. I also began to experience doubts about attending a wedding in Portsmouth the day before a race in Gateshead, especially if my selection for the Olympics was not certain. I could see a situation developing where I would have been under pressure to prove my fitness either in Gateshead or Zurich. Weddings, although most entertaining, are never the most relaxing of affairs and about the worst possible preparation for athletic competition. I do not think I have ever attended a wedding without returning home exhausted from the socialising. To attend Tom and Vicki's wedding, dash to Heathrow to catch a flight to Newcastle and then attempt to run in a race that could influence my participation in the Olympics was, I thought, cutting it rather fine. I therefore could have been faced with a difficult choice – running or attending the wedding.

My brother Tom and future sister-in-law Vicki are both runners and therefore understand my dilemma. Tom competed in the AAA Championships over the weekend, reaching the final of the steeplechase. He and Vicki have decided to curtail their athletic plans for the summer and get married instead!

I intend to travel down to Portsmouth on Saturday morning with Kerin. I shall attend the wedding and then drive to Heathrow to catch a flight late Saturday afternoon and run in the mile at Gateshead stadium on Sunday. Unfortunately I shall miss the reception, but perhaps that is not a bad idea if I want to avoid the social temptations of rich cuisine and champagne.

The mile in Gateshead will be a tune-up before my most important race of the summer so far, a 5000m in Zurich next Wednesday. The Zurich Weltklasse is probably the best meeting on the European circuit. The standard of competition is always exceptional, and a useful guide as to who will be the athletes to watch in Seoul. As it is my first 5000m this year I am not expecting to provide any upsets, but a good solid run would do wonders for the confidence.

August 14: Race, 1 mile, Gateshead. As I was intending to leave for Heathrow immediately after the wedding service yesterday, Kerin and I travelled down to Portsmouth to spend some time with Tom before the great occasion. Unfortunately the traffic intervened and we only arrived thirty minutes before the ceremony. Living in Loughborough, you are unaccustomed to the level of congestion found throughout the South-East. I suppose eventually you become oblivious to the constant stream of traffic everywhere and learn to keep calm despite waiting at every road intersection and traffic light for several minutes.

The wedding was a happy, family celebration. It was awful having to leave so quickly after the ceremony. A few snapshots, good wishes and then farewells, back to the car, through the traffic, on the plane and up to windswept Gateshead. Someone once remarked to me that the only occasion the wind has not blown in Gateshead was when Brendan Foster opened the track with a world 3000m record. My experience of the North-East cannot contradict that statement. Every track race I have run in the Gateshead stadium has been slow, aggressive and disappointing.

Today merely added to the catalogue of jog three laps, sprint one lap, mile races I have run there. I finished ninth in an overcrowded, ill-tempered field. During such races, unless you run at the front of the pack, you can find yourself in all sorts of difficult situations. It is like rushing to catch the last train home in a large crowd of people moving in different directions. You find yourself near the back and realise you must move forward into a better position, but as you move wide someone else has the same intention, so you are forced out into the second or third lane. You then try and accelerate out of trouble but there is no space to cut back into the inside lane, so you slow down and return to your original position having wasted precious energy. This melee continues throughout a slow mile race. The art is to move into the gaps that develop rather than fighting to improve your position. It is an art I have never mastered, chiefly because I do not possess the acceleration of pace necessary to exploit any openings that emerge. By the time I have lengthened my stride to try and nip through a gap between two runners, someone else is there ahead of me and I am forced to slow down and try some other tactic.

My problems in this type of race are not helped by being only five feet eight inches. Unfortunately, I do not cut an imposing figure on the track. I cannot therefore indulge in what some commentators refer to as 'tactical awareness'. This phrase was often used in reference to Steve Ovett's running in the early 1980s. As some poor athlete was bounced into lane six by the powerful Ovett his 'tactical awareness' was frequently praised. I am someone who by virtue of size is more likely to be on the receiving end of 'tactical awareness' than doling it out myself.

I cannot though blame today's run on 'tactical awareness'. The fault lies with basic speed or rather lack of that precious commodity. I am too slow. The comment often levelled by armchair pundits following such races is why didn't you go to the front early on and make it a faster race? Such a tactic on a typical Gateshead day with a number of faster milers than myself breathing down my neck and at my current level of fitness would be as likely of success as England against the West Indies in a test match.

A crumb of comfort from the race. At least, before the last lap burn-up began I felt comfortable with the pace. I am fitter than I was a couple of weeks ago in Edinburgh. There is slow, but distinct progress.

After the race I made a crucial mistake. I had just showered and visited the physiotherapist when Andy Norman approached me. 'They' would not let me receive my agreed £3000 subvention for that race. I would have to accept some reduction. Tired, and slightly disconsolate, I acquiesced. I should have said nothing. The last time to engage in such a conversation is immediately after a bad race. Nobody will increase the subvention if I run well, so why should I accept a reduction if I run badly? I do not want the aggravation of money intruding at this stage of the summer. I should have told Andy Norman to speak to George. When promoters renege on financial arrangements it is understandable that athletes resort to agents and managers.

The other and potentially much greater problem is the state of my Achilles tendons. They have been a permanent source of complaint for the last two or three years. For most of the year they grumble occasionally, but no more than any other muscle, ligament or joint in the fragile runner's body. Once I start racing on the track in lighter running spikes my Achilles tendons are not cushioned so well against impact and they do not like it. I do all I can to look after my tendons, but this year since my injury problems they have really been kicking up a fuss. After this afternoon's race I was hobbling around trying to keep moving and prevent the offending tendons from stiffening. Perhaps after a few races when they are accustomed to the shock of moving a little faster the pain will ease.

With a slow performance, aching tendons and my money cut, perhaps I would have been better off staying at the wedding reception.

August 16: To Zurich. It is easy to fall into the trap of moralising about the athletics Grand Prix. I am one of those who frequently criticise athletes who race around the European circuit all summer and end up exhausted when the serious championships begin. But through injury I have not competed in a Grand Prix event for over a year and I had forgotten the allure of the circuit, or rather the allure of Zurich.

The Grand Prix is a hotch-potch of events scattered around the athletics world. Unlike the motor racing Grand Prix where the same competitors contest each event, the standards in the athletics Grand Prix vary widely. Hardly any of the European athletes bother with the opening May–June US meetings in San Jose and occasionally Eugene, whilst the results of Prague rarely make the small print of the newspapers, and nobody really enjoys running in London because of the awful weather. But there are a selection of meetings where most athletes would like to compete. Brussels, Rome, Nice, Stockholm and Helsinki are all popular venues and two meetings take pride of place in the international athletic season – the Bislett Games in Oslo and the Zurich Weltklasse. Both are legendary for their fast tracks, enthusiastic crowd, high standard of competition and balmy summer evenings. Each year both meetings will produce some of the most memorable moments in the athletic summer, but Zurich has the edge. In Oslo there are a handful of great races whereas in Zurich every event is outstanding. Zurich is the richest event on the circuit, dazzling with Swiss efficiency and opulence. A feast of athletic abundance is guaranteed. The meeting is always sold out weeks in advance. The crowd are vociferous, appreciative and knowledgeable. There is no half-hearted clapping here. The entire twelve and a half laps of the 5000m are run to non-stop, rhythmical applause that follows the runners around the stadium.

Zurich displays the most attractive aspect of the Grand Prix circuit. In addition to the competition there are little touches of class that surround the meeting. In the hotel one television channel continually replays Zurich meetings in advance of the competition. The buffet, open at every conceivable meal-time, is lavish. Tables groan under the weight of food. Masseurs and physiotherapists are readily available. Instructions and details about competition are accurate and efficient. Such facilities are probably taken for granted by many top sportspeople but in international athletics there are very few events where the competitors' requirements are given the attention they deserve. Zurich is the model to which all other meetings should aspire.

Such surroundings are seductive. No wonder so many athletes fall into the over-racing trap. Picture yourself enjoying a meal and watching your mile race on the television. In a high class race earlier that evening you were dragged along to a personal best. A promoter approaches you. Would you like to run in Brussels in a couple of days' time? The flight will leave at 11am tomorrow. Of course all accommodation and food will be provided and the money will go into your trust fund. There will be the chance of another fast time and more Grand Prix points. After Brussels you can go to Cologne, then Berlin and either Koblenz or London, ending up with Rieti or one of the small Italian meets in early September. A summer of fast times, exciting races and boosted trust funds can seem very appealing. Why bother with all the pressure and tension of an Olympics? You can be on a nice little earner on the circuit and if you agree to be a pace-maker . . .

The hub of the Zurich meeting is the foyer of the Nova Park hotel. All the athletes stay there and wander down to the restaurant through the foyer, often meeting recently arrived fellow competitors. The foyer is therefore a haunt, not just of track-suited relaxing athletes, but also briefcase-carrying promoters, pen-clutching journalists, casually dressed agents and masses of autograph hunters. Amongst this amiable chaos it is the autograph hunters who have the greatest sense of purpose. They relentlessly hunt down their prey, equipped with piles of photographs and thick felt-tip pens. Even I had to sign a vast pile of photographs so I do not know how Carl Lewis and Ben Johnson ever made it through the foyer.

These are the two names on everyone's lips. Apparently the great clash between the world's two fastest men will take place tomorrow night and some US television company is paying each runner $250,000. It is not just Lewis against Johnson over 100m, more like Lewis versus Johnson the movie. The actual ten or perhaps less than ten seconds will be analysed, dissected, repeated, slowed down and enveloped by background colour, information, profiles, interviews, discussions and most importantly commercials. The whole package will be sold, marketed, promoted and screened world-wide.

As for me, I am in the 5000m against a high-class field including many potential Olympic finalists. It will be a tough race and I must not expect to perform at my very best. If I can manage a time close to 13.30 I should be satisfied.

August 18: 5000m, Zurich. The 5000m was the last track event of the evening at 10.30pm. On the positive side this meant the stadium was buzzing with excitement, but on the other hand it meant an entire day of inactivity. To psych myself up I was able to watch last year's meeting in my hotel room. Repeated approximately every two hours was the inspiring sight of me striding to victory in the 5000m, winning in a meeting record eight seconds ahead of Castro, the Portuguese runner who pipped me for second place in the World Championships. It was my best performance of 1987 and one of my best races ever. I was running confidently, comfortably and fast. On the last lap instead of glancing apprehensively over my shoulder as is my usual habit, my eyes were focused on the finishing line convinced that nobody could catch me.

I was not expecting such glories this year. If I could remain in contact with the leaders until the crucial closing stages of the race I should have a good base to build on for Seoul. The day drifted in a haze of rest, reading and eating. As the stadium is only a couple of minutes' jog from the Nova Park hotel I was able to witness the Johnson/Lewis clash in my hotel room.

Before the 100m was the men's 400m. Innocent Egbunike stormed through the opening 200m. A few metres back was Butch Reynolds who closed rapidly round the top bend. Reynolds, head back, stormed into the home straight. Unlike many 400m runners he does not wallow through the last metres of the race in the engulfing sea of lactic acid, but strides powerfully across the finishing line. Tonight Reynolds had devastated the opposition long before the tape, and all that mattered was the time. It was 43.29, a new world record eclipsing the 43.86 of Lee Evans in the 1968 Mexico Olympics. I could hear the roar from the stadium in my hotel room.

The 100m a few minutes later was exciting, but the headlining performer was eclipsed by the supporting cast. Johnson started quickest, but Lewis quickly into his ranging stride overtook him in the last thirty metres to record a decisive victory. Calvin Smith finished second, Johnson third.

Eventually I left for the stadium. It was another mild still evening. The smell of hot dogs and popcorn wafted through the air. I jogged around the grass warm-up area, but my tendons were stiffer than ever. Hopefully once the race began concentration would anaesthetise the pain. The 1500m finished and we were led onto the track. I gently strode along the back straight, cautiously testing my tendons, which were pain free. When the race began I dropped into last place. The pace was slow, unusual for a race of this class. Usually I would be disappointed by the cautious first 3000m, but tonight, in my first 5000m of the year, I was content to nurse my way along. Three laps left and I was still in contact. Two laps left and I even dared to move up amongst the leaders. This was a mistake. My lofty position did not last for long and once threatened I slipped rapidly back down the field. I faded dramatically on the last lap rallying faintly to finish ninth in 13.30. Up front Eamon Martin sprinted to victory ahead of Gonzalez, Castro and Paul Davies-Hale. Afterwards I hobbled back to the hotel. Once again I was disappointed with my performance. I felt I had allowed too many athletes past on the final lap. Once the prospect of finishing in the first three had gone I had lost interest. I was lacking in confidence and had been indecisive. If I can be blown away so dramatically in late August, how am I ever going to perform creditably in the Olympics a mere six weeks away?

August 21: More Injuries? On reflection, my run in Zurich was not too bad. Beforehand I admitted I would be satisfied with 13.30 – my final result. But as usual, once I have climbed one step of the ladder to recovery I am aiming higher. One of the problems with running is that you are rarely satisfied. You always feel you could have performed that little bit better. I was comfortable until the last lap of my first 5000m of the year on Wednesday night and I am hopeful of better things next time I compete over the distance.

What the results of the Zurich and Brussels 5000m have revealed is that there is no clear favourite for the distance in the Olympics. Assuming Said Aouita is serious in his intentions over shorter distances the 5000m is wide open. The fastest time in the world this year is only 13.15 by Sydney Maree, who currently seems determined to run himself into the ground racing in just about every meeting possible throughout Europe. Hopefully he will continue this destructive strategy for a few more weeks and that might wreck his Olympic chances. Maree is a very talented athlete, but he has yet to harness his ability in a major championship.

There is still everything to run for in Seoul. If I can keep training and my results improve, and if my tendons shut up, I might still reach the Games in reasonable fettle. It is the final 'if', my Achilles tendons, that are my main concern. I have embarked upon a serious course of tendon maintenance to try and prevent them from deteriorating further. When I climb out of bed in the morning they are at their stiffest. I hobble around for several minutes before I am able to extend them to their normal range of movement. I then spend at least fifteen minutes on a wobble board. This is a device like a miniature see-saw that you stand on and attempt to manoeuvre from side to side without allowing the edges to touch the ground. The wobble board promotes circulation and hopefully strengthens the areas around the tendon. Wobble-boarding is followed by stretching and the morning run. After the run and over breakfast ice-packs are applied and more stretching. The ice-pack treatment and yet more stretching is repeated later in the day. A final therapy, if I am feeling brave, is for Kerin to rub the tendons vigorously. Kerin completed a massage course a couple of years ago and since then she has relieved my sore muscles with her soothing touch. Unfortunately the friction she gives my tendons, on the suggestion of my physio, is far from soothing. This tendon rubbing is accompanied by complaining grunts from me.

All this effort is simply to keep me training. I can run steadily without too much difficulty; it is running on the track that really causes problems. The hope is that through regular care I can limit the discomfort to track running and races. I have exhibited the tendons to various physiotherapists and doctors recently and all agree I must try and nurse them until after the Olympics. Once the season is over I can think of a more long term solution – perhaps surgery will be required.

Tendons permitting, I shall race again in a week. Firstly, a two miles in the meeting at Crystal Palace next weekend and then another 5000m in Rieti the following Wednesday. After that I shall have two weeks' training before I depart for Japan and then Seoul. I would like a couple more races, but competition is very limited during September.

11

Improving Results?

August 24. After all the problems of this year I am eager to grasp any positive indication of improvement, so yesterday's respectable track session is cause for more optimism than usually would be accorded to my training performances. My tendon care also seems to be working. Perhaps, one day, I shall return to my former standards. This weekend I am collecting my Olympic kit and then embarking on my final series of races before the Games.

On Sunday I shall run in a two miles at Crystal Palace, followed by a 5000m in Rieti on Wednesday and another 5000m in Essen on Friday. The idea behind this hectic schedule is to approach the demands of the Olympics where I hope to run three 5000m races in four days. By completing three races in six days I am preparing to confront the Olympic timetable. Essen will be my last race before the Games and I shall then have two weeks' final slog before departing for Seoul. It is a pity there is not more time as I would like another couple of races, preferably over 1500m.

Meanwhile as I am absorbed in my own efforts, the athletics world continues to be dominated by the controversy over Seb Coe's non-selection. Peter Elliott has been subjected to the sort of ill-informed flak from the popular press normally reserved for English football managers and cricket captains. Completely ignoring his outstanding record of the last two years he has been portrayed as the carthorse compared to Coe the thoroughbred. The issue has now extended beyond the question of selection policy and become a personality clash. There has been talk of Coe receiving a personal invitation from Juan Samaranch, the president of the IOC, to compete in the Games. This has inevitably stirred up antagonism from many quarters as the invitation smacks of preferential treatment, entirely at odds with the Olympic limit of three representatives per event for each country. The wide opposition to Samaranch's proposal may kill the affair once and for all.

August 25: The Pressure of Competing. As the Olympics approach it is inevitable that everyone who participates in the Games experiences not only personal expectation and hopes, but also the aspirations of others. At best the support and encouragement of family and friends can inspire and increase confidence. At worst the pressure on the athlete can be increased greatly by insistent cajoling.

I am the type of person who experiences little difficulty in motivating myself for my sport. I therefore prefer not to talk about the Olympics outside my training and discussions with George and Kerin. Once I am away from the running track I would rather forget athletics, especially as the next five weeks will be completely dominated by it. But there are many friends and acquaintances who are seeing me for the last time before the Olympics, and it is understandable if they want to discuss my hopes and prospects.

So for all athletics enthusiasts here are two ways of dealing with competitors before any Olympics; the first helpful, the second not. Yesterday we had some friends from our university days to stay. This couple are both keen sports fans. He teaches PE and this was the last occasion I would be seeing them before I left for Seoul. Yet during the entire evening athletics was not mentioned. When they left they wished me well and encouraged me to enjoy myself. I do not know if it was deliberate or not, but in such company athletics ceases to be a major concern, and success on the running track does not seem to be so important.

By contrast earlier this summer I attended a cricket match as a guest of the committee. One of the committee members, an elderly rotund gentleman carrying a glass, offered me his advice. 'Now, when you get to the Olympics' he urged 'you push yourself through the bloody pain barrier and keep going'. It was hard to imagine this red-faced drinker ever confronting the pain barrier except when he walked up the stairs. 'You never give up and bloody bring back the gold medal for us.' I smiled weakly and mouthed some reply about doing my best. 'I mean it,' he exclaimed, his complexion now a deep red. I hoped he was not going to have a heart attack. 'You have got to keep going. We want that gold medal.'

The committee member walked off, probably to refill his glass. He had done his bit for Britain's Olympic effort. He had imposed his own trenchant expectations, or perhaps inadequacies, upon me. In those situations, which must be brushed off, a polite reaction masks the anger and aggression felt. What does this person know about running? Has he ever experienced the fatigue of hard training? What does he know about pushing your body to its limits? I can imagine the reaction of such people from the comfort of their armchairs when the Olympics is over. Success will be met with a told-you-so attitude, failure with a never-had-it-in-him rebuke.

I am fortunate in having family and friends who match the first example rather than the second.

August 28: Race, 2 miles, Crystal Palace. Two miles at Crystal Palace – or rather my fictitious Olympic heat. A wet late summer afternoon. Autumn is already in the air. Yet another scrappy, inconsequential race. An instantly forgettable affair. I contested the lead with two laps left. Gary Staines refused to let me overtake him. I settled into second place and was, as ever, unable to accelerate with Frank O'Mara as he kicked decisively with 200m left. There was a separate contest down the home straight to see who was the slowest sprinter of four British contenders for the Olympic 5000m team – Gary Staines, Paul Davies-Hale, Tim Hutchings and myself. Tim proved the slowest in finishing fifth, I ended up fourth, Gary Staines third and Paul Davies-Hale outsprinted us all to finish second. This was the last British meeting of 1988. It seems a long way from the same event last year where I won the 5000m in 13.17, the fastest time in Britain for six years.

Elsewhere, the two stars in action over the middle-distances were Said Aouita and Steve Cram. Both won. Both looked composed, neither appeared awesome. Their confrontation over 800m and 1500m in Seoul could overshadow even Johnson and Lewis.

August 30: Travel to Rieti. I am not running in Rieti until Wednesday, but strangely the only flight available was late on Monday night. As most of the British athletes travelled out on the more convenient Tuesday flight it did seem odd that I and a few others were flying on Monday. Was this the luck of the draw or is my card still marked as a result of refusing to run in the AAA Championships?

The upshot is that I have an extra day in Italy to recover from last night's journey. We arrived in Rome close to midnight. Tim and Sharon Hutchings, George and myself were kept hanging around the airport whilst the involved travel and accommodation arrangements were made.

Eventually we were taxied to Rieti with only one minor problem. Our driver experienced difficulty in leaving the car park. The car park barrier was operated by a prepaid ticket mechanism. The driver did not realise this and made several attempts to deceive the machine with his unpaid ticket. Eventually he was persuaded by our protesting and the growing queue of impatient traffic behind to return to the car park and pay the ticket correctly. After several minutes of dramatic gestures, tooting horns, screeching brakes and rapid reversing the situation was resolved. We arrived in Rieti in the early hours and were in bed as it approached 2am.

Late this morning I opened the shutters to reveal a scene from *A Room With A View*. Beneath was the cobbled town square surrounded by whitewashed buildings. Beyond were tiled roofs, lines of washing, mountains and monasteries. Adjacent was the cathedral with ancient statues and canopied cafes with circular tables. The noise of motor scooters and pealing bells echoed around the little square.

Rieti is located on a hill above a muddy river and traffic streams through the narrow ancient streets. After a late breakfast I wandered around the town, grateful for the shade of the tall buildings. The bright window displays of the shops contrasted with the faded peeling frescos of the buildings above. The ground floor was late twentieth century, those above sixteenth. A provincial Italian market town seems an odd place to hold an international athletics meeting, but apparently it is the home town of Sandro Giovannelli, a leading official and promoter of the Italian Athletic Federation. Not that I am complaining. I am quite happy to sit in the shade of a cafe watching the world pass by in the town square.

Before long there is a collection of athletes assembled outside the cafe. There is a relaxed bonhomie that belies the intense competition we all display on the track. There is much banter regarding the British Olympic kit. It is a tradition to ridicule the team uniform as ill-fitting, unfashionable and much worse than the outfit of any other country. The British team kit is therefore condemned as impossible to wear even if it does fit. I keep fairly quiet as being an average five feet eight inches, shoe size eight, everything fits perfectly. I also do not want to admit it, and certainly would not amongst the cynical middle-distance boys, but I still feel a thrill of pride when I try on my team kit. I do not think this is connected with wearing British kit and therefore a sense of national identity, but rather the status that wearing the kit instantly confers. It is more a feeling of 'I have done well to achieve this' than 'I am proud to represent my country'.

The conversation skirts around running topics. For some, Rieti is the last stop on the summer athletics circuit before home and rest. These are the athletes who have missed out on the Olympics. For others it is the final step in preparations, a last signpost on the road to Seoul. Many of Britain's top runners are here each with individual motivation and hopes. There is Seb Coe who must want to prove a point, even if publicly he remains controlled. Peter Elliott is ready to justify his selection, Steve Crabb wants to defend his. Mark Rowland is tuning up for the steeplechase, Steve Cram is looking for a brisk 1000m. Tim Hutchings, my long standing adversary, is perhaps wanting to prove a point against me and Gary Staines in the 5000m. We eat and chat together. There is no public animosity and although on the track no quarter will be given, most of us will be happy to enjoy a gentle run together on Thursday morning.

The 5000m should be a good race. In addition to the British contingent, the Spaniards Anton and Gonzalez are reputed to be looking for a fast time. The Rieti track is fast. There have been some great 1500m races here. Coe ran 3.29.77 in 1986 and Ovett 3.30.77 in 1983. I last ran here in 1984 in the 1500m, the year after Ovett's world record. Painted on the track there were (and still are), two lines about ten metres apart in the vicinity of the 1500m start. There was some confusion over which of the two start lines we should use. Naturally we decided to line up on the one furthest round the bend and closest to the finish. The officials conferred and ushered us back the extra ten metres. One of the runners laughingly pointed to our preferred start line and said 'Ovett – last year?'

September 1: 5000m, Rieti. I jogged down to the track in the early evening sunshine. In the relaxed rural atmosphere it was impossible to feel too nervous. The open stands, warm friendly atmosphere, trees and grass reminded me of a country agricultural show rather than an athletics meeting. In the warm-up area adjacent to the track there was a vicious dog tethered to an abandoned barn. Beyond were fields and an impressive range of mountains silhouetted in the evening light.

The previous night I had been talking to Peter Elliott. He had asked me if I felt under any pressure. Perhaps he was making reference to the fact that I have been selected for the Olympic team without showing any decent form this year and tonight would be racing Tim Hutchings, one of my rivals for the third place, who must be eager to beat me. I replied I did not, although I would like to show sufficient form to justify my selection.

My situation might appear tense to some people, but it is nothing compared to the pressure Peter Elliott has experienced. He has been subjected to intense criticism and scrutiny since he decided to run both the 800m and 1500m in the Olympics. In both events he has earned his place, yet he has been the victim of the widespread pro-Coe lobby. He has received hate-mail and been the butt of cartoon jokes yet maintains his determination and dedication. Before my race yesterday evening Elliott won the 800m in his best time of the season.

As I was warming up, Steve Cram appeared to be cruising to victory in the 1000m. With about 200m left he jumped into the air as if shot in the back of the leg. He lay on the infield waiting for help. Were his Olympic hopes ended? I did not have time to wait and find out. I had to concentrate on running my own race. My stomach felt uncomfortable and I visited the toilet several times before the race began. Even on the track I would have liked to nip behind a bush but there were none on the infield! As I took my tracksuit off, the press were descending on Crammie like a pack of wolves as he left the stadium. There would not be much interest in the 5000m.

There was a pace-maker who was supposed to be running 64-second laps. After 800m the announcer shouted in English 'too slow'. I have never heard the announcer tell the runners to speed up before. Unfortunately, the announcer had the wrong lap times as the pace was exactly as intended. The Spaniards, Anton and Gonzalez, were following the pace-maker and after 2000m the field began to split. So far the race had gone according to plan. I was tucked in at the back of the leading group and felt comfortable at the steady pace.

As you become experienced in running 5000m races, you become receptive to slight changes in pace. To the observer watching the athletes lap around the track the race may appear a sedate procession culminating in a final sprint, but within the race the pace is rarely consistent. There are hardly ever two laps of an identical speed and most of the runners are aware of the changing rhythm of their event. If a lap changes by more than one or two seconds I can appreciate the difference.

During last night's 5000m, the pace was regular until 2000m when it suddenly slowed. The pace-maker was unable to maintain his schedule and the Spaniards who wanted a fast time were not prepared to take the lead. A potentially fast time was lost between two and three kilometres. The field that had stretched leaving only four runners in contention bunched together. I was reluctant to commit myself to a decisive move as I still lacked confidence, but after another pedestrian three laps I could restrain myself no longer and for the first occasion this year actually led a 5000m race.

I gradually increased the pace with three laps remaining and was aware of runners slipping behind. One of the most satisfying experiences in running is to take the lead in a race and to be aware without actually looking that other runners are unable to follow your change in pace. At long last this was happening to me again. At the bell only Gary Staines had been able to remain in contact. He overtook me, reversing our roles. I followed him round the final bend and sprinted past in the last 100 metres. My final time was 13.24, Gary Staines was second in 13.25, and third place was over 13.30.

It was not a spectacular performance, but appreciably the best of my year. I had beaten a good field and justified my selection for the Olympics. Afterwards I warmed down, nursing a blister on my foot, but without any pain from my troublesome Achilles tendons. A victory at last. Today I travel to Essen for my second 5000m race in three days, feeling more optimistic.

September 2: 5000m, Essen. I was hopeful of another respectable time in tonight's race but in early September there is a big difference between the climates of northern and southern Europe. The north Atlantic depressions sweep through the

Ruhr and the strong wind whistling through the trees has not weakened all day. The differences between Rieti and Essen are more than climatic. Apart from hosting athletics meetings within a couple of days of each other there are few similarities. Rieti is a traditional Italian provincial town where we stayed in an old hotel with high ceilings, marble floors and shuttered windows. Essen, by contrast, is a heavy manufacturing town, flattened during the second world war, and now attractive to modern high-tech industry.

Our hotel is located on an industrial estate around the corner from a large IBM factory. It is the typical modern business hotel, canned music in reception, leisure club for guests only, lunchtime meetings and expensive leather briefcases for sale from locked glass display cases. I wander in to lunch in a jogging suit. Amidst the cigar smoke, suits and portable telephones I feel distinctly conspicuous. One of the business conferences is for Omega – 'timekeepers for the last twenty years of the Olympic Games' – so the promotional literature proclaims. All around the room are pictures of athletes winning races beneath Omega timing gantries. George and I briefly look around the display before being quickly ushered out: it is for trade customers only. This after all is business. People want to sell watches here, not look forward to the Olympics.

The wind had not abated later in the day. As usual I jogged down to the stadium about an hour before my race. The crowd was small, huddled together as if for warmth in the cavernous stadium. It was a night for rugs and flasks of hot drinks. There was an end of season atmosphere. There were only a handful of international class events, the rest were races for local athletes participating in their last track race before hanging up their spikes for the winter. But, even in windswept Essen there were athletes who could earn their Olympic places. For Patrick Ilg, the West German former steeplechase world champion, and Markus Ryffel, the Swiss Olympic 5000m silver medallist, this was the final opportunity to prove fitness and be included in their respective Olympic teams.

Both are former champions and in the declining years of their athletic careers. Seoul would probably be the last Olympics for either of them. Who knows, perhaps in four or eight years' time I might be in a similar position, hoping for a final swansong, looking to compete centre stage on one more occasion before departing the athletic arena.

The steeplechase was immediately before the 5000m and midway through the race Ilg dropped out. The race was won by a Norwegian runner who narrowly failed to achieve the Olympic qualifying standard. Is it better to fail by inches or miles? Ryffel was eager to run close to 13.30 in the 5000m and alternated in the lead with Hartmann of Austria. It was a hard task to maintain a respectable pace in the wind. I nursed my way through the opening laps, feeling stiff and tired after the race in Rieti two nights previously. With four laps left I speeded up, overtaking the leaders. Only Ryffel followed and 600m later he drifted back, eventually dropping out like Ilg. I began to tire noticeably in the last lap but fortunately had sufficient lead over the second place athlete. I won by four seconds in 13.32.

Later I spoke to Ryffel. He was disappointed, but not depressed. He would take a rest and go on holiday. He would consider whether to retire and devote himself to his sports shops. He is in his mid-thirties and has had a long successful career. Like all athletes he is facing another set of decisions. Should he keep on running or should he retire? Is his body capable of another year of hard training or not? Athletics, like many other sports, involves difficult decisions. Sometimes these are purely sporting decisions, whether to follow a break or remain in the pack during a certain race. Other times they are off the track, whether to have an operation or not, whether to look for a different coach. Fortunate is the athlete not faced with hard choices.

September 5. During the last week I may not have set the world alight but for the first time in several months I am looking forward to the Games. I have, temporarily at least, overcome my problems and with a couple more weeks' training may yet reach Seoul in respectable condition. My lofty ambitions of last year have been dented by the traumas of 1988 but I am slowly reaching a satisfactory level of fitness.

Three races in six days was a hard but necessary preparation for Seoul. I think that the three rounds of the 5000m will prove too much for many athletes. Gonzalez finished a distant ninth in the Rieti 5000m and I cannot imagine him challenging in Seoul. The 5000m is still an open race. The current frontrunners must be Regalo and Domingos Castro from Portugal, Eamon Martin, Sydney Maree, perhaps Stefano Mei – and who knows what surprises the Kenyans can spring. Amongst other British distance runners, Peter Elliott and Mark Rowland continue to impress. The big question mark is over Steve Cram. He appeared relaxed after his injury and was hopeful of resuming training before too long. After his injury trouble he will find it tougher than ever to defeat the remarkable Aouita who is continually improving at 800m.

Since the weekend I have had difficulty in returning to my final training phase. Training is so boring compared to racing. I enjoy the challenge and excitement of competition. It is hard to maintain motivation in training, especially after a series of races. Fortunately, there is less than a fortnight before I leave for Seoul.

September 6: The Environmental Chamber. Loughborough University possess an environmental chamber. This is a small room where temperature and humidity can be accurately controlled. Various experiments involving wide ranges of environmental conditions are carried out here. For the last two years I have used the environmental chamber before attending the championships in Stuttgart and Rome.

The aim has been to achieve heat adaptation before leaving Britain. By sitting in the chamber for an hour a day over a fortnight at steadily increasing temperatures and humidity it is possible for the body to achieve some degree of acclimatisation prior to departure. The process is conducted under careful supervision with continual checks of heart rate and body temperatures. The required adaptation is best achieved by exposure to temperatures and humidity higher than those expected in the country to be visited. This makes for an uncomfortable hour, but the only alternatives are to spend longer in the chamber under cooler conditions (boredom prevents this) or to exercise in the chamber at lower temperatures (my training prevents this). Instead I prefer to sit and sweat. Last year my final environmental session prior to Rome was conducted at 95 per cent humidity and 44 degrees centigrade. It was almost unbearable but, unlike many athletes, I experienced no problem with the conditions in Rome.

This year the climate in Seoul is not supposed to be as fierce as Rome, but I might as well make the most of the technology available. Last year the local TV station spotting a newsworthy item filmed my first session in the chamber. The reporter conducted an interview with me inside the chamber, once the camera had stopped misting over. He sensibly took off his jacket, shortly followed by his tie. After about ten minutes in 70 per cent humidity at 30 degrees centigrade his shirt was sticking to his back and his face running with sweat. He bravely soldiered on with his task, leaving rapidly the moment it was completed. Fortunately, he was not required to read the lunchtime news.

This year I have no such diversions to disturb the boredom of sitting in a hot room for an hour, interrupted only by temperature and heart rate checks. I sit in the chamber reading the paper and adapting. However within a few days perspiration will render any paper reading impossible and I shall sit, dripping, waiting for the hour to pass.

September 11. The pre-Olympic hype has begun in earnest. Newspapers are filled with Olympic stories, the Sunday papers have produced their pull-out guides, and the TV channels are vigorously promoting their all-night coverage. After much debate, many of the Olympic finals take place around midday Korean time. The US network NBC, who paid $300 million to cover the Games, wanted the Olympic finals to be scheduled for early in the day to coincide with peak viewing time. The big events will therefore happen conveniently for US viewers who will be able to eat their evening burgers and french fries in front of the athletic finals. In Britain it will be either a case of setting the alarm clocks for between 3 and 4am or staying up through the night.

The only effect the hype has on me is to increase my impatience to leave for the Far East. When George and I were deciding when to leave for the Games it seemed a sensible idea, in view of my injury problems, to complete all my serious training here in Loughborough and travel about ten days before I competed. I would then use the entire period before competition to wind down and recover from the jet-lag. This would be preferable to travelling earlier and attempting to resume heavy training in Japan or South Korea.

I still believe this is my best course of action, but as my event is one of the last in the Olympics, it means I am left in Britain training whilst everyone else has departed for the Games. Most of the British athletic team is happily ensconced in the luxury of the Nihon Aerobics centre in Japan but I remain here in Loughborough. My sense of missing out on the action is heightened by the lack of other runners with whom to train. For most, the season is over and if it were not for a handful of helpful training partners, who have been willing to sacrifice some of their well-earned end of season break to help me through a few of my harder workouts, I would be training completely on my own. Chris McGeorge, Bill Foster, Hamish McInnes and Dave Lee have all generously shared this task.

I am sure that my plan to leave for Japan on September 17, spend six days in the British training camp at Nihon and fly to Seoul on the 24th, four days before the heats of the 5000m, is my most sensible build-up to the Games. I am maximising the precious training time available in the UK and allowing myself sufficient days to wind down in Japan and Seoul. But I still feel as if I have received an invitation to a party and somehow have missed the bus, or in this case the plane.

September 13: Books. During the athletic season when it is important to relax between demanding training and racing programmes, I read. Wherever I travel I am weighed down by a large selection of books. This week I have been compiling a small library to carry to Japan and Korea. It is difficult to choose books that are as appealing on the journey as on the shelf in the bookshop. My usual problem is that in an effort to be educated I select some profound non-fiction work on the history or culture of the country I am visiting. When I arrive I would prefer a lighter novel to while away the hours.

This summer one of the books that has absorbed me has been *Native Stones* by David Craig. The book relates his experiences and emotions about climbing and mountains. Although there is not the same element of physical danger in running, many of the challenges of fear, risk and tension are as present in my sport as his. In running there is the same sense of achievement when or if you reach your summit.

In running as in climbing, your ambition is exposed, you can only achieve by harnessing your strength and determination towards a single purpose. You are not risking life and limb on the athletics track but there is the same intense confrontation with the unknown. The prospect of competing in a fast race against runners of equal and superior ability can be as intimidating as tackling a rock-face. The challenge in both is to overcome your fear. The best way to do this is to progress step by step. The climber can concentrate on the next foothold rather than looking up at the distant summit above. Likewise, the runner, when being dragged along faster than before, can focus on survival lap by lap and not think about the overall pace he is being forced to maintain. In both pursuits, surrendering to panic at the scale of the task will result in failure.

I also find the precious moments of competition more exciting and addictive than anything else in life. The thrill of success justifies all the effort and commitment. When Craig reaches the top of a mountain and can look down exhausted from the climb, savouring the panorama beneath him and perhaps wanting to express the intensity of what he has just lived through, he writes. When an athlete wins a race, whether edging past rivals in a desperate lunge for the line, or striding relaxed to victory with the opposition trailing behind, he or she celebrates. The victorious athlete can dance a lap of honour, wave to the crowd and express joy in a primitive display of self-congratulation.

Unfortunately, in running, there is only the one winner.

September 16: Autumn. Only one day left. Twenty-four hours before I leave. The weather has turned. Last week calm, mild September days signalled the lingering decline of summer. There was a serene stillness, a hint of autumn cool in the warm sunshine, a warning to enjoy these last, late summer days.

This week summer has been swept away in chilly northerly winds. I am feeling the cold. There are three reasons for this. First I am acclimatising to the conditions in Seoul during my daily environmental sessions; second, I have had a drastic haircut to convince myself I am a serious athlete; and third, I am running early in the morning to prepare for the time change.

The early morning running follows some advice from the BAAB. Apparently when you travel eastwards round the world you can help your eventual adjustment to the new time zone by advancing your body clock in the days before travel. Kerin and I are therefore attempting to rise earlier than usual. As I am leaving the minimum time possible to overcome the effects of jet-lag in the Far East, I am sure this will prove to be a good idea. However I am not enjoying leaving the warmth of bed at 6am on these chilly mornings.

I have adopted my full winter training garb, woolly hat and all, to combat the cold and protect my shorn head on these early morning jaunts. I have also switched on the central heating for the first time in many months. I am looking forward to the warmth of Japan and South Korea. I am counting the hours to departure as is Kerin for rather different reasons. In my complete absorption with my impending trip I have not considered our imminent separation. Kerin is staying behind in Britain whilst I do battle in Seoul. A few months ago we could not decide whether she should accompany me to the Olympics or not. When I was injured through June and my prospects of attending the Games were bleak, we decided not to gamble on my recovery. It would have been difficult to arrange her travel and accommodation only to cancel it owing to my failure to make the team. She will stay behind and visit her parents to watch my races. We shall both miss each other, but at least I shall be engrossed in competition.

This morning was my last hard track workout before the Games. It was awful – pathetic. I fell apart completely on the last set of repetitions. There are plenty of reasons for my exhaustion. Primarily, the training of the last fortnight, the environmental chamber and the general hassle of preparing for departure. I suppose I was hoping for too much from the morning's training. I cannot always expect to produce outstanding sessions. George did not appear unduly concerned and I am sure that after some days relaxing in Japan I shall notice an improvement in my performance. I do not intend making any changes in my training programme and am looking forward to the remaining recuperative phase of training.

The hard work is over. The injuries, races, disappointments and training are all behind me. Tomorrow at long last I am off to first Japan and then South Korea – the Olympic Games.

12

To Seoul via Japan

September 18: Arrival at Nihon. The tourist looks for new and different experiences. On holiday, one of the aims is to sample unaccustomed cultures and lifestyles. The sportsperson travelling abroad is the opposite. He or she wants to prepare in an environment that most closely resembles home.

Like most other Olympic competitors I shall be seeking to minimise the disruption to my domestic regime before competition. During the ten days before the first round of the 5000m I shall be avoiding all ethnic foods, not visiting Japanese or Korean tourist attractions and not sampling the night-life.

When I travel abroad to compete I am often envied for the opportunity to visit exciting places. Unfortunately I rarely capitalise on my travels. Usually it is a case of flying somewhere, checking into the hotel, resting, racing, eating and returning home. For the Olympics, I shall be away from home for two and a half weeks. Assuming I reach the final I am only anticipating playing the tourist role for the last three days of the trip. In the meantime I shall maintain my usual lifestyle. First stop on the trip is the Nihon Aerobics centre.

The BAAB organised the pre-Olympic training camp at the Nihon Aerobics centre near Tokyo to help the athletes prepare for competition in as suitable an environment as possible. George and I were the last two arrivals at the training camp and most of the athletes are already preparing to leave. We arrived this afternoon after a journey of about twenty hours – Heathrow to Tokyo via Anchorage. I had not relished the prospect of the seventeen and a half hour flight, but managed to sleep for a substantial proportion of the journey. My rest was helped by obtaining a seat at the front of the section where it was possible to extend my legs further than the usual distance available. The worst aspect of long flights for me is being cramped up in a small seat with no room to stretch my legs. On this occasion I was fortunate to obtain a decent seat.

From Tokyo, Narita airport, George and I were whisked to Nihon. The BAAB had been circulating reports about the luxuries of the Aerobics centre all year, the lavish facilities, excellent food and ideal environment to relax before the Games. The only reservation I had about the centre was the availability of a suitable area for steady running. Apparently the centre is surrounded by hills and there is hardly any flat ground suitable for distance runners.

Driving into the grounds of the complex the ecstatic BAAB reports seem justified. We passed through lush landscaped grounds on our way to the reception in the main complex. This is a huge building that I shall investigate tomorrow. Adjacent to the centre is the track, and opposite the golf courses. After checking in, we were driven to our accommodation in one of the cottages of Canadian cypress logs that are scattered in the woods around the complex. This evening's meal was excellent. So far, no complaints. I shall find out more in the morning.

September 21: The Nihon Aerobics Centre. 'A precious time nestled in nature will surely refresh your bodies and minds. Start the day listening to the forgotten respiration of nature.' The Nihon Aerobics centre is based on the philosophy of Dr Kenneth Cooper, one of the founders of the aerobic fitness system. An hour's drive from Tokyo, the centre was built as a relaxing haven for stressed executives, hence the emphasis on peace and quiet. Membership of the Aerobics centre is limited, exclusive and very expensive. All sorts of astronomical figures have been quoted. From what I can gather membership is usually purchased by companies and is in the region of $250,000 per year. The most accurate information I have so far obtained was from Les Jones, the assistant manager of the British men's athletic team. He told me that a round of golf on one of the three nine hole golf courses costs more than the annual membership of his club at home.

Given these prices and the demand for the facilities, it is an unexpected, pleasant surprise to find that the Japanese management have closed the centre to their usual clientele for the weeks prior to the Games. The British and US Olympic teams have had the complete run of the facilities. Most of the athletes have now left as battle commences in a couple of days, but for the remaining Olympians there is free use of a magnificent facility with hardly anyone around. George and I have a large log cabin to ourselves. There is plenty of space, comfortable beds, shower facilities and a kitchen. The log cabins are hidden in the trees about fifteen minutes' walk from the centre. Shuttle buses run between the two every thirty minutes, although the service has become more erratic since the main party of athletes left yesterday.

The centre itself is a huge three storey building alongside the athletics track. I have never seen a landscaped athletics track before. Within the perimeter is a little copse of trees. Around the trees is a selection of strange exercise apparatus and next to this is a putting green. With trees and rocks behind the track, the aesthetic effect is pleasant but I am not so sure about the practicalities of timing repetition sessions with the trees obscuring vision. The top floor of the Aerobics centre is devoted to exercise. There is a 200m indoor track and rows of gleaming stationary cycles, treadmills and weights machines. On the second floor are the washrooms and changing areas. To my mind these are the most impressive facilities in the building. I have never seen so much space devoted to the comparatively simple task of cleaning your body after exertion. There are jacuzzis, saunas, a swimming pool and sunbeds. There are all sorts of showers, ones that squirt water at you from different angles, ones that are arranged at sitting level so that you do not have to stand up to use them, and even conventional showers. Then there is the drying area, a room the size and style of a beauty salon with hair dryers, mirrors, handbasins, deodorant and after-shave provided. Finally there is a lounge, where presumably you recover from all the hard work involved in cleaning yourself up.

The restaurant on the ground floor serves ample and delicious meals so, unusually for an athlete, I can find very little to complain about. Actually, there are a couple of minor gripes – too many hills and too much security. There is a connection between the two as it is because of the hills that we are forced to take a mini-bus to a nearby park to run. This means we leave the heavily guarded Nihon complex and are escorted by armed personnel to the park. The tight security arrangements are considered necessary as the Japanese are concerned about any incidents regarding their guests, the British and US Olympic teams. This means that a half an hour run drags out over most of the morning as first we have to take a mini-bus to reception, then have our names checked out, wait until everyone is ready and trundle off to the park accompanied by our escort. After we have run we go through the same procedure in reverse. When we reach the park some of our guards cycle to different corners to make sure we never run beyond their range of vision. In future I think I may put up with the hills.

September 22. My birthday. I am twenty-seven years old today. I do not feel as if I am a genuine adult, perhaps because I am still enjoying my running career and not working in the real world. I have not celebrated my birthday in style. I opened the handful of cards I had brought with me from home, but otherwise I have concentrated on completing my last track session before the Games. The celebrations can wait until I return home.

We have been watching the Games on the television. There are often complaints about the nationalism of the Olympics –

the flags, the ceremonies and the medal tables – but the most nationalistic aspect of these and any other games is the television coverage.

Today in Japan we have seen Japan versus USSR in women's volleyball, the Japanese gymnasts in full flow interrupted by the occasional Rumanian and Russian, Japanese cyclists and Japan versus West Germany at handball. It appears that Japan provides half the competitors at these Games. Japanese television is as biased in its coverage of a major sports event as most countries I have visited. The worst example of this I have seen was at the European Championships in Stuttgart. In the final stages of the men's marathon the camera remained resolutely focused on the battle for third and fourth between two West Germans whilst up ahead the duel for first and second between the Italians Pizzolato and Bordin was completely missed. I have also been told that any non-American watching the Los Angeles Olympics in the US could have thought the Games were confined to US entrants. I am sure some overseas visitors would be equally critical of British TV. After all, the Olympics are as much about how our boys and girls are doing as who wins.

As we receive so little information from Japanese TV, news about the performances of British competitors in the Games filters through Nihon by word of mouth. I have heard more stories about Seoul from phoning home than anywhere else. I have yet to see Adrian Moorhouse's gold medal performance. There have also been some unfavourable reports concerning the Olympic village. It is supposed to be very noisy with queues up to an hour long for food. Here in Nihon it is blissfully quiet. George and I are the last remaining British personnel in the complex and we have the entire place to ourselves in the company of a handful of Australian and US marathon runners.

Apart from having slight problems with jet-lag I am totally relaxed. How could anyone not relax when you can lie in a jacuzzi overlooking acres of beautiful mountainous countryside and then amble downstairs for a bite to eat? At the same time I think six days will be enough here at Nihon. The last bus from the complex to the cottages leaves at 9pm and endless games of cards are not my idea of entertainment. Japanese TV, once the Olympics are over for the day, comprises games shows, martial arts based oriental soap operas, and whisky advertisements. I am amazed by the whisky adverts. They are male dominated and usually take place in a panelled club bar where everyone is dressed in sports jackets or suits. What is surprising is that often the men are seen drinking heavily. To me the advert seems to be saying why not go out with your mates and do some serious drinking? The adverts appear to be condoning excessive alcohol consumption. I cannot imagine such commercials being shown in Britain. Edwina Currie would have a fit.

September 23: The Japanese Countryside. This morning I sneaked past the security guards and went running on the roads around the camp. We are in the depths of the Japanese countryside here in Nihon. The hills are thickly wooded. I am surprised at the lush vegetation. Since we arrived in Japan the weather has been humid and damp. If it rains while you are running your T-shirts will not dry in the oppressive atmosphere. Insect life flourishes. Huge colourful butterflies and enormous dragonflies flutter around. On the less savoury side, one runner nearly stepped on a snake, and a couple of female distance runners were walking around with eye-patches. They had caught eye infections, possibly as a result of running into spiders' webs on the golf course.

Outside the complex the rice harvest is in operation. The paddy fields are edged with rice grasses drying on wooden poles. I can only see women working in the fields. Likewise in the park it is the women maintaining the grounds. Most noticeably, all the caddies on the golf course are female. There appears to be a clearly defined traditional role for women in Japanese society. They do all the hard work! I also notice that the regular cartoon in the *Asahi Evening News*, the only English language paper we receive here, is that symbol of the British northern working class, Andy Capp. Perhaps the Japanese can identify with Andy Capp's attitude to the fairer sex.

Gradually I am overcoming jet-lag. It has taken me four nights before I have slept without interruption. I have managed to avoid sleeping during the day which has helped my adjustment to the new time zone whilst here in Japan.

Tomorrow I leave Nihon for Seoul. As one of the coaches termed it, I am going 'into the cauldron'.

September 24: Seoul. One of the stories that reached Nihon from Seoul was of long delays in Seoul airport. I made sure I was carrying the correct accreditation, wore my tracksuit and was whisked through customs and immigration with impressive efficiency. As I was travelling on my own, a car hurried me off towards the Olympic village. George was taken off to the Olympic family town, another apartment block complex two miles away from the athletes' village, where spectators and officials were staying.

The airport and downtown Seoul were festooned with flags and banners. The bright colours in the afternoon sunshine were a distinctive welcome to the Olympic city. Flower beds with the Olympic rings picked out, banners on balconies, wherever you looked there were reminders of the Games. The taxi sped along the Han river past the Seoul sports complex and the main stadium. There was no mistaking the distinctive sweeping curves of the magnificent arena. Seeing the huge stadium dwarfing everything around it I experienced that familiar tingle of excitement and anticipation.

The journey from the stadium to the village took twenty minutes. I was swept through security checks and began mingling with athletes from all over the world. It was impossible not to feel excited and to appreciate what is meant by the Olympic spirit. I was met by one of the British team officials and shepherded through accreditation. The British team quarters were in one of the anonymous apartment blocks beyond the central concourse. This was a tiered greenhouse style construction built in the shape of the Korean symbol of the Games. The symbol is reminiscent of a horseshoe with one prong severed near the base. It did not strike me as a functional design but the building housed all the essential services for an Olympic village. The restaurant occupied a good third of the space and elsewhere there were telephone services, a post office, department store and lots of rooms full of computers and large piles of paper.

After another security check I reached the team accommodation. I then encountered my first problem. The room list had been altered. As I was one of the last athletes to arrive I had been shunted from room to room. Accommodation at major games is usually arranged so that athletes who are in broadly similar events and competing at similar times in the programme share rooms together. It is not sensible to have a shot-putter, competing on the opening day of the Games, sharing a room with a marathon runner who races on the final day. A better idea would be to put the shot-putter in a room with a javelin thrower and the marathon runner with a middle-distance athlete. This had happened, but by arriving late I had missed out on the various room manoeuvrings that had subsequently taken place.

An hour later I found my room. I was sharing with Stewart Faulkner, a young long jumper, in a flat of athletes all of whom had been knocked out of competition. Stewart was competing the next day and was not expecting to reach the final. I had another four days before I even began competing and I did not want to share with a group of athletes who no longer had any interest in resting up. It is not a personal slight, but athletes who have finished competing at the end of a long hard season are going to want to sample the attractions of the Olympics more than those who are still in action. I know if I had competed early in the proceedings I would enjoy the festivities, watch other sports and capitalise on the opportunity of attending the greatest sports festival in the world.

I tried to change my room with no success. There were no beds available in the middle- and long-distance runners' flat. I would have to stomach the arrangements or look elsewhere. Part of the Olympic experience is meeting other athletes, but at the same time, when you have spent so much effort in reaching the Games, you want to do everything possible to assist your chances. The British team officials could not help me. I decided to look for a room in the Olympic family town where George and my friend and training partner Bill Foster were staying.

Later this evening after various phone-calls and conversations I found myself in a quiet room in an almost deserted flat in the Olympic family town. This is ideal accommodation. A free shuttle bus or eighty pence taxi ride connects the two villages, so I can easily eat and visit the physiotherapist in the Olympic village. The arrangements were sorted out by Graham Botley, a friendly and helpful tour operator who also resolved my problems in Rome last year.

Amidst all this organisation I have missed the most exciting day of the Olympics. As I trooped through the various security checks and lugged baggage between the airport, Olympic village and eventually the Olympic family town there were only two athletes' names discernible in every language – Lewis and Johnson. As the day progressed Johnson's name became the one most frequently uttered. In the evening I heard about the greatest 100m ever. Ben Johnson had beaten Carl Lewis in a time of 9.79. Lewis was second in 9.92, and Linford Christie third in 9.97, the first European under ten seconds for 100m. It must have been a tremendous race. I may have to wait until I return to Britain to see it. The other stories rapidly circulating amongst the British team were less glorious. Steve Cram and Tom McKean both out of the 800. Crammie looked 'like Rome' was one observer's comment, whilst Tom McKean was disqualified for blatant pushing. If today is representative of the next ten days there will be some dramatic sport to come.

September 25: Instant Impressions of the Games. Today is a South Korean national holiday – the equivalent of American Thanksgiving. This morning I ran around the Olympic Park, the area adjacent to the village where many of the more exotic stadiums for swimming, cycling and fencing are situated. The Park also contains a selection of sculptures, a variety of walks amidst landscaped grounds and various outdoor snack stalls. The Park was thronged with people, mostly Koreans enjoying their day out. It was like Hyde Park on a summer Sunday, except many of the Koreans were wearing their national costumes. Amongst the vivid silk colours, the billowing flags, sunshine, chatter and smiling faces it was hard to imagine the Seoul I had expected. There were no student riots and the security, although ever present, was not overpowering. Children were rushing around laughing and posing for photographs. There was a friendly open atmosphere.

Twenty-four hours in Seoul and I am convinced this was a great place to stage the Games. There is so much cynicism around the Olympics. The controversy over drugs and the obvious commercialism are the two most blatant criticisms. The Olympic movement has its faults but mixing with so many people for whom these Games mean so much is an uplifting experience. I shared a taxi firstly with an American couple whose son was about to compete in a swimming relay and later with a supporter of the Australian basketball team. Outside the village Koreans were having their picture taken by a group of Italian competitors. There was a delegation from a Middle Eastern country, I think it was somewhere in Arabia, who told me how unbeatable Aouita was. All these people and thousands of others are caught up in a movement that transcends sport. It is healthy, invigorating and exciting and justifies the Olympics.

Back to the sport. I managed to see some athletics even if it was on a TV set; Ed Moses beaten in the 400m hurdles. George, to his credit, had been tipping Andre Phillips all week. Yvonne Murray's bronze in the women's 3000m. Tomorrow is the men's 10,000m and 800m final. Peter Elliott, as ever, has gritted his way to the 800m final. Aouita will be there; also Cruz, the reigning champion, and two Kenyans. The only way I can see Aouita being beaten is if someone goes off very fast. I suspect the Brazilians or rather Barbosa will do this, intending to help Cruz. The 10,000m is a very open race. Eamon Martin must stand a chance if he can remain in contact until the last lap.

Tomorrow I have a complete rest day. For two days before a major championship I like to have twenty-four hours without tying on my trainers. It is too late for any last-ditch training. I cannot improve my fitness any further.

September 26. This morning I visited the stadium for the first time. I wanted to familiarise myself with the layout so that when I come down for the first round of the 5000m on Wednesday, I do not turn up at the wrong entrance or fail to find the warm-up track. It is also useful to see how long the journey takes. There is the awful story of two US sprinters amongst the favourites for the 1976 Olympics who missed their heats and were therefore eliminated without even running.

I had only observed the stadium from the Olympic expressway alongside the Han river. Closer up you lose sight of the elegant curves and become engulfed beneath its vast concrete pillars. I wandered underneath the walkways and caught glimpses of the bright orange-red track between the gaps in the seat tiers. The stadium was almost empty even though the competition began in under an hour. Talking to some friends they told me how quickly the stadium could fill because of the easy access. Apparently the only occasion my friends had seen the stadium full, apart from the opening ceremony, was for the men's 100m. They reckoned that fifteen minutes after the race it was half-empty again.

I noticed the lack of shade in the warm-up area. As my races were in the early afternoon I would try to keep out of the sun as much as possible. The British team physios had secured a canopied area for their work. The physios' area is always a natural meeting point at a major games. Athletes gravitate towards physios like moths around a light.

I did not stay long at the track and arrived back in the family town before the men's 800m. I was correct. Barbosa stormed through the first lap and Aouita was struggling to stay in contact. Cruz was still in contention, and down the back straight both he and Aouita began to move up. Round the top bend seven of the eight runners were in the hunt for medals. For a fleeting moment Peter Elliott popped up on the outside straining for position, but Aouita was still fighting as was Cruz who might yet hold onto his Olympic crown. Then striding through the mêlée came a powerful Kenyan runner. The NBC commentators were baffled. They paused and exclaimed 'Kiprotich' as the fluent figure flew past the finish line. Cruz was second and Aouita held off the gallant Peter Elliott for third. NBC were wrong, the Kenyan was Paul Ereng, a twenty-year-old former cowherd, currently a student at the University of Virginia. He jogged around the track waving a Kenyan flag. For the first time in these Games a Kenyan runner has shown his ability.

Referring to Paul Ereng as one of the Kenyans adds to the mystique of these phenomenal runners. A few years ago the British middle-distance runners were spoken of collectively in awe. Now it is the Kenyans. Last year in Rome it was Konchellah, Kipkoech and Wakihuru. This year Ereng is the first to emerge. Later this afternoon the Kenyans were once again to the fore driving hard in the 10,000m. Antibo from Italy threw in a couple of vicious laps early on and split the field. Eamon Martin dropped out. The pace was fierce and soon after 5000m Boutaib the twenty-one-year-old Moroccan training partner of Aouita took the lead. He was never caught and won in an Olympic record. Another African distance victory. How does that continent do it? Every year great runners emerge. Phenomenal talents and yet so young. Boutaib has been living in the house the King of Morocco gave the great Said after he won the 1984 Olympic 5000m. Perhaps Boutaib will be given a house of his own after this. Produce a few more Aouita clones and the King of Morocco could be giving away an awful lot of houses.

Between the 800m and 10,000m the British team picked up a couple of silvers: Fatima in the javelin and Colin Jackson in the 110m hurdles. Jackson was a clear second behind the favourite Roger Kingdom. A good performance by Jon Ridgeon in finishing fifth after a year as successful as mine! This far the athletic competition has shown there will be no easy medals and the overall standard is even higher than at last year's World Championships.

September 27: The Ben Johnson scandal breaks. I walked down to breakfast and before I had my first mouthful of sugar-free muesli I heard the story of the Games. After the news there was, for once, a delay in resuming the serious task of eating, as the consequences of the Johnson scandal were discussed. Ben Johnson has been positively tested following his victory and world record in the Olympic 100m final. He has been stripped of his gold medal. The biggest star in world athletics has been banned. It is a shock that will ruin the Games.

Whatever else happens in these Olympics, the Johnson story will dominate. It will be the scandal of the Olympics, probably the sports scandal of the year. It may become one of the legendary stories of Olympic history alongside Jesse Owens' four gold medals in 1936 and Zatopek's triumphs of 1952.

On one level I am pleased. Johnson's positive test indicates that the IOC are prepared to face up to the problem. They have caught the biggest fish in the pond which must frighten and hopefully deter anyone else who is taking drugs. If athletics and sport wishes to tackle the drugs problem the authorities have to be prepared to ban any athlete who is tested positive.

On the other hand, it is a tragedy for athletics. It is awful that Ben Johnson has been tested positive for an anabolic steroid. Nobody knows the extent of the drugs problem in athletics, and from the rumours circulating around the Olympic village today there could be more positive tests. What will be interesting is if Johnson, now officially banned for life, is reinstated by the IAAF after two years. All athletes who have appealed against a ban after the mandatory two years have so far obtained a reprieve.

Johnson's positive test once again throws the spotlight back on the problem of drugs in sport. No doubt there will be endless discussion and suggestions on what action should be taken. What I find most frustrating is how every athlete is smeared by the drugs story. There will be widespread pontificating on the immorality of modern sport, yet I and thousands of other Olympic athletes would hardly know the difference between an anabolic steroid and a packet of Smarties. I find it irritating that the drugs story, which for me is the least interesting and relevant aspect of these Games, will dominate the Olympics. Already Radio Leicester have been in touch with George. The purpose of their enquiry was not to find out how one of the few local athletes attending these Olympics is preparing for his 5000m heat tomorrow. Radio Leicester are not really interested in my performance. They want an 'expert' to sound off about the Johnson story.

But although the continual emphasis on the scandal of sport, as opposed to the genuine drama of the competition infuriates me, I realise there are very real and disturbing issues to be considered. What is the best way to tackle the drugs problem? How can the sport develop ways of catching the cheats? At another level, which drugs should be banned? Where should the line be drawn between substances that are legal or illegal? These are all problems that must be addressed if sport is to maintain its credibility. It is all very sad and depressing.

For the meantime there are other priorities in my sporting life. It is a tragic day for athletics, but the heats of the 5000m are tomorrow. I am still waiting for the heat draw. I think the qualifying conditions may be the first seven in each of the three heats plus nine fastest losers. Thursday's semi-finals would then comprise thirty athletes with the first six in each semi-final plus three fastest losers qualifying for Saturday's final. The next four days will be the toughest I have ever experienced in athletics. It is an exciting prospect and whatever happens I am looking forward to the challenge.

13

The Olympic 5000m Heats and Semi-Finals

September 28: Olympic 5000m heats. There is an Olympic newspaper published daily. The *Olympian* appears at various points around the Olympic family town. The paper, as well as containing all the results from yesterday's sport, also lists the programme and start details for the day ahead. Unfortunately whenever I try to buy a copy the vending machines that are supposed to contain the newspaper are either empty or out of order. The *Olympian* is very popular and it is annoying to see large numbers of visitors to the Games reading the paper at breakfast when I cannot do so myself. I must be rising too late in the morning.

This morning I was eager to obtain a copy and find out the composition of the 5000m heats. As usual I had to endure seeing masses of copies of the paper before eventually borrowing one from a friend. He also informed me that the *Olympian* can be purchased from the store complex in the family town. In my ignorance I have been scouring the vending machines for the last few days when I could have popped across to the store in a couple of minutes.

When at long last I found the details I was almost satisfied with the heat draw. You can never admit you are completely satisfied, you must always moan slightly about how yo have the toughest heat and how hard it will be to qualify, but on this occasion I suppose I have been reasonably fortunate. As expected there are three heats of about twenty athletes. The first seven in each heat plus the nine fastest losers will qualify for tomorrow's semi-final. I am in the third heat which is a big advantage. The third heat is probably the strongest on paper containing the Europeans, Stefano Mei, Jose Regalo, Vincent Rousseau, Pascal Thiebaut, Hansjoerg Kunze from East Germany, Eamon Coghlan and my old adversary Evgueni Ignatov from Bulgaria. There is also one of the Kenyans, Charles Cheruiyot, and Terry Brahm from the US. Several of these runners are quick finishers, so the last lap could be fast. Running last is an advantage that outweighs the quality of my heat. I can watch the first two heats and calculate how quickly I need to run. If the first two races are slow most of the fastest qualifiers could come from my heat. As seven fastest losers reach the second round I might be able to finish outside the first seven and still be sure of a place in the semi-final.

The aim should be to qualify with the minimum effort possible. Tomorrow will be hard for everyone. On the two previous occasions – the 1983 World Championships and 1984 Olympics – when there have been three rounds of the 5000m, only a handful of runners have survived the demanding schedule and been able to produce worthy performances in the final.

After an idle morning watching the athletics courtesy of NBC's less than riveting coverage, I caught a taxi to the stadium. As NBC's coverage in South Korea is primarily aimed at the US armed forces stationed here, it is difficult to avoid the fervent military messages that interrupt the sports coverage. There seems to be a commercial break every five minutes. Most breaks contain some patriotic advertisement or reminder to US personnel to check their customs allowances when travelling home. It is hard to enjoy the excitement of the Games and watch the unfolding drama of the longer distance races when you are battered by military commercials every two or three laps. I managed to see Steve Lewis beat Butch Reynolds between 'messages' before I left.

Arriving at the Olympic stadium reminds me of the scene in the film *Airplane* when the hero, on entering the airport, fights his way through hordes of religious fanatics and peace-loving hippies who are trying to give him flowers. At the Olympic Stadium zealous evangelicals are continually trying to give you books and messages about different religions. They look at you with empty smiling faces urging you to accept their gift. There are also more materially motivated entrepreneurs offering T-shirts and a multitude of Olympic souvenirs. Once you have fought your way through the crowds there are the security checks and then you are in the Olympic stadium complex.

It is a relief to reach the shelter of the main stadium as it is a hot afternoon. There is a covered walkway beneath the Olympic stadium linking it to the warm-up track. The walkway is littered with the discarded paraphernalia of the opening ceremony, so in places it seems like being back-stage in the theatre. I find a quiet corner and sit down. Fifty minutes before my race I jog gently keeping in the shade. Twenty minutes later I shuffle down to the report area. At an Olympics the whole performance of reporting before a race has a sense of drama that adds to the tension. For most events, even national championships and Grand Prix meetings, you jog along and check your name off ten minutes before the gun goes. You are free to warm up in private, often avoiding your rivals until the start line. At a major games the process is extended. After the men's 800m, Johnny Gray, who finished a disappointing fifth, was complaining on NBC that he could not handle the waiting before the race.

The first call is fifty minutes before the race. Usually an official will check your name off at this stage. Thirty minutes beforehand the athletes have to report in under a covered canopy at one end of the warm-up area. When everyone has arrived the contestants are led off into a report room under the stadium. Here you are kept together for a few more minutes before being taken to the final room. Your spikes and bags are checked. Lastly your photo-finish numbers are allocated and about ten minutes before the race you are led onto the track. There is a short area of synthetic track outside the call room. At some time during the twenty minutes' wait the athletes will put on their spikes and run some gentle accelerating strides on this strip of track.

I have experienced this prolonged reporting drama before and it does not disturb me. There is a TV monitor in the final report room and I watch the first heat. There is a more relaxed atmosphere today than there will be tomorrow. Today there is a communal desire to qualify. Our rivals are the runners in the other heats rather than each other. Tomorrow, in the semi-final, the real racing will start. Garry Staines wins the first heat in 13.47, an average time for the first round of the 5000m. I was expecting quicker performances.

We are led onto the track as the second heat begins. This is the first occasion I have stepped inside the Olympic stadium and despite the vastness I can locate individual faces and hear reassuring wishes of good luck. I am surprised by the heat. I am sweating heavily. I take my tracksuit off early and splash water over my face. The second heat is slow. Eamon Martin wins in a time close to 14 minutes. I calculate I can run as slow as 13.55 and, as long as I finish in the first thirteen, I will qualify for the semi-final.

The race begins. My Olympic Games have started. It does not seem a particularly dramatic occasion. I dawdle at the back of the field watching the clock and checking that our heat is ticking along quicker than the other two. It is. Stefano Mei and Vincent Rousseau are alternating in the lead. At 3000m we are nearly ten seconds up on the opening heats. This should be a formality. I know I can afford to relax. I watch my adversaries for tomorrow. Mei looks comfortable, so do Rousseau and Thiebaut. Eamon Coghlan accelerates rapidly through the pack with about 200m left. I do not attempt to follow and allow myself to be dragged along by the leading group of eight. I raise sufficient sprint to finish tenth. Sprinting is an effort. I do not feel composed when I strive for the extra yard of pace.

Perhaps that is because I am trying to relax and conserve energy or, more worryingly, perhaps I am still lacking the elusive acceleration that has been lacking all summer.

The heats are over. I have qualified comfortably for the semi-final, even if one of the TV interviewers is surprised to see me finish outside the top seven automatic qualifiers. All three British athletes reach the semi-final, Eamon Martin despite dropping out of the 10,000m. There are some surprises. Pierre Délèze finishes eleventh in the first heat in 14.12 and is knocked out, as are Frank O'Mara and Millonig from Austria. Otherwise all the fancied runners are in the semi-final. All the runners I expected to qualify from my heat did so. Names to watch for tomorrow, in addition to those I have already observed, are Ngugi and Ondieki from Kenya, Sydney Maree from the US, John Doherty from Ireland; Antibo from Italy, the silver medallist from the 10,000m; and above all I reckon, Castro from Portugal, silver medallist from the World Championship 5000m. There are a large number of potential medallists who will be fighting for fifteen places in Saturday's final.

I should not fret. It is a waste of time worrying about names. Amongst these runners, only a handful will be sufficiently fit to run another 5000m tomorrow at a much quicker pace. After I have checked the results I hurry back to the warm-up track. In the open foyer you pass through to reach the warm-up track, Stefano Mei is holding forth to the Italian press. I jog a couple of laps to warm down and receive a massage from one of the British team physiotherapists. I am not feeling too stiff. My Achilles tendons are not painful, nor is my hip. I catch a taxi back to the village hoping to miss the crush at the end of the day's athletics.

Back on the track, Daley was fighting hard in the decathlon whilst Mark Rowland was cruising comfortably through the steeplechase semi-final. I hope I find it that easy tomorrow.

September 29: Olympic 5000m semi-final. This morning for once I managed to buy a copy of the *Olympian* from one of the vending machines. That was the good news. The bad news was the paper contained no details about the 5000m semi-finals. Confident that if anyone knew what was happening this afternoon the press would, I phoned a journalist friend, Andy Etchells.

I had been correct in my assumption and he reeled off the complete list of the two 5000m semi-finals. The qualifying details were as expected, first six in each race plus three fastest losers. I was in the first semi-final. Until this morning I have always had the good fortune to be in the second semi-final in any major championship in which I have competed. Just as yesterday it was an advantage to run in the third heat, so today it would have been beneficial to have drawn the second race. I half expected my luck would run out this year.

Both 5000m semi-finals are equally matched. I am hopeful that either Antibo, a committed front-runner, or one of the two Kenyans in my race, Ondieki and Cheruiyot, will keep the pace respectable, otherwise I could have problems with the faster finishing of Castro, Maree, Thiebaut and Dieter Baumann, a West German 1500m runner who is having his first serious attempt at 5000m. If the pace is not reasonable I shall have to make some effort myself, so that if the worst happened and I fail to finish in the first six, I stand a chance of qualifying as a fastest loser.

Even though the semi-finals of the 5000m were later in the afternoon at 5.30 it was still hot down at the track.

Jackie Joyner-Kersee was the centre of attention in the shaded area under the stadium walkway. I relaxed in the tunnel adjacent to the warm-up track. It was pleasantly cool and dark. The action on the track could be watched through the enormous barred gates. The men's 1500m heats were in progress. I stretched gently and half watched Crammie winning his heat. I wandered over to the physios for a soothing leg massage. In the adjacent canopied tent Salvatore Antibo was engaged in a more unusual method of race preparation. He was passionately entwined with his girlfriend, also an Olympian, embracing her with all the enthusiasm of teenagers on the dance floor when the romantic records are played at the end of the evening. Antibo has already won a silver medal in the 10,000m so he has plenty to celebrate about, but I would have thought he might have delayed his ardour until after our 5000m semi-final in forty minutes' time.

Steve Cram returns from his successful heat. He warns me that his race, the first of the heats, was kept waiting for almost fifteen minutes on the track, most of the time without tracksuits. Usually when officials ask you to remove your tracksuits there is only a couple of minutes before the gun goes. Cram reckoned there was almost ten minutes of waiting without tracksuits. These small details appear trivial but in the tense situation of an Olympic Games, familiarity with the pre-race procedure helps the athlete to keep calm. An athlete before a big race likes to operate with minimum disruption, leaving the mind free for the task ahead. Therefore to know that there may be ten minutes between taking off my tracksuit and the start of the race means I need not rush to complete my warm-up strides when the officials give the request to remove track-suits.

As it is still very hot I only jog lightly before reporting. The report procedure is quicker than yesterday, and as Cram indicated we are on the track fifteen minutes before the start. The stadium is fuller than yesterday, but lacks the buzz I expected of the Olympics. After experiencing the World and European Championships, I thought the crowd at the Olympics would be even louder and more involved in the athletics. So far despite the importance of the occasion the atmosphere has not been as animated as either Rome or Stuttgart. This does not detract from my nerves. For the first time in these Games I am feeling genuinely nervous. The semi-final is a no-win situation. If I qualify it will be an expected relief, if I am knocked out a disaster. But what about my lack of races and feeble last lap performances this summer? Do I have the fitness to survive an Olympic final?

I pour water over myself and lie in the shade of one of the long jump scoreboards. The two Kenyans, Ondieki and Cherui-yot, join me. It surprises me that they are concerned about the heat. There is a victory ceremony. Everyone stands up and the stirring East German national anthem reverberates around the stadium. I am reminded of the moments in Rome before the World Championship final when a victory ceremony took place. Once again, a year later, I try to appreciate the experience of participating, despite the apprehension I am feeling. The ceremony finishes, we are summoned to the line and the first Olympic 5000m semi-final begins.

Alongside the track digital clocks indicate the lap times. I use these and the large electronic scoreboard at the end of the finishing straight to check on the progress of the race. The electronic scoreboard projects pictures of the race and it is a useful method of observing the positions of the runners without having to turn round. I am hoping the race will be run in laps of between 64 and 65 seconds. The digital clocks are not working. This is crazy. How can anyone judge the pace if the clocks are not functioning? After four laps they flicker into action. Relief, but the pace is not quick enough. Antibo is loitering near the back of the pack alongside me. I was hoping he would be pushing the pace along. Perhaps he is exhausted from the 10,000m. The laps are ticking away. Somebody had better take the initiative soon. Antibo moves up. I follow him. There are too many athletes in contention. Maree and Castro are very relaxed. Antibo has taken the lead, but is grimacing. At 3000m the race is too slow. I check the scoreboard and the time. Unless I pick the pace up I could risk being run out of the final on the last lap. With four laps left I overtake Antibo and steadily increase my stride.

I am telling myself to run hard but relaxed. Do not panic. Maintain a smooth powerful pace. I am concentrating hard. This acceleration must trouble some of the runners. I cannot believe that more than a handful will survive my injection of pace. I keep on glancing at the scoreboard. Come on, drop behind. This is much harder than I thought. I am struggling, but I must maintain composure. Two laps left and at last a group of four are escaping. I have made the necessary break. Domingos Castro is doggedly matching my every stride. He is like a little terrier snapping at my heels. He will not let go. He is very fit. The other two athletes in the detached group are Sydney Maree and one of the Kenyans. The bell, I must surely be through. I glance up at the screen. Four of us are still significantly clear. Several metres behind is a small group of three chasing athletes. I can even allow two of them to overtake me and still finish in the top six.

Three hundred metres left and Castro overtakes me. I am genuinely tired after my efforts of the last three laps and cannot stay with him. Maree and the Kenyan pass also. I am struggling to increase my stride. I cannot sprint with them, but I am still in fourth place. I should qualify. 200m left and I am exhausted. Do not worry, I have a rest day tomorrow. Everyone else is probably equally tired. I cannot run any faster. I glance at the electronic scoreboard. Can I ease up? NO I CANNOT! Quick. Help. Come on. Like a nightmare when your legs are lead weights and you cannot move quickly enough to avoid the approaching disaster, I struggle desperately to accelerate. Three athletes are sweeping past me. I gaze at the screen. Come on fight, fight. I try to force my weary limbs to extend that extra inch.

It's no good. It's too late. The race is over. My Olympics could be over. I was seventh. Caught by Baumann, Kunze and Thiebaut who ran the last lap in 54 seconds compared to my 61 seconds. I stagger off the track ignoring the TV requests. My time was 13.23.17. I will be out of the final unless the eighth place runner in the second semi-final is slower. I pull on my tracksuit in the changing room. Kunze and Baumann are laughing. I do not want to talk to anyone. This whole year has been a disaster. How could I not run any faster? Who cares what happens in the second semi-final? If I cannot finish in the first six of the semi-final I am going to have no chance in the final.

Mel Batty rushes up to me. Mel, as well as working for ITV, coaches Eamon Martin who is running in the second semi-final. He urges me on to the track to watch the race. I reluctantly follow and slump silently near the finish. The second semi-final is in progress. The pace is almost identical to my race. I try and forget about it. If I am knocked out I can enjoy the rest of the Games. I can watch other sports. I do not really care about running in the final do I? I am disillusioned with the sport. The second semi-final passes 3000m in an identical time to ours. I might as well give up this stupid activity. There are plenty of better things to do in life. Why waste all this energy on a futile race? On the track the runners are passing the point at which I increased the pace. There are a group of one, two, three . . . nine athletes in contention. Too many, but they are fractionally slower. John Doherty tries to take the lead, Ngugi holds him off. I shall definitely retire. Mel Batty is yelling at Eamon Martin. He is grimacing and fighting to hang on to the leading group. He is suffering from running both the 5000m and 10,000m. The bell. Eight athletes are bunched together. Eamon Martin has been dropped. Garry Staines is comfortable. The time will be very close. I shall retire and do something less stressful in life. The eight athletes are close together. I do not watch the race, only the clock. As every digit changes, hope returns. 13, 14, 15, the seconds slowly flicker past. The runners are closing rapidly on the finish, but the figures continue to pulse onwards. 18, 19, 20, they are not going to beat 13.23. I have made it. Stefano Mei has crossed the line, followed by a mass of runners. It does not matter, the time was slower. 13.24 for the winner. Wonderful. What a fabulous result. I am in the Olympic final. Fantastic. What an achievement after such a difficult year!

There are the interviews. There is the need to present a public face. Gary Staines has qualified from the second semi-final and the two of us face the cameras. Was I concerned? No, not really, I made a stupid mistake, I eased up too soon. Yes, I felt fine. Gary Staines is delighted to have reached the final. There are not many who would have expected this of him a year ago. He looked comfortable throughout the second semi-final. His was a great run.

Back past the press. I am laughing, buoyant. Caused a few hearts to beat a little faster there didn't I? Judged it perfectly . . .

of course I knew what I was doing . . . just a slight miscalculation. I meet George. We can both afford to laugh. I am in the final by the back door. Peter Elliott is receiving treatment from the physiotherapist. I banter with him. He has had his narrow escapes from semi-finals in the past. Last year in Rome he squeezed through by the thickness of his vest and came second in the final. I have almost two days to recover and some of the other 5000m runners will be as tired as me.

My feet are sore. I have a large blister under the outside of my left foot. I have been too absorbed in the drama to notice it before. It is painful, but after strapping I can jog lightly on it. The athletics is over for the day except for the decathlon. There has been a delay. Daley broke his pole during the vault. Someone says you could hear the crack echoing around the stadium. He is battling on despite this and other setbacks. Apparently he has his thigh and groin heavily strapped. The final event of the decathlon, the 1500m, will take place later.

I catch the bus with George. We are joking. I feel light-headed as if I have been drinking. The delight and relief of reaching the final obscures my limitations that were so nakedly exposed in the last 400m of the race. This evening the euphoria of survival means more than the proximity of defeat.

September 30. The last day of September – the Games finish on Sunday. Tomorrow, Saturday, is the last day of the track and field competition. My 5000m final is the last individual track event at 1.30 tomorrow lunchtime. It is the evening and I am aimlessly flicking channels on the TV. The Koreans appear to be approaching victory in the Olympic table-tennis tournament; there is some football on another channel. I am looking for something to divert my attention, preferably something mindless, nothing to do with the Olympics or sport.

Conflicting thoughts run through my mind. On the one hand bold, positive and courageous. It is only another race against athletes I have beaten before. There is nothing to worry about. It is simply a matter of relaxing and committing myself like so many others have done in the last fortnight. I have fought hard to reach this far and have nothing to lose. But then, contradictory fears intrude to prick my determination. This is the Olympic 5000m final, the biggest and most important race of your life, on the last day of the Games, in front of a worldwide audience. Everyone who has ever followed my athletics career will probably be watching tomorrow. I've only reached the final as a fastest qualifier. I have been injured for most of the summer so how can I expect to succeed after a hard heat and semi-final? I might as well forget about it.

I wish Kerin was here. I have missed her company all week. We were deciding whether she should attend the Games when I was injured in June. At the time, as I was doubtful of my prospects of even attending the Olympics, it seemed a better idea for her to stay behind. When the British team was announced I thought it better for us to save the money and go on holiday later in the year. I did not want her to travel to Seoul unless I was confident of running at my best. This was a mistake. I wish Kerin had accompanied me to Seoul. Regardless of my performance it would have been a great experience for her to witness an Olympic Games. Furthermore I miss her.

I rapidly dispel these sentimental thoughts and try to boost my confidence. Whatever happens tomorrow it will be one of the most exciting experiences in my life. I have trained for years in this sport to reach an Olympic final. Now I am here I am not going to panic. I may never reach such heights again. I shall not be overawed and shall savour every moment of the experience. I am not risking anything. However I perform I can return to a secure comfortable happy home. I have nothing to lose. There are so many sportspeople who would love to be in my position of stepping onto an athletics track to compete in an Olympic final, so I must stop whingeing and enjoy myself.

Look at the courage and commitment shown by other British athletes. This afternoon there was Liz McColgan's gutsy silver medal in the women's 10,000m and Mark Rowland's magnificent bronze medal in the steeplechase. He smashed the British record in only his second year at the event. His run was the fifth fastest ever and he defeated some outstanding athletes. Or look at the heroism of Peter Elliott. He has been running with pain-killing injections all week. He has a serious injury to his pelvis. Pubis symphysis is suspected. It can take months to heal and may require an operation but Elliott is determined to struggle through tomorrow's 1500m final. These are all examples of athletes who have displayed great courage. I must go into the arena, be grateful for the opportunity and show some grit. It is a straightforward and simple task.

Back come the doubts. Perhaps I am happy with merely attending these Games. If it does not matter whether I succeed or not, why bother? I do not need to achieve any more. I have recovered superbly from injury to reach this far, why go any further? Surely I am a mature enough person to realise that sporting success is trivial.

All these deliberations flick through my mind in an instant. They are habitual pre-race ruminations. The same absorptions that have tormented and teased me for years. There is nothing new here at the Olympics. I have speculated like this about English Schools cross-country races over ten years ago. I have considered and pondered before school sports days and long forgotten athletic meetings. It is an integral part of running. All my thoughts about tomorrow's Olympic final run along well worn tracks. Eventually that is what is most reassuring. I have reviewed it all before many times in the past. Tomorrow may be that extra bit special, but the work is finished and worrying about the race will not help.

On the television the table tennis is over. The Koreans have won and it is almost time for bed.

14

The Olympic 5000m Final

October 1. Two hours before the Olympic final and for the first time today my placid demeanour is disturbed by jumpy impatience. I am stuck in traffic. The taxi carrying George and me to the main stadium is stationary in a mass of jammed vehicles. So far this morning I have controlled my emotions. I have remained in that blissful state when it is possible to orchestrate your adrenalin so that you arrive on the start line ready to produce your best performance. The idea is to harness your nerves, neither allowing them to run rampant nor to lie dormant. The taxi journey is threatening to upset my composure. I lean forward trying to impress upon the driver a sense of urgency, to no avail. He does not understand my gestures and even if he did he cannot progress any quicker in this static fuming chaos.

I relax back in my seat, pulling my sunhat down over the back of my head and wait. The taxi judders slowly forwards. There are only a couple more kilometres to the stadium and if we make little progress in the next fifteen minutes we shall have plenty of time to walk. What about the race? I reckon Castro, Maree, Mei and the Kenyans especially Ngugi are the runners to watch. Amongst the rest, Gary Staines and John Doherty could have good runs while Regalo has the ability but what about the temperament? The three athletes Kunze, Baumann and Thiebaut who stormed past me on the final lap of the semi-final should be more exhausted from their efforts than me. The minutes tick past. The taxi edges towards the stadium. George and I decide to walk. We arrive at the warm-up track seventy minutes before the race. My blister needs redressing. It was painful the morning after the semi-final but since then has been punctured and treated. It will not bother me in the final and I do not care how it feels afterwards.

The weather is warm but not as bright as earlier in the week. The sunshine is hazy, almost smoggy. Queues of spectators are waiting to enter the stadium and my favourite warm-up area beneath the walkway is more congested than usual. Trucks are trundling around moving the closing ceremony props. There are bells, drums and large Lego-like pieces of bridge. Thiebaut and Ngugi have been jogging for several minutes already. I am eager to begin the reassuring ritual of my warm-up but force myself to wait another five minutes.

My blister is much more comfortable after treatment. I visit the toilet yet again. I always like to drink plenty of water on the day of a race even if this means several trips to relieve myself in advance of competition. Gary Staines is jogging. We acknowledge each other but do not stop to talk. We are both absorbed in our pre-race routines. I run slowly and gently through the covered walkway. I had expected to feel stiff after the two races in three days but my legs although weak are supple.

I ignore the weakness. Thirty minutes before an Olympic final I would be surprised if I experienced anything other than nervous fragility. It is time to report. Of the fifteen runners only five were finalists in last year's Rome World Championships, Domingos Castro, Sydney Maree, John Ngugi, Evgueni Ignatov and myself. We are all absorbed in our own private worlds of hopes and doubts. In the report room nobody looks at each other. It is easiest to busy yourself with the small tasks of checking your numbers and lacing on your spikes. Twenty minutes before the 5000m final and all the contestants are engrossed in the mundane distractions of putting on vests, zipping up tracksuits and fiddling with bags. This is our way of preserving order and security amongst the inner turmoil. In a few minutes we shall be exposed on the track, committing ourselves to each other's defeat in front of most of the world. In the meantime we fuss with clothing and make sure numbers are stuck on shorts.

The TV monitor is showing the men's 1500m. Peter Rono from Kenya winds the race up from two laps out. A queue of runners follow, but none have the strength to pass him. He is holding on ahead of the striving pack. Peter Elliott is closest but he cannot quite catch Rono. Another Kenyan and African victory. Elliott is second, Herold third and Steve Cram fourth. The race has been watched in silence in the call room, a temporary distraction from our own approaching struggle. The officials usher us on to the track. Rono is jogging his lap of honour carrying the Kenyan flag. The stadium is packed and although the crowd is vociferous there is not the air of excitement I had been expecting.

When you are competing in an event like the Olympics you are aware of the crowd as a distant distraction. The noise of the crowd intrudes into your self-absorption. I have never found the size of an audience intimidating and look to the crowd to heighten the drama of the occasion. The audience in the Olympic stadium is disappointing. There are 100,000 spectators attending but the noise and level of excitement is not as great as at many of the European meetings I have attended. I think this is because the South Koreans are not great track fans. They do not identify as easily with track as they do with judo or the martial arts.

I run a couple of strides along the back straight. It is reassuring to stretch out and move fluently after all the waiting. The electronic scoreboard lists the results of the 1500m and then displays the names of the 5000m competitors. We line up on the start line. The announcer is following each name with his credentials. I am next to Stefano Mei, the European 10,000m gold medallist and 5000m silver medallist from 1986. As his record draws applause Mei mutters 'a long time ago'. In the second semi-final I thought he was struggling, but he showed a good turn of speed on the last lap. Is he exhausted or only bluffing? The announcer continues listing every finalist in English and then another language – is it Korean? Legs are being shaken, arms twitching. I am looking straight ahead. I stand still, mentally relaxing. I breathe slowly and deeply. The starter barks his instructions. A moment of silent tension. Bang.

I must conserve energy and do not compete for position. As usual I am near the back. We shall see who has survived the earlier races. The gamesmanship of the opening rounds will be exposed in the next thirteen minutes. Have I recovered from my traumatic semi-final or not? Ngugi is loping along in front of me. Suddenly he bounds through the pack. He gallops past the leaders and is off. Three laps of the race have gone and Ngugi has swept past and away. Another lap and he is almost out of sight. He is running in a different race. In the pack I am fighting to keep my place. I am tired and heavy. I am concentrating early in the race. When I am running well concentration becomes unnecessary until the end of a race. I can switch off, secure in the knowledge that I cannot lose contact with the leaders. Today, or rather this entire year, I have been concentrating early in the race. I should not have to work this hard only to be amongst the leaders.

Ngugi has split the race apart. The compact procession of runners is now a stretched line. Nobody is catching Ngugi. I do not have the strength to lead the chase. I have battled into the first half-dozen. John Doherty leads the race for second place until near 3000m when Domingos Castro takes over. Ngugi is six seconds ahead at 3000m. I thought Castro might chase Ngugi but he will not enjoy leading the pursuit. He does not like front-running. Castro prefers to tag along following other runners, but he realises that someone has to try and haul back the powerful Kenyan. If I could stay with Castro I could still have a chance of a medal. Castro is scampering away from the second group, but I cannot chase him. My strength is fast ebbing away. My upper body is relaxed but I feel as if I am hauling my legs reluctantly around the track. My only hope is to keep plodding away and see if others tire more dramatically than me.

Approaching 4000m and there are two runners clear of a group of six. The loping Ngugi heading for Olympic gold leads. In second place the diminutive Castro chases hard. Doherty leads myself and four others, six seconds back. Doherty and Ignatov are tiring. The group is down to four. Maree, Kunze, Baumann and myself. Kunze and Baumann must be tired. As I anticipate their demise, they repeat their double act of the semi-final. They sprint, faster than I have run all year, and my dwindling hopes of a medal disappear. It is the last lap and I am left to chase Sydney Maree for fifth place. I close on him over the last 200m, but cannot overtake him. I cross the line dizzy and faint with exhaustion. Baumann is sprawled across the track. Ngugi is waving the Kenyan flag. Castro is crying. I stumble towards the changing rooms. It is all over. I feel empty, flat, vacant. I do not know what happens next. I have only thought about life up until the Olympic final. What happens now?

Down in the changing room Domingos Castro is sobbing. He was a clear second place with 400m left. He lost firstly silver and then bronze within the space of ten metres. The two Germans, the surprise performers of the final, overtook him in the final strides of the race. Castro is completely inconsolable. A Portuguese coach tries to comfort him but he continues to cry. Athletes try to console him. He is heartbroken. I congratulate Kunze. He looks sheepish, almost guilty. He has won a bronze medal nobody would have expected. He has not worn the correct East German tracksuit, he had not thought he would be attending a medal ceremony. Gary Staines looks exhausted. I shake hands with Stefano Mei. We both know we can run better than today. Finally there is Ngugi, the Olympic champion. Kenyan officials are clamouring around him. The Kenyans have won the 800m, 1500m, 5000m and the 3000m steeplechase. They have also won a silver in the steeplechase and a bronze in the 10,000m. Africans have once again won all the men's track distance races.

I leave the changing rooms. George is catching a flight to China later this afternoon. He is spending a fortnight lecturing in Shanghai. I look for him, but he has had to leave already. I chat to the British journalists who are waiting to talk to Peter Elliott and Steve Cram. I spot Crammie in the distance. Elliott and Cram are walking together, the one happy and smiling, the other tight-lipped and disappointed. I repeat the same story to different people. I emphasise how I should be delighted after all I have been through this year. I have had a terrible few months, but have still finished sixth in the Olympic Games. I have struggled all season, I am really very pleased.

Inside I am lost and distracted. Andy Etchells lends me a telephone card in the press room. I telephone Kerin. It is the early hours of the morning in Britain. She congratulates me. She knows how I am really feeling. I am disappointed, not with the race itself but with the whole year. I realise that sixth today is a tremendous achievement. I only scraped into the final as a fastest loser. Ten weeks ago I could not run. I have salvaged sixth place in the Olympics after a miserable year. At one stage I did not think I would even reach the Olympic Games. If my injuries had not healed I would have packed up for the year. I must be pleased. It has been a heroic effort. Fantastic. Great. All that could be expected in the circumstances.

But running is never that satisfying. I started 1988 with high hopes of at least a medal and all through the year those expectations remained. As I experienced defeats, injuries and poor fitness I had faith in my ability to recover. All along I have been deluding myself that when it came to the crunch I would rediscover my elusive form. All year I have been shoring up inadequate fitness with dreams of glory. I could not conceal my lack of fitness in an Olympic final.

Even after the semi-final when it became crystal clear I was not ready to reproduce my running of 1986 and 1987 I ignored the evidence and continued to aim high. This is how an athlete should behave. You cannot afford to dwell on the negative aspects of your running. You must keep clutching at whatever straws you can find. After my semi-final I consoled myself with the thoughts that Kunze and Baumann must be tired after their last lap efforts, refusing to acknowledge my own exhaustion. Today I could not hide. Kunze and Baumann had survived. I had not.

Those hopes are now dashed. The year will not end in surprise glory. There is no dramatic change in fortune. I had hidden my disappointments behind mental doors. I had prepared for the Games focussing only on what I dreamt for. The doors in my mind have been ripped open revealing my limitations. I can see the year more clearly.

So I feel disappointed and flat. Yes, I repeat to my friends back at the Olympic family town, it was a great effort, but it has been an awful year.

October 2. I lie in bed the morning after the Olympic final. I hardly slept last night. What do I do today? In 1986 and 1987 after the European and World Championships I was swept along in the euphoria of success. But, this year there will be no trimmings of glory.

Twenty years ago I would have retired. Twenty-seven years old and sixth in the Olympics I would have entered the real world and looked for a normal job. Today the sport is different. I am a full-time runner. There are races all year, every year. 1989 is supposed to be a quiet year, but there is the Grand Prix circuit, the Europa Cup, the World Cup and a full complement of domestic fixtures.

So what are my options? Retirement may seem instantly attractive after the traumas of 1988, but is quickly rejected. What else could I do anyway? Also Olympic disappointment is already fuelling my motivation. If I gave up running now I would spend the rest of my life wondering what I might have achieved if I had continued. I could flog myself around the European cross-country and road race circuit. I have hardly raced all year so I could make the most of my fitness and earn some pocket money for the winter. Alternatively I could take a complete rest and eventually resume training for next summer determined once again to run as I know I can.

It is the last option that appears most attractive. I do not have the enthusiasm to keep plugging away all winter without a proper break from the sport. I want to let my hair down for several weeks and indulge in the types of activity that many would consider natural, but to me will be decadent. I intend to lead an active social life and indulge in gluttony. First stop is breakfast. No fresh fruit and muesli. It's pancakes, syrup and Danish pastries all the way!

15

Seoul Searching

It is only when I arrived home from Seoul that I saw how the rest of the world had reacted to the Games. When you are involved in the everyday drama of the Olympics you cannot step back and observe the whole picture. It is different if you are watching the Olympics on television (preferably in a language you can understand) as you have instant access to the best pictures and expert opinions. What television coverage can never capture is the unique experience of living through an Olympic Games and mixing with so many different people for whom this is the most important occasion of the year.

When I arrived home from Seoul I caught up with all the Olympic stories I had missed. I saw the men's 100m final for the first time and Greg Louganis' diving. I had heard all about the British hockey team's gold medal. Some of my friends had attended the final, catching a bus to the match following the last day of the athletics and returning jubilant later that evening. I had not seen a single moment of men's hockey action until I watched the recorded highlights back in Britain.

Back home I could also catch up on the experiences of friends who had followed my progress. My semi-final had taken place at 5.30 in the afternoon Korean time. This equated to 8.00am

Greenwich Mean Time. Many of my friends were hoping to watch my semi-final and then travel to work. But, as I was sitting nervously beside the track in Seoul waiting for the outcome of the second semi-final to see if I had qualified for the final, so family and friends were watching tensely beside their television sets in the UK. I delayed lessons in one school and caused several late arrivals to work that morning. An ex-University friend went into a betting shop following my race to put some money on me for the final. He was advised not to as, to quote the bookies' words, 'he doesn't know what he's doing'.

In Britain I could also observe the overall reaction to the Games. In April of this year I read an article in the *Independent* by Sir William Rees-Mogg entitled 'The Decline of the Olympics into physical and moral squalor'. He listed fifteen reasons why he would not watch the Olympic Games. These included the loss of idealism, vulgar nationalism, racial intolerance, blatant commercialism, corrupt administration, the threat of terrorism, widespread use of drugs and manipulation by television. In April I was exhausted from hard training and it offended me to see the ultimate goal of my efforts so criticised.

I sent a letter to the *Independent* as follows:

> 'Sir William Rees-Mogg will unfortunately not be watching the Olympic Games. He deplores the commercialism, politics, nationalism and bureaucracy of international sport. In fact he deplores almost every aspect of the modern Olympic Games, apart from one he overlooks – the athletes themselves.
>
> This is an important oversight. The Olympic Games although burdened with many of the problems that beset both sport and society are still at heart about the competitors. All over the world thousands of sportspeople are pursuing their aim of competing in Seoul. To qualify for the Olympic Games demands as much sacrifice, dedication and determination as it has since 1896. These are qualities admired throughout sporting history and are still present amongst today's sportsmen and women. I am not claiming that contemporary sportspeople are in any way superior to their

predecessors, merely that it is incorrect to assume that there will be "little fair play, no international citizenship, little sportsmanship, no open field, no harmony at Seoul".

Sir William should talk to the athletes who are striving to gain a place in the Olympic Games. Talk to them and learn of their commitment and diligence, the difficulties they face and their acceptance of a healthy sporting challenge. With some perhaps motivation involves wealth and fame, but for the overwhelming majority, the "taking part" outweighs any considerations of commerce and nationalism.

On the drugs issue Sir William should also listen to the athletes. Two hundred and fifty-four top British internationals have just signed a declaration requesting stringent controls far beyond the scope of current IAAF regulations. This is a positive move in the fight against drugs and although there will be a minority in any area of society prepared to break the rules for personal gain, there is a willingness amongst competitors to confront the problem.

If it is accepted that the pursuit of self-improvement and the attempt to achieve a healthy physical aim is still a noble quest, then it is worthy of support, encouragement and applause especially when all that may entail is nothing more energetic than switching on a television set.'

Of all the comments Sir William Rees-Mogg directs against the Olympics and sport, it is the drugs problem that alarms me the most. The letter was sent when I was involved in the IAC anti-drugs initiative. Subsequently one athlete, Jeff Gutteridge, who signed the declaration has been tested positive under the BAAB random out of season programme. With hindsight I realise that perhaps the IAC declaration is hoping for too much in expecting rapid concerted action in the war against drugs. Since the declaration was signed there do not appear to have been any drastic new anti-drugs measures at international level. The IAC declaration is a small plea for stronger action against drugs. That an athlete who takes banned substances could sign the IAC letter, indicates how ineffective the declaration is perceived to be amongst drug-takers. What chance that the athlete's voice is heard in the sport's corridors of power?

The story of the Games was, of course, the Ben Johnson scandal. The Olympics were elevated from the back to the front pages by his positive test. The Johnson affair threw the drugs issue into the spotlight once again. The traces of the anabolic steroid Stanozolol that were found in his urine sample, and his subsequent disqualification, have made the need for positive action against drug-takers more urgent than ever. It is impossible to escape the effects of the Johnson affair. Cliff Temple explained this in an article in the *Sunday Times* entitled 'Age of innocence is truly over and cynicism is here to cloud our joy'. He argued how difficult it has become when an athlete produces a great performance to celebrate the achievement rather than cynically query the legitimacy of the result.

At the Seoul Olympics there were rumours circulating every day. Ian Wooldridge wrote in the *Daily Mail*: 'If I were to list the names openly mentioned, in some cases because they have muscles bulging in unusual places and in others because of nothing more than a furtive countenance, I could lay this newspaper open to £20 million in libel damages.' Will a great athletic performance ever again be welcomed with unreserved applause or will the sly innuendo of drugs be ever present?

The actual disqualification of Johnson showed that the IOC are prepared to ban the world's most famous runner, but will the IAAF show similar determination in enforcing the life ban? It is clear that international athletics needs more powerful drugs testing procedures along the lines of the IAC declaration.

There have been suggestions to allow the legitimised use of drugs. This cannot be permitted, but there should be a distinction between the use of drugs for medicinal purposes and those used to enhance performance. To allow a drugs free-for-all would remove from sport all the values of realistic excitement and drama that are so widely cherished. Effective action against drug-users needs to be taken to protect the vast majority of innocent sportspeople. The fear is that as fast as the legislators act the laboratories invent.

The drugs problem cast a shadow across an otherwise tremendous Olympics. My experience of attending my first Olympic Games reinforces my belief that the Games have not declined into 'physical and moral squalor' as Sir William Rees-Mogg suggested. I am not disputing that the Olympic movement faces problems, only that these problems are subordinate to the efforts, achievements and enjoyment of the competitors and spectators.

The closing ceremony epitomised the success of the 1988 Olympics. Competitors from 160 different countries streamed into the stadium, laughing and mixing together in friendship. For two weeks the competition was fierce but there was no rivalry during the closing ceremony only warmth, comradeship and admiration for the wonderful display provided by the Korean hosts. Where else, apart from the opening and closing ceremony of an Olympics, do people from all corners of the world meet in such companionship? I found the closing ceremony an exciting and moving experience. The Koreans managed the show perfectly. They allowed the spontaneous dancing and frolicking to proceed unhindered but maintained control of the complex organisation of the ceremony.

I was standing in the centre of the arena when the lights went out and a bridge was 'built' under cover of darkness. The Koreans needed to clear a large space in the centre of the stadium amongst crowds of milling competitors. This was a potentially awkward moment as none of the athletes knew what was happening and many were cavorting, oblivious of the ceremony around them. I was in the path of the bridge building and like everyone else was ushered out of the way with brisk but friendly efficiency. It could easily have gone wrong. Someone could have fallen over. Athletes could have remained in the path of the bridge. Officials could have been over zealous in their efforts to move competitors. The bridge might not have been completed in time for the next stage of the ceremony. None of these disruptions happened and the closing ceremony proceeded with the correct balance of glittering choreography and impulsive fun.

I had feared the Olympics would be overburdened with security. The threat of terrorism and the political unrest in South Korea are valid excuses for stringent security checks. It is in everybody's interests that security at events like the Olympics should be foolproof but I found these Games no more restrictive than the Rome World Championships. On the last day of competition there were lines of police motorbikes outside the stadium waiting to accompany the marathon runners around the city. I had my camera and asked one of the policemen if I could have my picture taken on one of the bikes. He willingly agreed, encouraging me to put on a helmet correctly and use the radio. So much for the authoritarian security of the Olympics.

So long as you cooperated and obeyed rules the Koreans were impeccable hosts. If you did not they were justifiably angry. Some American swimmers found themselves in trouble when they stole some flags. They were sent home and a statement was issued saying that any stolen flags found at the airport would be confiscated. For most of my two weeks in South Korea I existed in the cocoon of Olympic organisation that separated the athletes from the Korean people. On the few occasions when I stepped beyond the insular world of the Games my limited contacts with Koreans were amicable. One evening a group of us were returning late from a restaurant (after I had competed needless to say). We were trying to catch taxis back to the Olympic family town when a private car pulled over. The driver offered his services free of charge! There were lots of stories of Korean tailors whisking made-to-measure suits out to the Olympic village within forty-eight hours.

The only off-putting encounter I had in South Korea was with kimchi. Kimchi is the Korean national dish. It is eaten with any meal and is a garlic smelling concoction of pickled cabbage and spices. I usually enjoy garlic and am not averse to sampling exotic cuisine but kimchi was too much for my taste buds. Kimchi, I found out afterwards as my mouth was burning, contains in addition to garlic an assortment of chilli peppers, ginger and pickled anchovies. The smell is overpowering. If I had eaten some before my race I could have overwhelmed the opposition.

Kimchi was one of the few aspects of these Olympics that left a bad taste in my mouth. Another was the curious relationship between the US and South Korea. The US, military protector of South Korea, also paid the largest sums to televise the Games. Whenever the NBC coverage was critical of the Olympic organisation the Koreans were incensed. The Koreans are striving to project their national identity on the world stage and are sensitive to criticism. They appear to resent the paternalistic attitude of the US. In some sporting arenas the US competitors were booed.

A more heartening nationalistic aspect of the Games was the diversity of countries that won Olympic medals. The East Germans, USSR and USA gained the bulk of the medals, but overall fifty-two countries won medals ranging from Surinam to Senegal, the Virgin Islands to Mongolia, Thailand to Djibouti. Sporting success is not just about countries that plough in vast sums to promote nationalistic self-assertion, but the achievement of outstanding talent in spite of more limited resources. On the track, the most powerful symbol of the poorer countries proving their athletic superiority is the uninhibited running of the Kenyans.

But the performances of individuals linger in the memory longer than waving flags. Ahmed Saleh desperately surging in the marathon – too early, caught and overhauled by Gelindo Bordin in the final kilometres of the race. Paula Ivan who front-ran to victory in the women's 1500m and Debbie Flintoff-King's sprint off the last hurdle to snatch gold by one hundredth of a second. The Olympics, as I argued in my response to the newspaper article, are firstly about the athletes. Seoul showed that despite the changes in sport the Games are worth preserving.

As for my own performance, I still have mixed reactions. It is too soon to appraise my run in the Games. In ten or fifteen years' time when I have hung up my spikes I shall be able to view the events of 1988 from a safer distance. I have invested too much effort into my running of the last twelve months to conduct a balanced examination. I need the buffer of time and more running before I can see the Olympics in context. The Olympics is too close. It dominates the landscape of my memory, a huge mountain dwarfing surrounding experiences. When I have struggled up other hills and through more valleys I shall be able to look back and see the Olympics as one landmark in a broad horizon.

I prefer to look forward. What shall I aim for next? I have not run a step since the Olympic 5000m final. I have imposed no discipline on my life. I have lain in bed when I wanted and have eaten what I wanted. I have become a lazy, self-indulgent slob. The novelty of this existence has worn off within two and a half weeks. It happens every year. I look forward to throwing off the yoke of running but as soon as I am accustomed to my freedom I am missing the sport. I miss running in the crisp autumnal air. I miss the morning mists and the crunching leaves. I miss the quiet solitude of the woods in the twilight.

Next week I shall start running again.

RACE RESULTS

Date	*Race*	*Place*	*Time*	*Winner*	
6/9/87	World Champs 5000m	3	13.27.74	Aouita	13.26.44
13/9/87	Crystal Palace 5000m	1	13.17		
15/9/87	Lausanne 2000m	3	4.53.06	Spivey	4.52.5
20/9/87	Westminster Mile	9	3.57	Elliott	3.53.6
27/12/87	Zurich 8k road	1	22.42		
6/3/88	Nottingham 10k road	7	29.28	Chorlton	29.17
6/4/88	Newcastle 5k road	14	14.05	McLeod	13.43
30/4/88	Lucerne 8k road	2	23.14	Délèze	23.00
20/7/88	Derby 3000m	1	8.05.5		
29/7/88	Edinburgh H'cap Mile	11	4.04.5	McInnes	3.57.2
14/8/88	Gateshead Mile	9	4.03.5	Passey	4.02.2
17/8/88	Zurich 5000m	9	13.30.27	Martin	13.25
28/8/88	Crystal Palace 2 Miles	4	8.26.52	O'Mara	8.25.65
31/8/88	Rieti 5000m	1	13.24.3		
2/9/88	Essen 5000m	1	13.32.99		
28/9/88	Olympic 5000m Heats	10	13.43.69	Mei	13.42.96
29/9/88	Olympic 5000m Semi	7	13.23.17	Castro	13.22.44
1/10/88	Olympic 5000m Final	6	13.23.85	Ngugi	13.11.7

World Championship 5000m

Rome, September 6, 1987

1	S Aouita	13.26.44
2	Domingos Castro	13.27.59
3	J Buckner	13.27.74
4	P Délèze	13.28.06
5	V Rousseau	13.28.56
6	E Ignatov	13.29.68
7	T Hutchings	13.30.01
8	Dionisio Castro	13.30.94
9	F O'Mara	13.32.04
10	S Ovett	13.33.49
11	S Maree	13.33.78
12	J Ngugi	13.34.04
13	J Tracey	13.41.03
14	A Anton	13.43.58
15	C Nelson	13.43.81

Olympic 5000m

Seoul, October 1, 1988

1	J Ngugi	13.11.70
2	D Baumann	13.15.52
3	H Kunze	13.15.73
4	Domingos Castro	13.16.09
5	S Maree	13.23.69
6	J Buckner	13.23.85
7	S Mei	13.26.17
8	E Ignatov	13.26.41
9	J Doherty	13.27.71
10	J Danielsson	13.30.44
11	P Thiebaut	13.31.99
12	Y Ondieki	13.52.01
13	G Staines	13.55.00
14	P Arpin	14.13.19
15	J Regalo	dnf